THE WEDDING OF MAGDEBURG

GERTRUD VON LE FORT

The Wedding of Magdeburg

First English edition translated and annotated by Chase Faucheux

Foreword by Christopher Check

IGNATIUS PRESS SAN FRANCISCO

Original text:
Die Magdeburgische Hochzeit

Cover art
The Sack of Magdeburg
Cover based on an original engraving on paper by
Daniel Manasser (d. 1637)
In the collection of the Ludwig Maximilian University of Munich
Wikimedia Commons image in the public domain

Cover design by Pawel Cetlinski

ISBN 978-1-58617-819-2 (PB)
ISBN 978-1-64229-267-1 (eBook)
Library of Congress Control Number 2024942792
Printed in the United States of America ♾

CONTENTS

FOREWORD

Is there a Catholic home in America that does not display an Infant of Prague watching over the family from the top of a bookcase or from the corner of a dresser or from the center of a mantle? Of the good souls in so many homes, how many can give an account of the origins of the devotion?

Fair enough. Piety does not insist on historical literacy. Nonetheless, the cataclysm at the center of the story of the Holy Infant Jesus of Prague is remarkable for the altogether inverse relationship between our conversancy with the event and its impact on the modern age. I am speaking of the Thirty Years' War (1618–1648). The conflict gave Europe the nation-state, saved Protestantism in central Europe, and reduced Spain. During and following the conflict the tactics of modern warfare and modern diplomacy matured. Some eight million perished, although more recent estimates claim as many as twelve million.

The reader will recall, however, that while there was a good bit of fanfare in 2017 to mark the five hundredth anniversary of Martin Luther's rebellion, one year later—the four hundredth anniversary of the Defenestration of Prague, the moment that set the match to the touchhole of one of the most sanguinary and destructive wars in all history—came and went without notice. Yet it is in the midst of this conflict that the Infant of Prague—a nineteen-inch Christ Child doll of wood and wax with a near universal reach—enters the popular imagination: the doll is lost, then is found on a trash heap, and then is invoked by the faithful to protect Prague from a siege prosecuted by the relentless Protestant soldiers of Gustavus Adolphus, king of Sweden.

It is not without explanation that American ignorance of the Thirty Years' War is near total. We are a former British colony, after all, and James I laudably kept England out of the conflict, though not a few of the future Roundheads and Cavaliers of the subsequent English Civil War would cut their teeth as freelancers on the Continent's battlefields. Moreover, our knowledge of Continental history, especially east of the Rhine, is near blank. Until one of today's masters of silver-screen brutality (Ridley Scott? Mel Gibson?) commit the event to celluloid, English speakers who have given up reading will have to make do with the compelling if problematic (and with carnage enough) 1971 picture *The Last Valley*, written and directed by *Great Escape* screenwriter James Clavell. Michael Caine and Omar Sharif play a Protestant mercenary captain and a Catholic schoolteacher respectively, who broker a separate peace during the Thirty Years' War in a secluded farming village protected by mountains. Caine, who read the picture as an indictment of religious turmoil in contemporary Northern Ireland, felt he delivered one of his standout performances. The photography is striking, clearly influenced by Jacques Callot's baroque engravings *Les grandes misères de la guerre*. The masterful score is the work of none other than John Barry, composer of the James Bond soundtracks. Catholics looking for a "we were the good guys" narrative of the Thirty Years' War will be disappointed. So will they be by *The Wedding of Magdeburg*, penned by the great German Catholic novelist and convert Gertrud von le Fort.

To le Fort's masterpiece in a moment. First, a fool's errand: summarizing the causes, action, and consequences of what may be the most involved war in history.

Since the Protestant rebellion, wars between Catholic and Protestant princes flared and quieted, but a century later, the Habsburg Empire, at strength in Spain and Austria (and Africa and America), seemed positioned to impose by political and cultural influence, and by military might if needed, a thoroughgoing restoration of the Catholic Faith throughout Europe. Indeed, any observer of the time would have reason to doubt the future of Protestantism as a serious political and cultural force.

The office of Holy Roman emperor had been for centuries filled by election. Indeed, the great princes and prelates of Europe were called "electors". Long had the Imperial throne been a Habsburg possession, but Protestant holdouts in Bohemia feared the potential rule of the heir apparent, the fervent Ferdinand II. The aforementioned tossing out the window of Ferdinand's ambassadors by the Bohemian Protestant nobility provoked the Catholics. Quick victories in Bohemia and the Palatinate (southern Germany) might have put the matter to rest, but the devout and enthusiastic Ferdinand, who was at last elected in 1619, pressed—*overpressed*—his advantage.

His generals, who both feature in le Fort's novel—Albrecht Wenzel Eusebius von Wallenstein and Johann Tserclaes, Count of Tilly—vanquished Protestant armies as far north as the Baltic Sea. Ferdinand did not extend to his Protestant subjects the religious tolerance that his predecessor, Rudolph II, had codified in his Letter of Majesty of 1609. Backed into a doctrinal corner, the German and Bohemian Protestant princes formed an alliance with King Gustavus Adolphus of Sweden and, alas, Cardinal Richelieu, working for the long-standing Habsburg rival Louis XIII.

For more than a generation Christian Europeans tore at their own collective throat. Europe, Germany especially, became a wasteland of slaughter, plunder, and rape by mercenaries whom neither side could afford to pay and by religious fervor gone mad. Notorious among these soldiers of fortune—and villains of the novel—were Croatians. Le Fort's portrayal is not ahistorical, much less unjust, but one wonders whether it was not also without contemporary inspiration. She was writing as the Nazis in her own country were ascendant, and she cannot have been ignorant of the Ustaše Croatian racial and religious purity movement, whose foot soldiers just a few years after *The Wedding of Magdeburg* was published would perpetrate under Nazi alliance the genocide of as many as half a million Serbs.

In decades of horrific slaughter, it is ridiculous to speak of a nadir, but the siege and destruction in 1631 of Magdeburg, Saxony's capital city, site of the death of Saint Norbert and resting place of Otto I, the first Holy Roman emperor, must be the most infamous. Ferdinand's 1629 Edict of Restitution (the "Imperial Edict" in the novel and central to its moral crisis) proved too much for the Protestant burghers of Magdeburg's Rathaus. They resisted the edict and invested vain hope in Gustavus Adolphus. How le Fort portrays the heartbreaking failure of both sides to seek the better part in the other should make run ice-cold the blood of any American who has ever uttered "unconditional surrender" and meant it. Two-thirds or more of Magdeburg's thirty thousand citizens were shelled, burned, or starved. Four-fifths of the city was laid waste.

Count Tilly's culpability for the war crime is in doubt. The Jesuit-trained officer was a man of moral principle. Le Fort is sympathetic. She does paint his number two, Gottfried Heinrich, Count of Pappenheim, as more of an enthusiast for bloodshed in the service of the Catholic cause. While we know that Pappenheim ordered the burning of two buildings, historians in search of an accurate account have argued that the strong winds of that fateful day (also in the le Fort work) and the mercenary mob gone out of control (foreseen by Tilly, according to le Fort) carry much of the blame.

There were no winners of the Thirty Years' War, although, as with war today, a few people in power became extraordinarily wealthy. The most harmful and lasting effect of the war was the privatization of religion that began with Martin Luther a century before. Germany did not recover until well into the eighteenth century. Magdeburg's recovery wasn't until the nineteenth. The Catholic Church knows, especially in the modern age, that once the dogs of war are let loose, horrible human suffering will follow. I'm not hopeful that American military institutions will regard seriously the Church's just-war doctrine, when Christian princes set it aside with abandon in the seventeenth century. Still, perhaps *The Wedding of Magdeburg* could be required reading at Annapolis and West Point. More than for military officers, however, le Fort's novel should be required reading for the staffs of those think tanks and journals ever advocating for more American funding of, and participation in, perpetual war.

The rest of us need to seek something more: redemption. "Who can understand the human heart?" asks Jeremiah (17:9, GNT). In times of tragedy especially, its best and worst qualities are made manifest. Better than any historian, storyteller Gertrud von le Fort brings her unique genius for laying bare the human heart in making sense of and finding redemption amid the horror of human suffering. She stands with Gironella and Manzoni in this regard—and, in my mind, ahead of Dickens. All due praise and thanks to Ignatius Press for bringing this and other of her works back into print for English readers.

—Christopher Check
Feast of Saint Clare of Assisi, 2024

Christopher Check is president of Catholic Answers. He served as an artillery officer in the United States Marine Corps from 1987 to 1994.

Part I

Maiden's Eve

On the fifteenth of October 1630, the day Colonel von Falkenberg's courier arrived in Magdeburg, Dr. Reinhart Bake,[1] first preacher at the archbishopric's great cathedral, had a peculiar experience. As he prepared to walk over the threshold of the great cathedral in the grayness of that early morning, he could have sworn he heard someone shout—but in what sounded like a convincing imitation of his own voice—the words that Dr. Martin Luther was said to have cried out in the last, difficult years of his life as it became clear to him that there was no way out of the fraternal strife that raged between Christians in the German lands: "Come, dear Last Day!"

Hearing these words alarmed Bake in a most peculiar way, for he had just come to the great cathedral quite confident that with the Swedish succor this Colonel von Falkenberg[2] would deliver, all danger of physical and spiritual ruin threatening this good, exceedingly steadfast city of Magdeburg might be averted. Indeed, he had hoped this meant that the greatest day of all was now approaching, when after a century of struggle, she would be secured once and for all, and the protesting, rebelling, triumphing city of Magdeburg could finally have peace! It was this hope that he had been prepared to fortify and enflame in the hearts of the people gathered at the great cathedral with the sermon he planned to preach later; he'd given Dr. Gilbert, the great preacher of Saint Ulrich's, his word.

[1] Reinhart Bake (1587–1657) was a Protestant theologian who in 1617 became the pastor of the cathedral in Magdeburg.

[2] Dietrich von Falkenberg (1580–1631) was the German officer in the Swedish army who commanded the defense of Magdeburg.

Startled, he looked about, but there was no one to be seen from whom the shout could have come; the streets were still gray and deserted in the early morning light. Only the stone figures above the Paradise Portal of the great cathedral (also called the Bride's Portal)—the wise and the foolish virgins on either side of the Virgin Mary as she is assumed into heaven, a holdover from the Papist days—gazed down on him in the full dawn of that autumn morning, still so obscured by darkness that it was not possible to tell the wise ones from the foolish ones.

This alarmed Bake for a second time, as he was by nature a tender and easily distressed soul. To him, this inability to distinguish the figures appeared to be yet another ominous portent concerning this momentous day; for the city of Magdeburg bore in her coat of arms a beautiful young maiden, and Bake had always thought of her as one of the wise virgins who took care to preserve her oil.

Nevertheless, there was still not a soul to be seen in front of the great cathedral, so Dr. Bake concluded that the shout he had heard must have been a temptation from the wicked Enemy, trying to trick him into thinking he was hearing his own voice as it had sounded on the Tenth Sunday after Trinity Sunday. That was the day on which the ostracized former administrator of the archbishopric had reappeared and been welcomed by the people with honor and distinction, bringing with him the first promise of military aid from Sweden. Dr. Bake could still hear his own voice at the service, how it had suddenly grown so oddly discolored and faded as he read the Gospel about the destruction of Jerusalem, the reading for the Tenth Sunday after Trinity Sunday. At the time, he'd thought all the people must be as frightened for their lives as he was. But then the crowd out in front of the great cathedral had started singing the old Magdeburg *Trutzlied*, the song of resistance against the Interim[3]—except it was almost as though they sang their defiance against the destruction of Jerusalem:

> Though soul and body perish,
> We'll never bow to Rome;
> Our liberty we cherish;
> Pope, Emperor, go home!

And so, the protesting, rebelling, triumphing city of Magdeburg had, as it were, leapt right into the great cathedral and over the frail voice of its preacher, leaving it as lonely, as powerless, as forsaken among the enormous crowd that filled the great nave as the voice of Our Lord Jesus Christ outside the walls of Jerusalem. And that was exactly how the voice he'd heard had sounded—just as powerless and forsaken, as if to indicate that the city of Magdeburg had nothing to look forward to now but the Last Things.

But it was precisely in such despondency that the deceitful wiles of the diabolical Adversary could be made out, and there was no doubt that he was involved here. For the city of Jerusalem had fallen because she had turned a deaf ear to the voice of her Lord, but the city of Magdeburg had embraced God's Word in all truth! As if to put the lie to the wicked Enemy, Dr. Bake thus said confidently in his heart: What happened to obdurate Jerusalem can never befall us—we're the city they call Our Lord God's Chancellery, after all. We're the protesting, the rebelling, the triumphing city of Magdeburg!

[3] The Augsburg Interim of 1548, decreed by Holy Roman emperor Charles V. The Interim established a temporary doctrinal compromise between Catholics and Protestants in Germany. However, the Interim was viewed by Protestants as being too Catholic, so much of Protestantism rejected it.

By now, however, he had entered the great cathedral. The enormous space within was still quite empty, the deep darkness which seemed to stretch out in front of the great crucifix that towered above the rood screen illumined only by a delicate, pearly gleam that trickled down from the lofty windows of the choir like a train of gray tears. Everything apart from this spot appeared to be covered in ashes; it appeared as though the only thing in all the world that could be made out was this great cross which seemed to span the distance between heaven and earth. Dr. Bake prostrated himself before it, seeking to fortify his soul in prayer, that he might utterly defeat the temptation of the wicked Enemy and ascend to the pulpit as a faithful and courageous servant of the Word, where he would enflame the hearts of the people in favor of the accord with Sweden.

But in prayer he did not receive the strength he sought; rather, the longer he prayed, the more any strength he needed to enflame the people eluded him. He felt as utterly powerless as he had on that day when he'd preached about the Lord Christ's lament over Jerusalem. Today, as on that day, this powerlessness pushed him ever closer, indeed irresistibly close, to Christ; it was almost like the powerlessness he felt was the power of Christ Himself in disguise, pulling him toward Himself. He felt an ineffably intimate longing henceforth to embrace the Crucified One alone, to persevere with him faithfully, even in the most difficult trials of faith, to bid a firm farewell to all matters of politics and to place all help—whatever happens will happen, he thought—in the hands of the Almighty God and say, along with the Lord Christ, "Not my will, but thine be done."[4] Thus all things, as it were, were transformed for him in

[4] Lk 22:42.

prayer; even the shout that had previously alarmed him so much now seemed to take on an entirely different meaning: it was not a lament over the fate of Magdeburg but a cry of longing for the New Jerusalem. Surely, he said to himself, there can never be anything that a Christian soul could not accept from its heavenly Bridegroom and Lord, even if it were the earthly end of all our affairs, indeed the earthly end of our faith itself—for what is an earthly end, anyway? In God's name, I say, Come, dear Last Day—yes, come, Lord Jesus!

Meanwhile, the doors of the cathedral were continually opening and closing, and now when Dr. Bake looked up, no longer was there an impenetrable darkness stretching out in front of the great crucifix, but the church had grown bright and cheerful; and where before everything had appeared to be covered in ashes, there were already a sizable number of people sitting in the pews, filled with confidence and expectation, ready to hear God's Word preached to them by Dr. Bake. So, getting up in a hurry, he headed to the sacristy to put on his clerical robes, in the meantime telling himself that he would have to give a completely different sermon than the one he'd planned to give.

But as he was walking through the nave of the church toward the pulpit, he at once felt that he would be unable to get this other sermon past his lips; for he saw before him all the headstrong and impetuous men who, nine months ago, had thrown out the old Council and its leader, Johann Ahlemann, for not taking a brave enough stand against the Imperial Edict—the Edict, after all, commanded that the archbishopric be handed over to the Papists! And then he saw all the strapping blond women who people joked sang their little children to sleep with the old *Trutzlied* against the Interim. And indeed, just as he ascended to the pulpit, appearing lank and delicate in front of all the sturdy townsfolk—not like a pugnacious theologian at all, but more like a lissome schoolmaster or even a poet—he saw coming into the cathedral the maid Erdmuth Plögen, who as a little girl had been his best pupil in catechism class. She entered through the Bride's Portal, for today she and Willigis Ahlemann were to have their banns read for the third time, or as they said in Magdeburg, today was the day they would "jump from the pulpit". Everyone looked at Dr. Bake, and it was as though his own words and sermons were staring back at him. They couldn't possibly have all been wrong, for that would mean everything that had happened in Magdeburg over the past hundred years was wrong as well. And so, once more, all things were transformed for him—not like before, in prayer, for he was no longer praying now anyway, nor was he looking at the Crucified One. Rather, what he now saw was the ardent longing and incredible potential of this steadfast and combative city and its capacity to accomplish great things. He saw the glory of the old Lutheran stronghold and its holy fury for the Gospel. He saw, as it were, the Word of God fashioned into a sword and placed in the hands of the rebelling, triumphing city of Magdeburg: for truly, the Christian soul could bear any burden, but the one thing it could never tolerate was the embrace of the Papist whore! So, for the second time that morning, Dr. Bake believed he saw quite clearly that there was indeed a devil, whose cunning was beyond all measure; it was he who'd tried to convince him that the despondency he'd felt earlier was actually the power of faith. And so he made up his mind, cast the wicked Enemy down from the pulpit, and in the name of God, began his sermon:

"Then will you stand there, you proud, maidenly city, like the fair virgin in your coat of arms: upon your head, the slender wreath which you victoriously defended against His Roman Majesty Carolus Quintus,[5] and held high in your hand, the same wreath after you steadfastly denied it to the Duke of Friedland.[6] Thus with joy you shall open your chamber to the proper bridegroom, the one whom God has chosen for you, the Hero of Midnight,[7] who now approaches to safeguard your most precious jewels: the liberty of the Imperial Estates and the purity of the Gospel in German lands!"

On finishing this sentence, Dr. Bake paused for a moment and looked around. His eyes fell once more upon the young Erdmuth Plögen, who was sitting with her bridegroom, Willigis Ahlemann, directly below the pulpit, whence they would soon "jump". From his place up in the pulpit, Dr. Bake had a clear view of her head; so proud and blond did it gleam against the dark church pews, as if made of gold. It was a proper Magdeburg head, the face somewhat broad and full but nevertheless fair and sweet in its own particular way, like the faces of the wise and the foolish virgins out there in the embrasures of the Paradise Portal. Indeed, Erdmuth looked as though she might have just come down from there; she looked like the fairest and the proudest of the wise virgins, the one who must be the bride herself—so thought Dr. Bake, for her whole face seemed to glow with a triumphant splendor. And at that moment it was as though the sun had at last risen over the dark portal outside, and he was finally gazing into the face of the benign omen he'd longed for this day. Thus, with confidence, he continued his sermon:

[5] Charles V, Holy Roman emperor from 1519 to 1556.

[6] Albrecht von Wallenstein, Imperial army generalissimo in charge at the attempted siege of Magdeburg in 1629.

[7] King Gustavus Adolphus of Sweden, referred to later as His Royal Majesty of Sweden.

"Yes, then will you stand there, you fair, maidenly city, like the wise virgins above the portal of your great cathedral, your face filled with laughter and rejoicing, just like those maidens as they go in with the bridegroom to the wedding!"

The maid Erdmuth Plögen, however, with the youthful haughtiness typical of a young bride, was actually thinking—for she had indeed noticed that Dr. Bake kept looking at her as he spoke—Yes, then you will stand there like me!

Up in the pulpit, Dr. Bake said "Amen" and closed the Bible. He then announced that it was time for the young Erdmuth Plögen and Willigis Ahlemann to "jump from the pulpit".

But when he called out the bridegroom by name and looked in his direction, he was suddenly unrecognizable. Willigis Ahlemann, like Erdmuth, was one of those sturdy, thriving citizens of Magdeburg, but the man whom Bake now saw in his place was pale as a corpse, like a man who was gravely ill—or one who was filled with wrath. And he was no longer sitting at the side of his bride, where he was supposed to be sitting while the banns were read, but had stood up from his seat like a man who could no longer contain himself, and he was now striding all alone through the great nave of the church toward the door, whereupon he slammed it shut behind him, causing it to thunder and quake in every last corner of the cathedral. Everyone inside stared at the beautiful bride with astonishment and dismay.

Meanwhile, Dr. Bake had descended from the pulpit and gone into the sacristy. He was about to signal to the sacristan that he should go and find out just what exactly had happened with the bridegroom; but then another messenger arrived from Dr. Gilbert, the great preacher of

Saint Ulrich's, who requested his presence: the gentlemen of the city government, who would be assembling today at the Rathaus,[8] were in need of spiritual assurance, and he needed to consult with Dr. Bake about this.

Bake did not find this particularly uplifting, as he was easily intimidated by the secular authorities, knowing well that they did not like it when the clergy interfered in worldly affairs. But alas, Dr. Bake thought in his heart, such interference was often necessary; for even the ruling gentlemen of the city are but poor, frail men, always in need of God's Word to motivate them, to rebuke them, and even, if necessary, to punish them. Readying himself, he stepped outside the great cathedral.

There, in the deep golden light of the autumn morning, lay the city of Magdeburg; regal in bearing, she rose up from the banks of the broad, billowy Elbe, proudly rolling along like a great highway of destiny, whereupon none but the fair Virgin of Magdeburg was in command; each and every wave of the proud waterway seemed to kiss the feet of the maiden as it knelt before her and offered a silver mirror that she might gaze each day on her magnificent and mighty countenance and her glorious abode. Her towering home was like a crown, its numerous prongs formed by the slender spires of the six stately parish churches and the copper spires of the handsome Rathaus towers, which gleamed in the sun as if covered entirely in ducats! Encircling the Virgin's mighty fortress was a dense, thorny maiden's wreath bristling with bulwarks, bastions, and redoubts, all equipped with towers and spires of their own; but instead of gleaming with splendor, they loomed with menace! Inside the fortress, however, was a bustling and cheerful scene, where stepped gables of glazed brick

[8] Town hall.

leapt gaily and jauntily into the sky, and honey-brown half timbers sagged with the weight of the city's amply filled larders. And every house was decked with bright and florid colors, festooned in all manner of emblems and images, after which they took their names—for in Magdeburg, every house had its own name. Scattered above the doors and cornices, one could see garlands of roses and apples, golden ears of wheat and grapes, silver moons and stars, all carved in wood and painted or exquisitely fashioned out of baked clay—the whole town looked as though it were forever decorated for a festival. Just then, outside one of the houses, two young, cheerful maidservants were hanging a thick wreath of green rosemary over the front door; this was the door of the Plögen house, known as *Zum Hohen Lied*, "The High Song". It displayed no image above its door but instead bore an inscription from the Song of Solomon: "For love is strong as death, and like unto a flame of the Lord!"[9]

No one in Magdeburg could say who had put this passage up there, though it had to have been done many years ago. The whole house was built the way they used to build them in the old days: it rose steeply, almost violently, up from the street, as if those who'd built it had meant to leave the earth and force their way into heaven! It was also clear to all that the inscription was utterly out of place; for the Plögen house was not a home in which Solomon's high song of love was sung. The inhabitants of the house had instead always gone their own way, in particular the fair Plögen maids, none of whom had found happiness in marriage for a hundred years. And so it would be a great miracle indeed if tomorrow the nuptials of the maid Erdmuth actually took place.

[9] Paraphrase of Song 8:6.

For now, however, the whole area around the Plögen house was filled with the distinct and comforting aroma of the sundry cakes and roasted dishes that made up the bridal feast that would be served to the guests, and there were already servants unloading casks of all kinds in front of the door. And there in the pointed archway stood Dr. Bake's own better half, a small, sprightly woman, still bearing the face of an innocent young girl in spite of her five young children, four of whom clung to her skirt, their little faces visibly peeping out from all the folds. The fifth was not yet visible, for Frau Bake still bore it beneath her heart; it could be seen only from afar, as if through the delicate veil of pallor and fatigue that showed in her own little face. So Dr. Bake stopped and reminded her not to exert herself too much; after all, she was to play the part of mother of the bride here at the Plögen house tomorrow since the young Erdmuth had no one else. He then asked her whether she'd heard what had happened at the cathedral with Willigis Ahlemann today—perhaps the young man had fallen ill?

Lifting her little, girlish face—nestled in her broad white ruff, it was as though she were presenting it to him on a little platter—she answered him: Oh no, she did not think that Willigis was ill. Who ever heard of a bridegroom falling ill at the reading of his own banns? No, there had to be something else entirely going on, for Erdmuth was bitterly aggrieved and incensed. Perhaps he would go and speak with her? She was always his best pupil in catechism class, after all; surely he would help her in her hour of distress and tell her what a Christian bride needed to hear at such a time! Then she looked at him as though she herself were a bride and had just promised to wait for him, even if it should take seven times seven years. He had always quite liked it when she looked at him in this way, but today her bride-like gaze made him feel strangely uncomfortable, though he did not know what brought this feeling about. Rather self-consciously, he suggested that perhaps she would like to speak with Erdmuth herself, then. Oh no, she replied, surely this was something that only the pastor himself could presume to do—young maidens in Magdeburg were quite proud these days, as though they'd let the virgin in their dear native city's coat of arms get to their heads. No, she could not possibly be the one to do it! She said this with a little smile, another trait of which he had always been quite fond but which today made him uneasy—indeed, it almost felt as though his wife were trying to implicate him in something. So he suddenly put on his schoolmaster's face and said, quite abruptly: "Now, dear, do have some modesty for once—I've told you that *you* should speak to the young maiden!"

Her face flushed red all the way up to her forehead, but then the children were jumping up on her and yanking violently at her skirt, as though they were trying to tear it apart. So she bent down to them and said: "Now, children, didn't you hear your father? We're to be modest!" Upon which Bake turned red himself and hurried off into the house to check on the maid Erdmuth.

He found her sitting in her room in front of her wedding ensemble, which was laid out sumptuously before her: the silken gown, three times as wide as the open arms of the fair maiden bride as she embraces her beloved bridegroom on her wedding day—so the dressmaker had said. And beside it lay the bodice, ornately decorated with golden lace and elaborate braids, quite like a glittering shrine over the bosom of the fair maiden bride, inside of which she carries the portrait of her beloved bridegroom on her wedding day—so the dressmaker had said. And then there was the high bridal crown of brass sequins, with all the pearls and stones on their trembling wires that inclined so sweetly, like the head of the fair maiden bride as she leans in close to her beloved bridegroom—so the wreath maker had said. And beside this lay the bridegroom's wreath of green rosemary, beautifully interwoven with cords of gold and silk: none but the fair maiden bride on the morning of the wedding may place it on the bridegroom's head, crowning him her king, as it were—so the wreath maker had likewise said. The groom, however, does not crown the bride; rather, he removes the crown from her head on their wedding night. With it she gives to him all her pride and all her own splendor, that she might thenceforth receive his—so the wreath maker had likewise said. Just this morning all this had sounded so joyful and festive to the maid Erdmuth; now the thought of it caused her bitter pain, for earlier that day her bridegroom had left her in the great cathedral at the reading of their banns! She had now been sitting in her room for two hours waiting for him to come back and apologize to her and explain himself. Surely she had every right to demand that much of him; after all, a bridegroom was supposed to remain with his bride during the banns, never leaving her side, even if the world was about to end!

But Willigis never came; the only one who came was the maid Ilsabe Fricken, who was supposed to be the chief bridesmaid at the wedding tomorrow. She poked her head through the door and said in her shrill voice that she'd heard that Willigis had gone to see his uncle Johann Ahlemann, the one they always used to say really ran things around here (surely he had an official position with the Imperials in Wolmirstedt by now)—what did she think, could that really be true? And then came the maid Anna Guericke with her pert, round eyes, who was supposed to be the second bridesmaid tomorrow; she'd heard that Willigis was saying he couldn't sleep another night in Magdeburg, even if it were his own wedding night, if there was to be a Swedish officer in charge there—could that really be true? And then chatty Agnete Brauns came and opened her big mouth: she'd heard that the reason Willigis had remained in Magdeburg after Johann Ahlemann had ridden out of town when the old Council was thrown out nine months ago wasn't because of his bride at all, but only because he wanted to stay and find out what was happening here so he could report it to his uncle at Wolmirstedt, and that he didn't really care about her as much as she'd always thought he did—could that really be true? And last came pointy-nosed old Frau Spitznase, who always had to be the first to know everything that happened in Magdeburg, and whose granddaughters were also supposed to be bridesmaids; she'd been informed that the wedding at the Plögen house would have to be postponed because the bridegroom was keeping the maiden bride waiting—could that really be true? Each time Erdmuth replied that yes, none of this was news to her. But no one believed what she said; they all just thought that she did not want to let them know how terribly aggrieved and heartbroken she was.

When Dr. Bake came in and saw her sitting there all alone before the magnificent splendor of the bridal ensemble spread out before her, her eyes a bit moist and her aching lips pursed like a small child about to cry, he felt painfully sorry for her in his tender soul. Adopting a gentle, fatherly tone, he told her how badly he felt about the terrible misfortune that had befallen her. But she could open her heart to him in confidence, as he was here to comfort her and to pray with her for patience; for patience, as she knew, was the sweetest refuge and the most beautiful adornment of a grieving bride. It is by her patience that she adorns all mankind, as it were; for alas, what would become of the human race if dear brides and wives did not exercise patience with their husbands? Surely then the whole world would be utterly bereft of it!

As he was speaking, the maiden had pulled herself together somewhat; she still had the same sorrowful look on her face, but in her bearing she now looked quite dignified and resplendent once more, rather like she had this morning at the great cathedral, as though she might be thinking in her heart: What exactly do you expect of me, then? I'm the fair Plögen maid; what need have I of consolation? Then she said as much aloud, with obvious condescension in her voice: "But I don't have to sit here and wait for Willigis—I can find my way on my own!" He was becoming increasingly aware of how bitterly aggrieved and incensed she was. And so he proceeded even more gently: one should not say such things when entering into marriage, he reminded her; he urged her to think of her dear departed parents, who had arranged for her betrothal to Willigis when she was still a minor child—the houses of the children are founded on the parents' blessing, after all![10] And then, he reminded her, she might do well to recall the beautiful Bible passage he'd selected as their wedding text, from the Book of Ruth, chapter 1, verse 16: "Whither thou goest, I will go; and where thou lodgest, I will lodge: thy people shall be my people, and thy God my God.... The Lord do so to me, and more also, if aught but death part thee and me."

Seeing that the maiden was again looking at him rather dismissively, he suggested that perhaps she did not understand what he was saying. Our Father in heaven, he explained, had created her to be a fine wife and destined her to be a bride, and surely there could be nothing at all that a loving bride would not be able to accept from her beloved. But as he spoke, he was suddenly struck by the

[10] Paraphrase of Sir 3:9.

same disquieting sensation he'd felt a short time ago with his own wife: again it was as though there were someone trying to implicate him in something, but this time it was Bake doing it to himself. He realized quite clearly that he was repeating to the maiden something that he had already said once today, but had then dismissed—

Bake fell silent, but that was when the maiden came alive. She began telling him about the terrible things those wicked girls had related to her: apparently it was the sermon about the Swedish accord that had prompted Willigis to get up and rush out of the great cathedral—what on earth did the Swedish accord have to do with a bridegroom at his own banns, anyway? And now, she lamented, Willigis had ridden off to his uncle Johann Ahlemann, as if he had more right to her beloved than she did. And, it was certainly no small thing to be given the chance to wed the maid Erdmuth Plögen—they had to know what was due to her! And, everyone had always thought that it was for her sake that Willigis had remained in Magdeburg, and now it turned out he'd wanted to stay only to find out more about the Swedish accord so he could report it back to Wolmirstedt! How could she possibly accept all this with meekness and patience?

She was again overcome with grief, and she gazed at him helplessly, as though she still expected, demanded, some sort of consolation from him. But now all of a sudden, just like this morning in the pulpit at the great cathedral, he found that he could no longer say what he'd meant to say: it was as though she had wrested each and every word from his lips.

As he came down the stairs, he found his wife still waiting under the pointed archway, except she had sent away the children, presumably as a way of demonstrating to him that they were all now behaving themselves with due modesty.

There she stood, all alone, defenseless before him, as it were, giving him a questioning look that he knew meant she wanted to know how his talk with Erdmuth had gone.

He responded abruptly, almost gruffly: It was nothing at all like she'd said. Erdmuth had every right to be as angry as she was. It was indeed on account of the Swedish accord that Willigis had rushed out and ridden off to Johann Ahlemann. Just imagine, he told her, what it would be like if her own husband suddenly left her side and ran off to join the Imperial Papists! Would she just let it happen without taking offense, or perhaps even go with him?

"Yes," she replied innocently. "Yes, my dear, for where else should I go if that was where you went? Would you expect me to leave you?"

At this he completely lost his composure, and he repeated, raising his voice but utterly helpless with dismay: "To join the Imperial Papists?"

She answered him truthfully, "Oh, but they too are but poor children of the Lord, and our Savior has patience with them, as he does with us."

To this, he had absolutely no response, but this happened to him quite often with his wife: she would sometimes say things that smacked of outrageous effrontery, though there was really nothing to object to—it just wasn't proper to say such things!

So he merely repeated that Erdmuth was quite right to be angry and resentful, and perhaps all she had to do was remain calm, and Willigis would come to his senses again. But now he needed to make haste, for he did not wish to offend Dr. Gilbert by keeping him waiting.

As he was hurrying along to the parsonage of Saint Ulrich's with his curiously uneven gait—it always seemed as though he sought an entirely different path than the one he was on—Dr. Gilbert himself came and met him halfway to the

Rathaus. He glared at Bake with his dark eyes, a common feature in the German south, for he had come to Magdeburg as a persecuted and displaced preacher after being expelled from the Imperial hereditary lands in Austria. Bake thus always felt a great sense of awe and reverence in his presence, as though he were looking into the eyes of a martyr.

Without a moment's hesitation, Gilbert said that he'd heard how manfully Dr. Bake had taken up his exhortation to promote the accord with Sweden at the great cathedral this morning—indeed, the entire city resounded with his sermon! When people heard the mild Dr. Bake speaking in such a combative tone, he touched their hearts in a completely different way than did a fighter such as himself. Bake, modestly and somewhat apprehensively—for now the look in those martyr's eyes was quite commanding—responded that yes, he had advocated on behalf of the Swedish accord to the best of his ability.

The other man grew fervid: And it was indeed sorely needed, he exclaimed, for the councillors of this good city were in great danger of pitifully capitulating! Ever since the courier had brought the news that His Swedish Majesty's commandant had been dispatched to Magdeburg, they'd been acting as though they'd been struck by lightning; they'd been unwilling to receive him, unwilling to recall what they'd previously promised, unwilling to take a stand and suffer for the Gospel! They'd had the nerve to explain to him that the Rathaus was not a sacristy, and that the noblest duty of Christian authorities was not to safeguard the Gospel; for belonging as it did to the nature of higher things, it was protected by a higher power. Life and limb, honor and esteem in this world, on the other hand—these things were not immortal, they'd said, but could indeed perish miserably, and it was with these things alone that they needed to concern themselves! He continued, fiercely remarking that the Council that now governed Magdeburg was essentially no different from the one that had been in charge a hundred years before; the councillors knew nothing of the Gospel but from the very beginning had seen it only as a means to break away from the archbishopric and become a Free Imperial City, the status which they believed had already been assured to them by the emperor Otto, called the Great.[11] This privilege was their idol and their highest good, and for its sake they were even now willing to hand over eternal bliss! But, he continued, those who served God's Word were still here as well, and it was now up to them to take over the leadership of the city, for what happened in the Imperial hereditary lands must never be allowed to happen in Magdeburg.

Bake thought to himself that perhaps the Council, in their concern for the privilege assured to them by Emperor Otto, did indeed mean to safeguard the Gospel as well, for if Magdeburg were a Free Imperial City, the Edict could do them no harm. To a Free Imperial City of Magdeburg, a Catholic archbishop would not be able to say, as its sovereign: "*Cuius regio, eius religio*";[12] instead, she would be able to say to him: "I am the protesting, triumphing city of Magdeburg, and it is I who rule here!"

But Bake did not dare reply, for Dr. Gilbert was always reproaching him for taking the side of the authorities.

So he asked, somewhat sheepishly, why the Council had received the administrator on the Tenth Sunday after Trinity Sunday—surely by doing this, they'd already gone over to the Swedish side, had they not?

[11] Otto I, who ruled from 962 to 973.

[12] "Whose region, his religion"; i.e., the sovereign's religion would determine the religion of the people. This principle was agreed upon in the Peace of Augsburg (1555).

Gilbert replied that the Council had not taken the administrator seriously, and that there was very good reason to fear that they were only using him as a toy to present to the clergy and the people in order to buy enough time to negotiate with Johann Ahlemann on behalf of His Imperial Majesty. This would all come to light when Willigis Ahlemann returned from Wolmirstedt.

He then said that it was now time to mobilize the people against the Council: the people had raised this Council up; the people could bring it down again. Bake had already laid the groundwork for this in his sermon that morning; the crowd had been so powerfully and gloriously enflamed in favor of the Swedish accord that they would now sweep away the misgivings of the Council like a heap of withered chaff!

Horrified, Bake objected that he'd been entirely unaware of this—he'd been under the impression that the Council stood behind his sermon! God forbid that he should incite the people to rebel against Christian authority—Dr. Martin Luther would rise from his grave to prevent it! The people were created by the Lord for obedience, not to rule, after all; like fire or water, the mass of people was indeed a useful creature, but also blind and a dangerous one—there was never any way to know when it might erupt out of control and when it might not; to release the people from the bonds of obedience was to call forth a demon! Holy Scripture itself even says that all authority is ordained by God, and that we are to obey not only those rulers who are benevolent and just but those who are unjust as well—the latter were simply part of the cross that the Christian must bear. He stopped abruptly, as though an entirely different and much deeper horror had occurred to him.

But then Gilbert said, almost sympathetically: "If that is what you think, Herr Bake, then you should have preached this morning not about the accord with Sweden but about obedience to His Imperial Majesty."

At that moment, they entered the Rathaus.

Inside, the ruling gentlemen of Magdeburg were seated in assembly. It was hot and sultry in the room from many heated speeches and counterspeeches, and the windows had been thrown wide open. Outside, the autumn sun shone down on the wide, bright market square, upon which stood the statue of the emperor Otto, who, seated on his horse and accompanied by his two female standard-bearers, was headed directly for the Rathaus where the gentlemen were assembled.

Just then someone spoke up, as the administrator had done in the same room on the Tenth Sunday after Trinity Sunday; it was not he who spoke today, however, but the Swedish ambassador Stalmann, who spoke in the same grandiloquent phrases and tones as the administrator, as though the men in the Rathaus were the audience of a traveling show booth and were beholding with their own eyes the general rebellion of the Empire's Protestant Estates, which had been waiting only on the city of Magdeburg to step up heroically, that they might burst forth like a mighty storm; they saw them taking up arms: the Electorates of Brandenburg and Saxony, Hesse-Cassel and Hesse-Darmstadt, Holstein, and the cities of the Hansa and the former ecclesiastical principalities, in addition to Bohemia and the Imperial hereditary lands, Upper and Lower Austria, and, far away, presumably even the land of Tyrol; behind this scene, as though painted in the background, they saw the torch of this cruel thirteen-year war, laid down once before and nearly extinguished, now raised high once again, blazing from one end of the Empire to the other, and there in the middle of it was the flame that fed it all, the city of Magdeburg! There could suddenly be heard the familiar crackling and creaking sounds from the woodwork in the old paneled Council Chamber where the gentlemen sat in assembly. But this was the same chamber where, nine months before, the people had thrown out the old Council; it was likewise the same gentlemen whom the people had triumphantly brought in to replace them. Yet today they looked quite different than they had on that day—they did not look at all like a council chosen by an ever-youthful, tempestuous people; instead, they looked serene and impassive, as though they were thinking: We are quite aware that our city is the key to everything in this country—we do not need anyone to tell us! But the one to whom we will give this key remains to be seen: it is we who rule in the mighty city of Magdeburg, and we will not allow ourselves to be drawn into an adventure; rather, we will wait.

To the ambassador, however, it looked as though they actually were waiting for someone, and he kept occasionally glancing at the door to see whether there was anyone not here yet who might still appear—but none of the gentlemen were missing save for Willigis Ahlemann.

The ambassador was not the least bit bothered by this; that Ahlemann fellow was always so steadfastly silent, and there was no talking with silent people; but if he couldn't talk, then he was indeed powerless! Thus it seemed quite clear to the ambassador that there was absolutely no reason for him to wait around for Willigis Ahlemann like the others, and that he should instead get through his business quickly, before the empty seat was occupied.

But then Burgomaster Brauns spoke up, asking him in his broad, ponderous voice: "Herr Ambassador, how many miles now lie between our city and His Royal Majesty of Sweden?"

To which the ambassador, smiling like a jack-of-all-trades performing his tricks, replied: "Miles will no longer be of any concern to His Royal Majesty of Sweden once the general rebellion is blazing!"

Burgomaster Brauns, speaking in the same deliberate manner as before, but now with a small, uncomfortable grin on his face: "And if the general rebellion does not blaze?"

To which the ambassador retorted: "Whether it blazes or not is entirely up to this mighty city of Magdeburg—the city of Magdeburg *is* the general rebellion!"

Then someone earnestly said: "Still, we really should wait and see what happens first!" At this the ambassador turned once again toward the door.

But Burgomaster Brauns continued, sober and unperturbed, seemingly intent on pushing the ambassador all the way against the wall: "You cannot tell us how far away His Royal Majesty of Sweden is, but we can tell you where Generalissimo Tilly and his marshal von Pappenheim[13] are: miles are of no concern to them either, if they wish to reach us, because their people are already gathering at Hamelin and Halberstadt." Thus the great show booth of the war suddenly appeared before them once more, now viewed from the other side, as it were, the side which the ambassador had not intended to show them; the scene they now beheld was quite different from the one before; they now beheld the ominous and terrifying spectacle of the city of Magdeburg standing on the chessboard of two hostile armies, checkmated, so to speak; they now saw, not a gloriously blazing torch, but a smoldering pile of rubble!

The ambassador, however, as if he alone of all those in the hall did not perceive the imminent threat of this spectacle, retorted: "But, my dear gentlemen, surely there

[13] Johann Tserclaes, the Flemish Count of Tilly, commanded the combined Imperial forces during the Thirty Years' War (1618–1648). Gottfried Heinrich von Pappenheim, a German cavalry officer, led the attack on Magdeburg.

can be no greater safeguard against Generalissimo Tilly and Marshal von Pappenheim than to receive His Royal Majesty of Sweden's seasoned commandant!"

Then another voice called out from the back, where the youngest of the councillors sat: "We do still have a better option: we can expel the ambassador from the city and bar the gates against his Swedish commandant!"

The ambassador turned a shade paler but nodded obligingly: "And then, my dear gentlemen, when you have expelled us from the city, will you submit to His Imperial Roman Majesty, accept his Edict, return the archbishopric to the Catholics, and renounce the great glory achieved by your fathers as you crawl back under the lordship of a prince-archbishop?"

That will silence them for sure, the ambassador thought to himself. But then again someone called out from the back, this time almost triumphantly: "And who told you we'd have to accept the Edict? Do you think Vienna isn't also aware of who holds the 'key to everything' in this country?"

The ambassador's thoughts began to race: Surely they do not plan to wait for His Imperial Majesty to come around, or to acknowledge them as a Free Imperial City? That could take a very long time—indeed, we'd never see the end of it! He looked around the room, aghast.

But then Burgomaster Brauns, as calm and unperturbed as ever, said that they had been waiting this whole time for Willigis Ahlemann; they expected him to come at any moment, and they could not decide on anything as long as one of their number was absent.

Meanwhile, at the Plögen house, Erdmuth was still waiting for Willigis as well. The golden October day was already drawing to a close, and it was approaching the hour known as maiden's eve: that is, the evening before the wedding, when the friends and companions of the beautiful young bride would gather at her home and take her into their midst to play and sing with her the happy songs and games of her youth. This would take about two hours. Then, at the stroke of seven, they would go out onto the market square, where the bridegroom and his groomsmen would come to meet them, and together they would sing and dance the lovely dances that were normally sung on maiden's eve. This would take one hour. Then they were all supposed to go their separate ways and go to sleep, according to the rules for maiden's eve set by the Council. Erdmuth's heart grew more and more restless and anxious, and she thought: What if we go out onto the market square for the dance and Willigis is still not there, and I have to stand there alone in front of all my friends as I did this morning at the great cathedral? What am I supposed to do then? I'd much rather be dead!

At that very moment Ilsabe Fricken came in and announced in her shrill voice that the girls were all gathered for maiden's eve, beckoning her to come down and join them.

Erdmuth thought once more: I really would rather be dead than have Willigis not show up this evening. But surely I won't have to go through that—he would never do that to me!

As she descended the stairs—Ilsabe Fricken always one step behind her—she passed the small door behind which her maiden aunt Itze, her father's happily unmarried sister, had lived when she was a child. Erdmuth could still see her quite clearly: a stern old maid with a withdrawn face, always dressed in plain, unassuming clothes. Twenty years before, Itze's bridegroom had run out on her on the day of their wedding because a clamor had arisen that she was a witch who'd used her craft to make herself more beautiful—this was in 1612, the year they'd caught a number of witches in the nearby town of Egeln.

In her heart, Erdmuth thought: I'm not a witch, though; I'm the fair Erdmuth Plögen! Surely I won't end up like my aunt Itze!

As she descended the second flight of stairs, she passed the heavy bridal chest of the maid Engelke, her grandfather's happily unmarried sister, whose bridegroom had run out on her on their wedding day after a clamor had arisen that Engelke had been making eyes at another man. In her heart, Erdmuth thought: I haven't made eyes at anyone, though; I'm the respectable Erdmuth Plögen! Surely I won't end up like my aunt Engelke!

Then, as she descended the third flight of stairs and stepped out into the hallway, there was an open door, behind which she could already see the table set for the wedding soup that she was to eat along with the guests tomorrow morning before the ceremony. There on the table stood the magnificent silver centerpiece that had once belonged to the maid Regula, her great-grandfather's happily unmarried sister, of whom nothing was known except that no suitor had ventured to approach her at all; and so, like the maid Regula, the silver centerpiece had remained at the Plögen house, where it now stood on the table, in the very spot where it had stood when the maids Engelke and Itze had sought to marry.

Then Ilsabe Fricken spoke up: "Oh, Erdmuth, there's no reason to think you'll end up like your aunts Itze and Engelke!" Hearing this, Erdmuth felt as if all hope was lost. What if Willigis never does come back? she thought. Then I really will end up like my aunts Itze and Engelke!

Meanwhile, her friends were sitting in her little maiden's parlor in their stiff dance dresses with wreaths set atop their curled hair. Before them were baked goods and sweets aplenty; but instead of reaching for these, they were leaning in close and chatting with one another. When Erdmuth entered the room, she heard one of them reminding the others that no Plögen maid had found happiness in marriage for a hundred years. Ilsabe Fricken quickly clapped her hands; their faces turning red, the girls jumped up and formed a circle around the maiden bride. But the bride's heart beat ever more anxiously, and she could hardly join in the cheerful songs and games.

So passed the first hour of maiden's eve. As the second hour began and the girls were already gazing out wistfully at the market square, Ilsabe Fricken began to sing, in her shrill voice, the beautiful "Ballad of the Ten Virgins", which is always sung in the last hour before the dance. The first of the maids would stand up and go out onto the market square to look for the bridegroom. Then she would come back and tell the bride that alas, he has not yet arrived, and ask her whether she could go on waiting. Then the bride would answer her: "Ah, dear maid, love makes all things possible." Then the second maid would go out and come back and give the bride the bad news and ask her how it was that she was able to remain so patient. Again the bride would answer: "Ah, dear maid, love makes all things possible." Then the third would go out, then the fourth, then the fifth, and so on, and each one would come back and the bride would admonish her to be patient, for love makes all things possible. The maid Erdmuth had a very hard time saying this line, and it became so dreadfully difficult with each turn that she wondered whether she would even be able to get it past her lips. None of this is true, she thought in her heart; in fact, this whole act is a lie—love can't do a thing! If love made all things possible, then surely my bridegroom would be unable to put me through *this* hour; if love made all things possible, then surely it would make him think of me! Or is this line I'm supposed to say not about the love of the bridegroom at all but about the love of the bride? That would mean it was not until today that I knew what love was. But surely that cannot be!

In the meantime, the maids had lined up alternately on her right and on her left, each playing her part in the story: those on her right side played the role of the wise virgins who accepted the bride's counsel of patience and stood waiting beside her, and those on her left played the foolish ones who shook their heads at her counsel and sat back down, pretending to fall asleep. Then Erdmuth thought in her heart: Would that I could join the foolish ones, for truly they have got it right. How I would like to close my eyes and see and hear nothing more! Oh, if only I could hide behind my aunt Engelke's bridal chest, or in my aunt Itze's little chamber—everyone is afraid to go in there, no one would come looking for me there! Oh, if only it were my turn to keep watch outside, then I could run away from it all!

But it was little Anna Guericke's turn next, and it took a curiously long time before she returned. This was on account of the young councillor Otto Guericke, her cousin, whom she had run into outside on the market square.[14] For they were still waiting for Willigis over in the Rathaus as well. When it had become clear that he was not coming, someone had mentioned that tonight was his bride's maiden's eve, and perhaps he could not resist going to see her first—that was just the sort of thing one might expect a bridegroom to do, after all. And so Otto Guericke had headed out to the Plögen house to inquire after him.

[14] Otto Guericke (1602–1686) wrote one of the primary accounts of the destruction of Magdeburg, which the author certainly used as a source text.

Now, as he stood there before his cousin Anna, his bold, slender face, all brown from the sun up on the city ramparts—for he was of course chief engineer of Magdeburg's defensive works—she recalled how fond she was of him, and she began to tease him: Come on and dance with me for heaven's sake, she pleaded with him; she was just dying at this miserable maiden's eve!

With a laugh—for he liked to joke around with Anna too—Otto replied that no, he could not dance with her, for whether she would believe it or not, they were acting out a story of their own over at the Rathaus, and just like her, he'd been sent only to keep a watch and had to return right away.

Oh, she asked, giggling excitedly, were the gentlemen over there acting out the "Ballad of the Ten Virgins"? Suddenly becoming quite serious, he replied that this evening could well be the maiden's eve of the city of Magdeburg herself. And at that, she nearly burst out laughing again.

But by now all the maids except for Anna Guericke had gone over to stand by Erdmuth, and when Anna finally returned, it was time for the finale. At this point, the bride herself was supposed to go out and look for the bridegroom, who would have meanwhile come onto the market square with his companions; and she would cheerfully return to the house and call to the girls: "My bridegroom is here!" Then the virgins on her right would go out with her to the market square to dance, while those on the left would stay behind until the groomsmen came and woke them up with frolic and mischief of all sorts, everyone playing their part in the story.

If Willigis doesn't show up now, Erdmuth thought in her heart, and I have to go before the girls alone, like this morning in the great cathedral, and say: "My bridegroom is not here," then I shall perish. I will not be able to go on waiting, nor will I be able to go on forgiving, for then Willigis will have insulted me too grievously. I am the much-sought-after Erdmuth Plögen, after all; surely I cannot allow myself to put up with such a thing!

At that moment the clock struck seven, and it was time for her to go out. As she took up the door handle, she could feel the curious eyes of the young maids behind her burning into her neck as they peered and strained to see just what in the world was about to happen. Literally fleeing them, she entered the dark hallway, where she again said in her heart: Now I shall perish indeed! How am I supposed to endure this? How did my aunt Itze, how did my aunt Engelke bear it when their bridegrooms did not show?

Just then she thought she heard a voice beside her in the darkness say: "Pride makes all things possible!" It sounded just like the voice of her aunt Itze, who had always been so quiet and indeed rather demure, even though people were constantly afraid of her. For a moment young Erdmuth was likewise overcome by a curious dread in her soul, yet at the same time she sensed in her blood that Aunt Itze was her closest and most faithful relation. And already she felt curiously safe and secure, as though all the things that had frightened and tormented her were about to change, and no one on earth would be able to offend her or harm her ever again. She could lie down to sleep in peace whether Willigis showed up or not; it made no difference. I'm done with it all! she said to herself; I no longer need to go on waiting, to go on forgiving—that's all behind me now; pride makes all things possible.

But as she said this to herself, she felt an entirely new, and much deeper, pain than before, as though not Willigis but her own heart were delivering her a fatal blow: it pounded relentlessly against her chest, as though it were trying to force open some door inside her. Truly, she thought to herself, I never knew I loved Willigis as much as I do now that I intend to leave him! The line does say that love makes all things possible, and I'm quite sure now that this refers to the love of the bride. Thinking this, she again felt curiously safe and secure, as though no one in all the world could cause her grief or make her anxious any longer. She no longer felt the need to slip into Itze's little chamber either; rather, she could take refuge in the great love within her own heart—that love could turn even the bitterest of things sweet. Tears fell from her eyes as she opened the front door and stepped out onto the market square.

Outside, the moon was already high in the autumn evening sky, spreading its soft light over the earth, as though it were a serenely gentle woman lowering her veil to envelop all things below, like the mantle of the Virgin Mary in the images of the Papists. The whole world appeared wondrously becalmed and pacified, as if no child of man had ever quarreled or acted in defiance in this place, or as if all quarreling and defiance had been wiped away by the delicate veil of heaven, like tears from the cheeks of an unruly child. Suddenly, there was nothing at all but the sweet meekness of profoundly patient things, lying together so willingly and peacefully, the small in their small way and the great in their great way, above them hanging the shadow of the two church towers of Saint John's like a silent hymn of praise to the Creator. To the maid Erdmuth, it seemed as if the whole world had become a place of bliss, and she felt that she herself was walking forward through a vast sea of soundless bliss as she drew ever nearer to Willigis, who was still nowhere to be seen. It was as though all distance had turned to nearness, all bitterness to sweetness, and she felt as if she herself had been given another spirit, one that transformed all things or created them anew. She said to herself: I feel as though Willigis kissed me for the first time this very hour.

She suddenly heard the sound of hoofbeats, bright and clear in the night, almost silvery, like a hammer striking a bell—it had to be Willigis' gray; no other horse sounded like that! And then she saw it with her own eyes, bursting out onto the market square from the darkness of the street behind Saint John's Church, as though she herself had drawn the rider here with the power of her love! And now, she thought, the sea of bliss through which she approached him would come crashing down upon the two of them—she could already feel his silent kiss on her lips, like an unbreakable seal.

The gray whinnied brightly—it had noticed her! She heard it rearing and scraping, as if it wanted to stop and the rider was giving it the spurs—but then it was already dashing past her on its way to the Rathaus.

Erdmuth stood all alone on the market square, still quite dazed; she'd been cast out of the sea of bliss and onto a naked, barren beach, a single thought occupying her mind: The horse noticed me—only the horse. Then, startled by the sound of faint whispering behind her, she turned her head and saw, in the open doorway of the Plögen house, the maid Ilsabe Fricken and, standing on her toes behind her and looking over her shoulder, little Anna Guericke. And beside them stood Agnete Brauns with her big mouth wide open, and at the windows, with their faces pressed against the panes, the other girls peered out after her; they had all been watching, had all seen the gray recognize her while its rider rushed right past her! Thus she watched as the whole fair moonlit night appeared to be swallowed by an abyss, and the great sea of bliss was as though it had never been, and nothing remained but the wicked girls standing in the doorway of the Plögen house.

The girls, however, had likewise been startled when Erdmuth had turned around all of a sudden, and Ilsabe Fricken, quite abashed, said: "Oh, Erdmuth, please forgive us for being out here, but we really didn't know that you were still waiting for Willigis." And Anna Guericke added: "Yes, forgive us, but we just couldn't keep waiting for Willigis any longer."

Before Erdmuth's eyes, everything suddenly became as black as before in the dark hallway of the Plögen house, and in a voice that sounded exactly like the voice of her aunt Itze, now suddenly become her own, she said: "Oh my, you've been waiting for Willigis all this time? Well, I'm not waiting for him at all. And now it's time for us to go to bed—good night!" At that, the door handle flew out of Ilsabe Fricken's hand and the door slammed shut so violently that the crash echoed across the market square, jolting all the houses, great and small, out of their evening tranquility. Erdmuth suddenly felt a deep sadness like she had never felt before in her life, as though a door inside her had also slammed shut, locking her out of her own heart, as it were, and she was truly left with no other refuge but Itze's little chamber. Without looking back, she ran around to the dark hallway and up the stairs.

The room was just as Itze had left it. Everything inside was as neat and tidy as in a proper old maid's parlor: there was not the slightest trace of anything sinister or unnerving—a black book, for instance, or a mysterious phial, or some symbol on the wall; rather, there were only such things here as one would need for the sake of one's toilette and good order. Nor did it smell of flowers, which Itze—so it was said—could supposedly conjure from thin air. Indeed, it smelled somewhat musty, like air that had been trapped indoors for some time. This, too, was perfectly natural. Only the moonlight that fell through the window appeared unsettling and strangely awry, no longer resembling the veil of a meek and gentle woman as it had over the hazy landscape outside; it instead appeared pale and yet vividly lurid, as though it were not the real moon's light at all but some other, ghostly kind of moonlight. Erdmuth could scarcely bear the sight of it, and she thought: If I don't close my eyes at once and forget everything, I'll either cry myself to death here or die of fright. She threw herself down on Itze's empty bed, closed her eyes, and fell asleep.

After a while she began to perceive a strangely enchanting fragrance, as if there were indeed flowers somewhere in the room, and she opened her eyes in a dream. She saw a big, ugly spider running along Itze's bedstead; but just as she was about to jump up in horror, it was no longer a spider but a flaming red carnation. And as she marveled at the sight of it—still dreaming—there scurried out from under the bed a mouse, which then transformed before her eyes into a golden yellow rose. And then she noticed—still dreaming—a ghastly bat hanging from the ceiling; it became a fragrant violet. And so it went, on and on, until the whole room was like an arbor filled with flowers.

Then Erdmuth—still dreaming—thought: What a curious sight—everything in here is being transmuted and transformed! Was Itze really a witch after all, then? I've always thought that was just something people said about her! But then the strange magic that was present in the room began to work anew: she heard, just like before, the hoofbeats of a horse in the market square. It sounded as bright and clear as the silvery hoofbeats of Willigis' gray—but suddenly the silvery hoofbeats were no more, and in their place the hoofbeats became quite heavy; the sound they made was dull and discordant, and it hurt her ears so much that she could scarcely bear it. In the dream, she wondered: What's the matter with Willigis' gray? Why, he's lost his silvery hooves, and now he's got stones on his feet! Oh, how I wish he would never arrive—having to see Willigis now would be the worst thing that could happen to me!

But then—still dreaming—she could already hear people running up and down the stairs, and she thought she heard the voices of the girls calling her name: "Erdmuth, Erdmuth, where are you? Are you really asleep?" Then came the shrill voice of the maid Ilsabe Fricken: "Erdmuth, Erdmuth, your bridegroom is here, you need not wait any longer!"

Then Erdmuth thought—still dreaming: Didn't I tell the girls that I would not wait for Willigis? Thinking these words, she felt no longer that unfathomable pain from before but rather an almost triumphant sense of joy, because now it was Willigis who had to wait for her. She said: "I was always under the impression that spite and bitterness stung like thorns, but they feel quite nice, in fact; they're sweet, they're intoxicating! Indeed, I feel as if I'm lying on a great bed of roses! Itze really was a great enchantress after all: I feel as though I have entered an entirely different world, and I can only wonder what's in store for me now."

Suddenly a voice beside her—much sweeter than that of her aunt Itze—said: "Here comes Lady Adventure!"[15] Hearing this, she noticed that there in the arbor into which Itze's chamber had been transformed sat a beautiful maiden, attired in a splendid yet quite demure gown, on her head a crown of brass sequins, just like Erdmuth's own bridal crown, its luster only somewhat faded. The maiden smiled at her and said: "I am Engelke, and tomorrow is my wedding day." But no sooner had she said this than she took on an entirely different countenance, oddly dangerous and at the same time alluring, and the splendor

[15] A well-known muse in medieval German literature.

of her gown took on something quite alien and strange, and suddenly she was wearing no longer a bridal crown atop her head but rather a flickering star. And when Erdmuth looked more closely, she saw sitting in the arbor not the fair Engelke but Lady Adventure, with one hand on a wheel of fortune and in the other a drinking cup, which she raised to Erdmuth: "Good luck, dear Erdmuth, good luck! If one suitor doesn't come, another one will, so good luck, good luck!"

She handed her the cup, but just as Erdmuth was about to lift it, Lady Adventure suddenly vanished as well, and now it was Erdmuth who sat in the arbor with her hand on the wheel of fortune. The wheel began to spin, and it seemed as though the whole world was in motion and everything was tumbling and toppling out of order: what was on the top to the bottom and what was on the bottom to the top, and what had hitherto been good and beautiful took the place of the irksome and the ugly, these things in turn taking the place of the proper and the beautiful—indeed, it seemed to Erdmuth as if the more irksome something was, the more beautiful and enticing it became, and she felt the urge to clap for joy because everything had lost its meaning. That was when she woke up.

There stood Pastor Bake's wife holding a candle and wearing a large apron, just as white and round as the platter of the ruff around her neck; nothing about Frau Bake had changed at all, even though she was here in Itze's chamber. As kindly as ever, with just a hint of urgency, she said: "Erdmuth, it's already eight o'clock—I was unable to come sooner because of the children. I prepared your bridal bed[16] this morning; your bridegroom need only pick

[16] "Bridal bed" refers not to the entire bed but to a removable top layer placed over the lower mattresses.

it up when he sends the bridal carriage for your trousseau. Now I need you to help me finish packing the bridal chest; we're still missing the small linens for your future children. And then we still need to pack the last things of all"—by which she meant the death shrouds and the winding-sheets; it was of course the maiden bride's responsibility to provide these things for herself and her beloved in the bridal chest as well.

Hearing all this, Erdmuth thought it sounded as though everything was as it had been before, and tomorrow was her wedding day; all she had to do was to get out of bed and help Frau Bake pack her bridal chest, and then everything—her whole future life and one day, her death—would be restored to its proper order. Nevertheless, she did not get up; she merely stretched languorously and said, almost confrontationally: "Frau Pastor, are you really not surprised to find me lying here in Itze's chamber?"

Oh no, Frau Bake replied, she'd known right away that Erdmuth would be here; there was nowhere else left, after all—the girls had searched every other room of the house in vain hoping to tell her good-bye! But now it really was time to think about the bridal chest: she wanted to hurry up and start packing it; otherwise Willigis would return from the Rathaus before it was finished, and surely it was not right that he should be kept waiting for his bride.

Erdmuth's blood ran hot: I wanted Willigis to have to wait for me just like I had to wait for him—I wanted everything I experienced in Itze's chamber to come true! She couldn't help but ask Frau Bake if she thought Willigis would be impatient and anxious if he were to come and find that she was not yet there.

Oh no, Frau Bake replied, she didn't think so at all. After all, Willigis was always saying that he'd been waiting for his bride since he was a young boy—why should a little delay make him impatient now?

This sent another hot surge of anger through Erdmuth, and an evil desire came over her. But I do wish to make him impatient, she thought—I want him to be just as anxious and furious as I've been!

And then she was once again overcome with the ecstatic shivers of her dream, only much more enchanting and much more intoxicating, bursting forth from the twilight into the brightness of her clear consciousness, and she could scarcely wait until Frau Bake had left the room and gone down the stairs. Thereupon, she rose from the bed and tiptoed after her—past the half-open door, behind which next to the bridal bed piled up high the pastor's wife was packing the little linens for her future children and the two death shrouds into the bridal chest—and out onto the market square in the now-eerie darkness of the night, lit only by the blazing windows of the Rathaus.

Inside the Rathaus, they had meanwhile given the ambassador an hour's leave so that they might speak privately with Willigis Ahlemann, who was due to return from Wolmirstedt at any moment with confirmation of their rights as a Free Imperial City. These rights, they maintained, had been awarded to them six hundred years ago by the emperor Otto, called the Great, and Emperor Ferdinand[17] could not withhold their freedom any longer now. They were entirely confident in their cause, they had been careful to choose the right hour to make their demand, and they would not suffer the same fate as their forefathers, who had been denied time and time again. For surely His Imperial Majesty knew as well as they did that the city of Magdeburg was the key to everything in this country, and

[17] Ferdinand II, the Habsburg king who ruled over the Holy Roman Empire from 1619 to 1637.

he could not allow it to slip from his grasp at this moment. Nor indeed could it have escaped His Imperial Majesty that the Swede was here on Imperial soil and was everywhere working to fan the flames of rebellion. No indeed, they said in their hearts, His Imperial Majesty cannot afford to let us become a Swedish city; he must pay the price that we demand; he must acknowledge our rights as a Free Imperial City and release us from the control of the archbishopric and all clergy, Catholic as well as Lutheran! The gentlemen of the Council cast a glance over to the side where the associated ministers of the church sat, amid whom Dr. Gilbert loomed menacingly like an angel of judgment. Soon Gilbert would no longer be able to leverage the Edict against the Council and use the mild-mannered Bake to stir up the people, for the Edict was of no concern to a Free Imperial City. The gentlemen of the Council were thus striking down two troublesome forces with a single blow, as it were, ridding themselves of their own combative pastors just as they had rid themselves of the archbishopric—the Free Imperial City of Magdeburg would at last be governed by its secular authorities and not from the troublesome pulpit. Then the Magdeburg Virgin would be mistress over her own house, much as today she dictated the decisions of His Imperial Majesty, in true reflection of her ancient splendor.

Willigis Ahlemann had now returned. They had expected him to announce the news he brought immediately upon entering through the door, and in any event they were sure they would be able to read it on his face at once. But now, as he stood before them—his forehead still glistening with sweat from the hard ride, his sturdy frame still redolent with the smell of the steaming horse—they could discern nothing at all in him; they saw only that the Willigis who had rushed out of the great cathedral this morning pale faced and furious now looked entirely calm and composed once more. One might even conclude that the emperor's yes or no, which they knew he carried, was of no particular concern to him. After a quick greeting, he sat down in his seat and began to unpack his valise. At last—they were dying with impatience—he pulled out a parchment and announced that the Imperial commissioner had given Johann Ahlemann a document explaining how the free status assured by the emperor Otto was understood in Vienna. At that, they almost had to laugh, for they were far better acquainted with their freedom than Vienna was; there was really no need for anyone to read it out to them—all they wanted from Vienna was the confirmation!

In the meantime, Willigis had unfolded the parchment and, in his deep and heavy voice, commenced reading slowly, clearly, and faithfully:

"Regarding the rights granted by the emperor Otto, called the Great, to the city of Magdeburg, or the privileged status conferred upon the same:

"Magdeburg means 'fortress of the maid'; this name dates back to the days of the emperor Otto, called the Great, who granted this city to his royal consort Edith as dower, as one gives a faithful and humble maid to a young woman to be her servant and protector. Thus Emperor Otto entrusted to the city of Magdeburg the most precious thing in his possession, his own heart's sweetest refuge, but in doing so also entrusted her, as it were, with his legacy, the future and the glory of his Empire, and this act of entrustment constitutes the first component of the great privilege conferred upon the city of Magdeburg by the emperor Otto."

Willigis read further:

"And when Queen Edith died, Emperor Otto, called the Great, chose the city of Magdeburg as the final resting place of her mortal remains, placing her, as it were, in the lap of her faithful maid, who now embraced her freely; thus he once again entrusted to the protection of the maid that which was dearest to him, the sweetest refuge of his now-grieving heart, and this act of entrustment constitutes the second component of the great privilege conferred upon the city of Magdeburg by the emperor Otto.

"Now, whenever the emperor Otto, called the Great, grew weary from fighting the savage tribes beyond the Elbe, he would return to Magdeburg and lay his head to rest in the lap of the faithful maid, who freely embraced him as she once embraced his beloved consort, and by resting in her lap as he once did with the one who now lay buried there, he entrusted to her care, as it were, the power and the glory of his Empire. And this habit of returning to the free and faithful maid to rest, as if she herself were his queen, constitutes the third component of the great privilege conferred upon the city of Magdeburg by the emperor Otto."

Willigis again continued:

"And when Emperor Otto, called the Great, was preparing for his own death, he commanded that his body be brought to Magdeburg and laid to rest beside Queen Edith; thus, in dying, he laid himself in the lap of the faithful maid, who freely embraced him as she once embraced his beloved consort; and he remained with her forever, as though, in his desire to rest with her even in death, he was entrusting her with the power and the glory of his Empire in perpetuity. And this final embrace and ultimate act of entrustment constitutes the privileged status and eternal bond, freely and mutually granted, between the city of Magdeburg and the emperor Otto, called the Great."

The ruling gentlemen of Magdeburg sat and listened, completely dumbfounded at what they were hearing. In their hearts, they thought: Ahlemann really must be an Imperial lackey to read us something like this! Surely this can't be an official document—it must be poetry of some sort, a mere flight of fancy! How can he waste our time with this sort of thing at this hour?

They assumed that Willigis would now come to the point at last. Just then, however, he folded up the parchment and fell silent. Still quite dumbfounded, they asked whether he was ever going to tell them what His Imperial Majesty's response to their request was.

Willigis replied that this *was* the response; Johann Ahlemann had received no other. The Imperial commissioner who had handed the document over to him had said that it contained everything they needed to know in Magdeburg. Indifferently, he looked about the room, his gaze falling on the grave-faced Burgomaster Brauns, whose broad, heavy hand suddenly flew up from the tabletop and began to tremble quite strangely, as though it had become the light and delicate hand of a woman. Looking over at the other burgomaster, the haughty Georg Kühlwein, he could see the throbbing blood vessels in his temples. And then he saw the gentlemen of the ecclesiastical ministry putting their heads together and whispering to one another; Dr. Gilbert had a triumphant look on his face, as if he knew that his cause was well on its way to being accomplished, or that all it would take was one little push to get it there. He stood up and exited the room along with the other pastors; only Dr. Bake, silent and distraught, remained seated.

Meanwhile, the gentlemen of the Council burst forth: "But we are the key to everything in this country, are we not? How can His Imperial Majesty deny us the rights that are due to us? We were granted privileges as a free city back in the days of Emperor Otto! Why, it sounds as though His

Imperial Majesty has absolutely no understanding of just how important our great city is! Or does the commissioner mean to suggest that we have misunderstood the privilege granted us by Emperor Otto, and that it refers not to a special right at all but to a special duty, a special loyalty, so to speak, which we owe at any cost? If that's the case, then it's Emperor Otto himself who betrayed us! And how can Johann Ahlemann accept such a decision and announce it to us in the first place? He knows full well the position that the Edict has put us in—has he already forgotten, then, how the people and the pastors deposed him and the rest of the old Council? What does he think about all this? What does he say?" They turned again to Willigis.

Willigis responded that Johann Ahlemann had nothing to say other than what he'd always told the old Council, that they must wait for His Imperial Majesty to come around.

"But that's just it!" they replied. "We cannot wait any longer—the Swedish commandant is right outside the city gates. We've got to choose now whether we're to remain with the Empire or not."

Willigis retorted: "Choose? But we do not have a choice whether we belong to the Empire or not—we *are* in the Empire!"

To which they replied, now somewhat less sure of themselves—for Willigis was suddenly glaring at them in the same threatening manner that so intimidated the ambassador: "What do you mean, we have no choice? Do you mean to say that with Tilly at Halberstadt and Hamelin, he's got us in his hands?"

"What does Tilly have to do with whether we belong to the Empire or not?" Willigis shot back. "You yourselves are always saying that Magdeburg is a Free Imperial City—well, that's a city of the Empire!"

To themselves, they thought: He really does view us the same way he views the ambassador—surely there is no point in keeping him here. Then, aloud, they informed him that they were granting him leave: tonight was his dear bride's maiden's eve, after all, and he mustn't keep her waiting any longer.

Willigis did not get up—it was as if he did not even hear what they said, or as though he were sitting on a lonely rock far out in the roaring sea of their disappointment, and there was no longer any way for them to get through to one another.

In the meantime, however, the hour's leave which they had granted the ambassador had now passed, and as he stuck his smooth face through the door once more, it was immediately apparent that the gentlemen had been disappointed in their expectations. Well, well, he said to himself, it looks as though the ruling gentlemen of the mighty city of Magdeburg have suddenly come down from their high horses—perhaps the "key to everything" has failed after all. Before, they had sat there as though they expected His Imperial Majesty to bestir himself personally to deliver them the rights they fancied were owed to them as a Free Imperial City; now, however, it seemed that His Imperial Majesty intended to keep them waiting. And thus there was no longer any need for the Swedish ambassador to hurry things—now it was time to punish them. He suddenly assumed an entirely different, quite restrained manner: Well, he announced, it appeared that the gentlemen would prefer to be left alone; he did not wish to disturb them any longer, and would instead bid them farewell—though he would have liked to know more about the rights they enjoyed as a Free Imperial City, for of course His Royal Majesty of Sweden would have to confirm them himself when he came to Magdeburg. But he could see that they would rather wait for His Imperial Majesty, and that was quite understandable, what with Tilly at Hamelin and Halberstadt, after all—

They retorted: What did it matter to them that Tilly was at Hamelin and Halberstadt? The elector of Saxony had spent several months pitched up outside their walls before having to withdraw again; the Duke of Friedland had done the same back in '29; even savage Pappenheim had been unable to subjugate Magdeburg—their situation today was no different than it had been many times before. Indeed, they had stood all alone against the emperor and the Empire often enough in the past!

The ambassador, remaining aloof, replied offhandedly that they were quite right: the situation was no different than it had been many times before, except that today the gentlemen would not stand all alone against the emperor and the Empire, but in a powerful alliance with a foreign potentate—

Willigis Ahlemann spoke up, loudly enough for everyone to hear: "With a foreign potentate—but that's not like before; that's . . . that would be—"

The faces of the two burgomasters suddenly went ashen pale, but even the ambassador appeared to be overcome by an abrupt sense of unease. He exclaimed, in a rush of enthusiasm: "Treason against the Empire, gentlemen? Surely the time for that has passed; you can no longer betray the Empire, for it has already been betrayed. Have you not yet heard of the great French Eminence[18] who stands behind His Royal Majesty of Sweden? Truly, you

[18] Cardinal Richelieu was the chief advisor to King Louis XIII of France from 1624 to 1642. Though Catholic, he backed the Protestant Swedes during the Thirty Years' War in order to curtail the power of the Holy Roman Empire.

have nothing to fear from the Empire; this war will smash it to pieces, and soon it will be of no more consequence than the old ghost that haunts your market square down below." He said nothing more, for Willigis had grabbed hold of him and thrown him out the door.

Meanwhile, the gentlemen in the hall were staring at the windows, as if they truly saw a ghost down there. What they saw was not a ghost, however, but the stone statue of an Imperial horseman, appearing as if it had suddenly come to life and were now riding across the market square and straight for the Rathaus, as though it were headed toward its most ancient and ancestral possession.

At once, big, heavy Burgomaster Brauns stammered like a stunned child: "What is to become of our Free Imperial City if the Empire is destroyed? We don't want to end up a city of the foreign Swedes, after all!"

And then haughty Kühlwein, as though suddenly weak in the knees: "We cannot commit treason against the Empire—for what are we, what is our city against the Empire?"

Just then the room was filled with a marvelous splendor, as though the red afterglow of the evening sky had reappeared in the dead of night; it was a rather distant glow, already quite faded. It was a broken and refracted splendor, yet still powerful, indeed overwhelming—it was a splendor they knew quite well, for it was the splendor of the fair Virgin of Magdeburg herself, who, they knew, had always shone brilliantly not with her own splendor but with the reflected splendor of the Empire. It was as though Emperor Otto, called the Great, had truly returned and were now coming to lay his head in the lap of the free and faithful maid as he once did in the lap of Queen Edith, entrusting to her care once more the power and the glory of his Empire. Spellbound, they sat and stared, like men utterly transformed, or indeed reborn, transfixed by an ancient reality once more become their own.

But they were suddenly startled out of this trance: somewhere in the distance, on the dark streets of the city, they heard the sound of many voices singing:

> Though soul and body perish,
> We'll never bow to Rome;
> Our liberty we cherish . . .

For a moment the gentlemen assembled in the Rathaus thought they were witnessing the hundred-year glory of the protesting, rebelling city of Magdeburg mustering and preparing to withdraw, like a company of proud landsknechts[19] leaving a stronghold after it had been forced into submission. "God help us," they said. "Why, it sounds as though our fathers have risen from their graves and are now preparing to abandon us." But then the singing seemed to make a volte-face, as though the defiant little company could not bring itself to depart from this place—the singers turned onto another street, and suddenly the hundred-year glory of the protesting, triumphing city of Magdeburg was surging straight toward the Rathaus. And then it was clear to everyone in the hall that the spirit of their fathers was not abandoning them but turning against them.

At the start of the session, when they were still certain that the emperor would confirm their rights, they had issued an order to all the guards in the city that if the Swedish colonel von Falkenberg came knocking at the gate that night, they were not to let him into the city but were to arrest him. The only soul to turn up that night, however,

[19] German mercenary foot soldiers.

was an unfamiliar boatman who appeared at Saint Ulrich's Gate asking to be let in. The guards in the tower shouted down to him that Magdeburg was asleep at this hour and he would have to wait until morning.

The boatman replied that he could not wait, for he had a job to do in their city that would brook no delay, so would they please hurry up and open the gate to him as soon as possible. Finding it unusual that a simple boatman would speak to them in such an imperious manner, the guards spoke to one another: "You don't suppose that's the Swedish colonel disguised as a boatman, now do you?" For there was talk that the Imperials had put a price on his head and blocked the passes of the Elbe to prevent his passage. So the guards decided they would feel this stranger out. They shouted down to him that they were waiting for a Swedish colonel to appear; perhaps he'd come across this fellow by some chance and could describe him to them? They were not sure what he looked like, for rarely had a Swede ever been seen in Magdeburg.

The boatman replied that from what he'd heard, Colonel von Falkenberg was not a Swede but a German mother's son, born in Herstelle in Westphalia; but he'd left house and hearth behind for the sake of the Gospel; for the Gospel, it was said, along with the liberty[20] of the German Estates, he cherished even more dearly than his ancestral homeland—just like the people of Magdeburg.

The guards shouted: "Hey now! Our Council is loyal to the emperor; we have orders not to let this Colonel von Falkenberg in!"

This seemed to displease the boatman, who retorted that even if the Council were loyal to the emperor, he could tell them all sorts of things that they really needed to know.

[20] "Liberty" in this context refers to the liberty of the Imperial Estates as political units.

The guards spoke quietly to one other: "That's got to be the colonel. We should arrest him and report to the Council." They shouted to the boatman that he could make his report to them, that they would come down now to hear him out.

Upon opening the gate, they saw standing before them a handsome man with a severe and at the same time rather dashing countenance, stern as death and resolute as a direct order. He eyed the guards up and down from under his shabby boatman's hat, ostentatiously pushed aside the one nearest him, and said: "As for Colonel von Falkenberg of Sweden, I can report that by this time tomorrow, everyone in Magdeburg will know what he looks like." With that, he unhurriedly passed them by and disappeared onto the nearest street.

The guards looked after him in astonishment, each of them thinking he should run after him and arrest him. But no one moved from his place.

Finally, one of them said: "The stranger said that Falkenberg was a German, a native of Herstelle in Westphalia, but that man looked as though he had no native land at all." Then the second one said: "He also said something about a mother's son, but I cannot imagine such a fellow even having a mother, much less a wife and child." Then the third: "And he also said that Falkenberg left behind house and hearth for the sake of the Gospel, but he looked like he'd never bowed his head in all his life."

Thus they all agreed with one another that the stranger could not have been Colonel von Falkenberg, climbed back up to their tower, and went to sleep.

The stranger, meanwhile, went deeper and deeper into the city, which rose up before him in the vast expanse of the night sky: in the darkness, the proud lines of the towers and walls appeared bold and massive, as though any foe who came here would be repulsed much more defiantly by night than by day. He continued walking at the same unhurried pace, not like a man whom the guards had just tried to stop from entering the city gates and who believed he might be pursued, but confidently and undauntedly—almost, in fact, as though he were making a silent but solemn official entry into the city. His steps echoed unmuffled through the deserted streets; one might have imagined he did not think himself alone in this strange city but believed there followed him many others who could not be seen—indeed, that he was being followed by an entire army. And that was how the stranger felt too. He said to himself: Now I take thee into my possession, O lofty city of Magdeburg! Now I shall lead the fair Virgin of Magdeburg into the arms of my master, and if I should die in this endeavor, then I do not fear my death—but neither do I fear thy death, proud maiden! Saying this, he was struck by a strange sensation, as though all of a sudden this great, magnificent city had become pleasantly small and cozy, like one of the quaint little rooms in his distant childhood home. All at once he saw not the bold, massive lines of the high walls and towers but all the small, dark windows behind which little children now breathed peacefully, and man and wife lay together lovingly in their beds. He said to himself: Just a moment ago I was preparing myself to die, yet now all of a sudden I feel the desire to sink the roots of my life deep into the soil of this city, to once more have a place to call home, to be like other men, with wife and child and hearth of my own! Dost thou tempt me with life, fair Virgin of Magdeburg, knowing that I have come here prepared to die? That would be an enormous mistake, for it is not for thee that I am to die, but for the Gospel and for German liberty. But do come and try!

With these last words, he reached the end of the street and turned onto another, whereupon he literally recoiled in surprise, for he actually saw, coming toward him, a beautiful young maiden! She was walking all alone down the completely deserted street—he could clearly make out the contours of her figure, lusty and sweet like those of the fair maiden in the city's coat of arms; it was a perfect likeness but for the lack of an outstretched wreath in this maiden's hand. The stranger found it extremely odd that the first person whom he should meet in the slumbering city this night should be this young maiden, and upon seeing her, he stopped dead in his tracks and stared at her as if she were an apparition.

Meanwhile, the maiden had come within a few steps of him. Her face—it was now illuminated by the light of a small lantern—was a bit too wide and too full when seen up close, but at the same time beautiful and very proud; indeed, there was something almost haughty and defiant about it; the message it sent was quite clear: See here, you lowly foreign boatman, don't think you can just stand here and stare at me because I'm out here alone on the street at night while the city sleeps! I am a lady of Magdeburg; I have my reasons for being here, and they are none of your concern! And to make this even clearer, at the exact moment she was about to pass him, she gathered her long cloak to herself in a graceful, grandiose flourish, lest it brush against the sordid-looking boatman.

But then the boatman stepped aside himself and gave her a deep, chivalrous bow. And now it was the maiden's turn to gaze at the stranger in utter amazement. For it was suddenly as though she saw, slipping out from under the shabby boatman's garb, a genteel, noble cavalier, who looked at her as if he'd been waiting for her there in the lonely stillness of the night, and as if she, though quite unaware of where she was actually headed, had arrived at some secret rendezvous. And then he spoke, as though it were completely natural that they should meet one another here—and yet there was nothing natural about it at all, it was most peculiar indeed: "Dear maiden, I am grateful that you have come this way. Would you do a stranger, who would otherwise become lost in your city, the kindness of guiding him to your Rathaus?" He bowed to her once more, as though already thanking her for granting his request, but at the same time he looked at her with the look of a man who need not ask or thank at all but can demand and seize what he pleases.

Troubled, and thus quite haughtily, she spoke: "What business do you have at our Rathaus at this hour? What right have you to be there?" She was under the impression that he wished only to follow her.

To which he replied, somewhat derisively, as if to confirm her in her childishly false impression: "And what right has the pretty young maiden to be walking here alone and without protection by night?" His face made his meaning clear: she had no such right and must therefore put up with being taken into custody for her own protection.

Furious, she replied: "What do you think you are doing, and who are you, really?" But at that moment the genteel cavalier whom she thought she had discerned before slipped out from under the shabby boatman's doublet once more and now stood before her quite unmistakably, his presence commanding and confident, as though he believed he was taking into his custody not just a proud young maiden but the entire city of Magdeburg. And then she realized that there was but one possible answer to her question: "Are you the Swedish colonel, von Falkenberg?" she asked hastily.

To which he retorted, a faint smile on his lips: "Are you the Virgin of Magdeburg?" And now he was really and truly looking at her, such that she felt he meant to take possession of her body and soul, and if she led him through the city now, it would in reality be he who led her wherever he wished, toward an oppressively unknown destination that beckoned as mysteriously and alluringly as the fair Engelke transformed into Lady Adventure. And suddenly she felt all her pride and her splendor faltering and fading, as it were, and her face changed color, as though caught in the reflected glow of a distant conflagration, such that the stranger's eyes darted about like a falcon's[21] to see whether the guards might indeed be hurrying after him with their torches after all. But there were no torches blazing, only the face of the young maiden.

And at that moment she said, "Come, then, I shall lead you to our Rathaus."

As they stepped out onto the market square, there hung a large flickering star above the city of Magdeburg, like the one Erdmuth had seen in her dream atop the head of Lady Adventure. And the whole square, which before had been enveloped by the still, white light of the moon like the veil of a gentle woman, now appeared blackened with people, as though here, too, the whole world were shifting about as it had behind the door of Itze's little chamber: what was on the top to the bottom, and what was on the bottom to the top. And indeed, to the gentlemen in the Council Chamber above, it seemed as though time were rushing backward all of a sudden, and they themselves were now the old Imperial Council that the people were again coming to topple, just as they had nine months ago.

When the crowd first entered the hall, however, the situation did not seem all that alarming; it was merely like when the fair, blond river Elbe—the very life-stream of the city of Magdeburg—would overflow its banks a bit: the people

[21] The German name Falkenberg means "falcon mountain".

who came in were all good, loyal folk, men and women whose names, ancestry, and occupations were well known to the Council, and all of them with such honest faces, clearly indicating that they'd left their evening beer tables and cozy bedchambers only reluctantly—just as the waters of the Elbe change color but a little when they first begin to overtop the banks, as though unwillingly. But that's when things suddenly do turn dangerous! For a river is home not only to the gentle, docile waters near the top but also to the powers and forces that proliferate in its depths: the wild river sprites and water faeries, similar to man in appearance but in reality quite different from him—ever poised to devour him and his work.

The gentlemen had hurriedly agreed that if the river did break in, the young councillor Otto Guericke would be the one to confront it—he was, after all, chief engineer of Magdeburg's fortifications and defensive works, before which even the waters of the Elbe, should they prevail, would halt. Guericke stood on the raised windowsill as though he were standing on the city's high ramparts, his hair moving slightly in the light breeze coming through the window behind him (as in the handsome portrait painted of him). From there, his clear, clever face was visible to all, eminent and dignified like the face of a scholar, and brown from the sun out on the city ramparts like that of a soldier. The crowd was still somewhat abashed at their own boldness, so Guericke began to joke with them as he had done earlier with his little cousin Anna, when she sought to dance with him at the wrong time—for when speaking to the people, one had to speak as one did with women or children. He said they could see for themselves that they were mistaken in coming here, and at this hour—it was almost midnight, he reminded them, and now it was time for everyone, councillors and guests alike, to go home and go to bed.

But then someone shouted back, still somewhat timidly: "It is not we who are mistaken, but the gentlemen of the Council, if they think we will allow them to betray the Word of God and the Gospel!"

To which Guericke, again speaking as he had to his little cousin Anna when she sought to dance with him at the wrong time, replied: "But nobody is talking about the Gospel here, my dear people—you are once again mistaken. This is the Rathaus: here we are concerned with worldly matters, with life and property, with the governance and the security of the city, with His Imperial Majesty and the Empire."

Another voice, already noticeably bolder: "But the Empire is no worldly matter! We're told it's a 'holy, catholic' thing, are we not?"

And then another: "And His Imperial Majesty is no worldly power either but a Roman and a Papist one!"

And then a third: "And you men at the Rathaus had better be concerned with the Gospel—for what are property and security compared to the Word of God? What is life compared to heavenly bliss? Surely no one here wants to spend eternity in hell!"

Guericke, still speaking as he had to his little cousin: "But, my dear people, don't you see that you're confusing matters? When we say 'worldly', you say 'catholic'; when we say 'politics', you say 'Gospel'—just let things remain in their proper order!"

To which they replied: "But it is the Gospel we are talking about, not politics. We're talking about the accord with His Swedish Majesty—and Swedish means Protestant!"

Then another: "It is not we but you who are confusing matters! What about the Edict? Is it a matter of politics, and not the Gospel, if we are to become a Catholic archbishopric once more, then?" Guericke felt as though he'd suddenly become caught in a whirlpool; in place of the matters that had just now occupied the Council—the power and the glory of the Empire—there was now only the Gospel in peril. In his heart, he wondered: Is there a demon on the loose in the fatherland of the German nation? Is that why no one sees just how mixed up the order of things has become? For truly, no one sees it! He began to feel as though he were staring into the face of an inescapable calamity. Shaken, he called out: "But, people, would you then have our dear native city perish on account of the Edict? Holy Scripture, after all, says that we are to subject ourselves even to an unjust master—you have to wait for His Imperial Majesty to come around!"

"Wait? When the Gospel and pure doctrine are in peril? Do you expect the Virgin of Magdeburg to fall asleep with her lamp like one of the foolish virgins? Pastor Bake preached something very different to us this morning at the cathedral—otherwise we wouldn't have come here at all! Do the men of our government think they can make us accept a foolish virgin in place of a wise one?" The fair, blond waters of the Elbe began to roar.

Guericke wanted to say that if the clergy exchanged a wise one for a foolish one, then yes. But he felt that he would then be reversing the order of things himself. Calmly and cleverly, he asked: "Is there no one here from the ecclesiastical ministry who can establish whether Holy Scripture says that we are to be subject even to an unjust master?" None of the pastors remained in the hall save for Bake, who was still sitting quietly and distraught in the same place where he had sat hours ago with Dr. Gilbert, not even realizing that the others had long since left to join the gathering storm of the crowd. That crowd now surrounded Bake on all sides, shouting at him to rebuke the deluded authorities and speak to them as he'd done this morning in the great cathedral! Amid the consternation brought on by the rush of the crowd, Bake had risen from his seat and stood up rather awkwardly, his pious, introspective face now bearing a look of deadly terror; for there really was nothing from now until the end of days that he could say to the authorities here in the Rathaus but that Holy Scripture says we are to subject ourselves even to an unjust master. But before he could utter a single word, there was a tremendous shouting and cheering down in the market square, such that everyone inside the Rathaus fell silent.

Suddenly Otto Guericke, who had been leaning out the window, turned back to the hall and said, his voice trembling slightly, yet remarkably clear: "Dr. Bake, your answer comes too late—the time for decision is over."

"What decision are you talking about? What is over?" they shouted.

"The maiden's eve of the city of Magdeburg," Guericke replied. On the stairs, someone was already crying: "The Swedish commandant is outside the Rathaus—" The last words were swallowed up by uproarious singing as the crowd in the market square broke out in their song of resistance. And now the fair, blond waters of the Elbe really did wash over all its banks, sweeping everyone in the Council Chamber down the stairs.

No one was left in the hall save Dr. Bake, who once again did not know which way he should go. And so he stood alone beneath the spent candles in the deserted hall, surrounded by a vague twilight like the dim light outside the great cathedral this morning, although—and this he felt clearly—it was he who had that very day been voice and guide to the people singing and rejoicing down there; it was his word that had decided everything. Indeed, he was still their voice and their guide, and even as he stood there in the empty Council Chamber, he was at the same time marching at the head of the rebelling, triumphing city of Magdeburg across the roaring market square. This realization, however, filled him not with cheerful confidence and high spirits but with a peculiar sense of trepidation. Quickly, as though he were rushing off with the others, he turned again to Christ, and he felt that at the same moment Christ was turning to him and looking at him—from a great, great distance—with a look of unfathomable pain. It was like this morning beneath the cross in the great cathedral: this cross was the only thing he could make out. Confused and frightened, for he had to keep pace with the relentlessly rebelling and triumphing people he was leading, he spoke: "Lord, surely it cannot be that we are mistaken, but if we nevertheless go astray, even in our error let us never fall entirely from Thy grace."

He was thus granted the certainty of unlosable grace—but it was the only thing of which he was certain.

Part II

The Dance of Honor

When Willigis Ahlemann entered the town of Hamelin and inquired where he might find the headquarters of the generalissimo, the soldiers—the place was swarming with them—shouted to him: "Our Father Tilly is staying at the Wedding House on the market square!" At the mention of the Wedding House, Willigis felt a curious, stabbing pain in his heart, and he thought to himself: I, too, could be staying at a wedding house today; I could be taking my dear bride home to be my wife, and instead I'm here in a strange city, having to ride in this storm! He would have preferred to turn back, but Johann Ahlemann had sent him to Hamelin to report to the Imperial generalissimo on recent developments in Magdeburg and to ask that his beloved native city be granted a stay of execution; this was not a mission he could afford to forsake. He thus rode on to the market square. Before him stood the famed Wedding House of Hamelin, the sumptuous lines of its three proud gables soaring up into the evening sky, as though the architect had sought to adorn the elegant structure with a magnificent triple crown. And no sooner had Willigis arrived at the house than there emerged from the door a column of servants bearing torches, illuminating the deputations from the regiments as they marched with their flags into the generalissimo's residence. A fierce wind, indeed almost a gale, blew across the darkened market square and caused the torches to flare up brightly as Willigis dismounted his horse. He again felt a stabbing pain in his heart, as he thought to himself: If I were now in Magdeburg at my own wedding house, it would almost be time for the dance of honor to begin, and the guests would be lining up with their torches too. Yet I'm not in Magdeburg, but in a strange city, and I cannot even think about my dear bride. For here in Hamelin there are none but men, and more men besides—one might imagine there was not a single woman left on the face of the earth. Who could think about the dance of honor with his bride in this place?

In the meantime, however, as the regimental deputations were passing Willigis and entering the house, they had begun to sing a dance tune; only, in the harsh throats of this band of soldiery, it sounded like a war song. Willigis could make out the words:

> The old and prickly maid the chance
> The Emp'ror did deny to dance;
> She dances with his men tonight,
> Oh, how it serves the proud girl right!

As the men sang, the flags they carried swished and swayed like a vast forest made up of naught but the victorious banners of Empire and League.[1] At the head of the procession were the handsome white-and-blue Bavarian flags emblazoned with the emblem of the Jesuits—they billowed like swollen sails, they surged as if they were filled with joyful impetuousness, they rolled like waves, they crackled like cannon fire, they quite literally strained against the hands of their bearers, as though struggling to break free and hurl themselves into the storm. Willigis noticed that the bearers could scarcely hold on to them; they stopped singing and began talking to the flags. One man was shouting at his: "Calm down, old girl, calm down! Yes, it's time again, but you've got to attend to Father Tilly first. Then you can fly on to victory when we march on Magdeburg!"

[1] The Catholic League, a military alliance of Catholic powers in Germany, formed in 1609 and led by the Duke of Bavaria, Maximilian I.

This startled Willigis; he simply could not fathom that people here were already talking about marching on Magdeburg. After all, Johann Ahlemann had sent him to Hamelin as soon as Willigis had told him of Falkenberg's arrival so that he could be the first to report it to General Tilly; yet it now sounded as though they'd already heard the news from someone else.

In the meantime, the flags had all proceeded into the generalissimo's house, and the door was now clear. Willigis walked in, handed his credentials from Johann Ahlemann to an orderly, and was admitted to the antechamber. Inside were several Imperial and League officers waiting to greet General Tilly, who had returned the previous evening from the Diet[2] of the prince-electors in Regensburg. Since then, it was said, he had been laboring day and night over the great maps in his chamber and had still not finalized his war plan.

The officers were impatient, but at the same time cheerful and in good spirits, particularly those of the League, who were filled with pride because their own General Tilly had at Regensburg been given supreme command of the entire Imperial army in place of the dismissed Duke of Friedland. They teased the Imperial officers: "Hope you fellows are ready to cross yourselves nicely before the banquet and go to Mass in the morning! The Duke of Friedland's not in charge anymore; His Excellency Tilly's going to make this a godly war again!" "*Cuius regio, eius religio!*" the Imperials replied; then, laughing: "Well, the war is certainly worth a Mass!" It seemed to Willigis as though the roaring outside filled them all with the same joyful impetuousness that moments ago had animated the

[2] Diet of Regensburg, July 30, 1630, where the prince-electors of the Holy Roman Empire replaced Generalissimo Wallenstein with Count Tilly.

flags. Each time one of the brief, violent blasts howled up the chimney, they threw one another triumphant looks and shouted boisterously: "He'll come through, you'll see, he'll come through—thank God, it's finally happening!" What they meant by this, Willigis did not know.

He stood somewhat apart from the others; no one paid him any attention. Indeed, no one even noticed him, for as his mouth kept silent, so, too, did his appearance, as it were. He had not removed his wind-battered raincoat since yesterday morning, and they probably took him for some simple courier. It was just as well for him that no one spoke to him, for although he had previously thought he would be unable to think of his bride here in Hamelin, he was in fact thinking of her constantly; it was as though he felt the need to shield himself from the thought that there was no one else on earth but soldiery. In his heart, he said: What does it matter that here in Hamelin there seems to be none but men? There is only one woman on earth as far as I am concerned anyway, and she shall never vanish from my sight. I carry her in my heart, for she is my bride after all, and I her bridegroom.

As he stood there speaking to himself, the door flew open violently, as though the tempest outside had suddenly burst into the room. It was not the storm that entered, however, but a young marshal, accompanied by the cavalierish music of spurs like the jangling of a distant cavalry squadron. In a bright voice—indeed, it was almost a bit too high—he shouted: "Gentlemen, I have news from Magdeburg! The rumors that were brought to us this morning are all true: Falkenberg is in the city!"

The officers cheered: "So the great Lady of Magdeburg has finally shown her true colors! We were afraid she might yet back down! Heaven be praised that she's finally thrown off her mask—now His Excellency can get his hands on her!"

The cavalierish music at the young marshal's feet clinked and jangled as though the distant cavalry squadron were mounting their attack. "Yes, let's hope His Excellency can get his hands on her before she manages to seduce the Saxon and the Brandenburger—that's all the Swede is waiting for! Gentlemen, why didn't the Duke of Friedland let me take the city back in '29? The Swede wouldn't be giving us so much trouble today, I tell you! Indeed, it looks to me as if Falkenberg has snatched the bride from the arms of our Imperial Lord just as he did with the bride of that young Ahlemann fellow—they say she's the one who led Falkenberg into the city by night." They crowded the marshal on all sides, eyes gleaming: "Upon my soul! There was a woman in the mix too? Who is this Ahlemann fellow, and what's this about his bride?"

"What do you think happened?" the marshal retorted dismissively. "The maiden went after a counterfeit bridegroom in place of her rightful one, just like her noble native city!"

Willigis felt as though someone had struck him in the face with a horsewhip; for the maid they spoke of was in fact his own dear bride, of whom he had just been thinking so fondly. Indeed, he said to himself, I'm quite sure I saw her myself amid the turmoil in the market square after I threw the ambassador down the stairs. But then I left the Rathaus to go and meet her for her maiden's eve—I was almost there when the people began cheering for Falkenberg. Why she was walking beside him amid the turmoil, I do not know; there was no time to ask her, after all, for I had to jump back on my horse right away and report to Johann Ahlemann that Falkenberg was in the city. Then he thought, coolly: But there was no need for me to ask her either; for she has been like a dear sister to me since childhood, and she is destined to be my wedded wife more certainly than my family's property and my own inheritance are to be mine; there is surely no need to ask if she does something strange! He began to ponder—these things always took time for Willigis—whether he ought to come to his bride's defense or not.

At that moment, however, the door flew open once more, and the orderly to whom Willigis had previously handed over his credentials shouted into the antechamber: "His Excellency summons Herr Willigis Ahlemann of Magdeburg!"

At the name of Willigis Ahlemann, all the officers turned their gaze toward the supposed courier. The young marshal, however, his face beet red, stepped quickly toward Willigis and said, in a chivalrous tone: "Herr Ahlemann, I did not recognize the nephew of our friend from Wolmirstedt; otherwise I would have chosen my words differently. My name is Pappenheim, and if I have been falsely informed, then to an Imperial-minded man of Magdeburg I am willing to make satisfaction." The cavalierish music of his spurs clinked and jangled as though the distant cavalry squadron had set out over an abyss.

Willigis understood that the celebrated marshal was treating him with honor and distinction in front of everyone present. So he replied politely—for he remained quite calm: "Satisfaction from my lord marshal? If my lord were indeed correctly informed, then only Falkenberg could give me satisfaction; nevertheless—" He was about to say: "My lord marshal has not been correctly informed," but the marshal was already shouting: "So then, Herr Ahlemann, between us there shall be not enmity but friendship and brotherhood! That makes me glad! No one save Falkenberg can give me satisfaction either. And by God, he shall give satisfaction: to you for your bride, and to me for your city!" He looked at Willigis, aglow with violent impetuosity, like a youthful god of war.

At this, the Magdeburger suddenly felt the same strangely oppressive sense of unease that he had felt before on seeing the vast horde of soldiery, when he'd thought there must indeed be only men left on earth. He felt that perhaps his heart, too, might one day be like the town of Hamelin, that on looking into the face of this bellicose young marshal he was looking into his own future, and it would truly be as the marshal had said: between them, brotherhood and a shared destiny. Only he had no time to dwell on these thoughts now, for he had to go with the orderly officer to see the generalissimo.

He passed the flags once more—they were now handsomely arrayed against the walls of a sumptuous meeting hall, wherein a table had been set, at which His Excellency Tilly would soon dine with his officers in celebration of his return. Inside His Excellency's chamber, however, there stood but a single flag; it could be none other than the famous personal standard of the generalissimo himself. The flag bore an image of the Virgin Mary; Willigis had heard it said that before every battle he fought, the Count of Tilly would hold a secret council of war with this Madonna. General Tilly himself sat bent over a table covered with charts and maps; they lay spread out before him like the borders of the Empire laid bare: first, the map of Sweden, who had already advanced deep into Pomerania; next to it the maps of Poland, Holland, and Denmark, all of whom had made secret agreements with His Swedish Majesty; all the way at the bottom was the map of Mantua, where Imperial troops were fighting over the succession; at the very top, the map of France, whose intentions were still unknown. It looked as though Generalissimo Tilly were trying to come up with a war plan against half the world! In the middle, however, lay the map of Germany and rebellious Magdeburg; one could almost see the red flames of insurrection already flickering toward the Electorates of Saxony and Brandenburg.

There was no one else in the room with His Excellency Tilly save for a young Jesuit priest, who stood beside the worktable like His Excellency's shadow, his figure slender and dark, his face animated by an intense passion that was nevertheless muted and restrained, appearing rather like a low-burning candle. When Willigis hailed His Excellency, the priest took a few steps back and stood silently against the window, as though he were the generalissimo's bodyguard.

Thus the young Protestant from Lower Saxony stood before the old Excellency of Wallonia, called Father Tilly by the common soldiery but known as His Catholic Excellency among the officers, so as to distinguish him from His Excellency the Duke of Friedland—of whom no one knew whether he was Catholic or believed only in his stars. His Excellency did not look grim or terrifying, as people in Magdeburg imagined when they thought of Johann Tserclaes, Count of Tilly. Nor did he look monkishly somber or scheming, as they imagined someone educated by the Jesuits would look; yet he did not look like the invincible commander and almighty generalissimo either; rather, he looked like an entirely ordinary old soldier, his face plain and honest, at the same time sober and rather austere, like a true lifelong bachelor. Only in his handsome, lonely eyes (so Willigis thought) was there anything "Catholic" about His Catholic Excellency; looking at them, Willigis could well imagine him holding a council of war with the Madonna on his personal standard.

Willigis gave his report on what had transpired in Magdeburg, his words cumbersome and at times halting, for like Willigis himself, His Excellency genuinely knew how to keep silent. He did not interrupt Willigis, he did not press him when he faltered, he did not show any surprise—it was as though he was hearing nothing that he did not already expect. When Willigis finished speaking, His Excellency remarked that this was probably bound to happen once the old Council that was loyal to the emperor had been deposed. He then asked whether Johann Ahlemann had anything else to say to him, so Willigis put forth his uncle's request that the city be granted a stay of execution. The new Council, too, he said, really did wish to remain obedient to His Imperial Majesty, only they had been overpowered by the people on account of the Edict. If His Excellency would grant them some time, they might be able to regain control over the people.

His Excellency suddenly showed great interest: Did Willigis get the impression that the Council itself was willing to accept the Edict and return the archbishopric to the Catholics, then?

Willigis looked confused—he had always thought that where the Edict was concerned, they could patiently wait for the emperor to come around, but now His Excellency himself spoke as though His Imperial Majesty could not wait. He said, hesitantly: "No, the Council is surely not prepared to do that. The archbishopric is Lutheran, after all; it cannot be put under a Catholic archbishop." Then, confidently: "But we can still be part of the Empire!"

His Excellency, likewise hesitantly: "What do you mean, Herr Ahlemann, 'we can still be part of the Empire'?"

Willigis, innocently: "I mean that if matters of faith are not interfered with, we can all work together to drive the Swede out of the Empire."

His Excellency was silent. Willigis thought he looked as though the Edict itself were causing him heart palpitations. But then, in a terse military manner, he said, "The archbishopric of Magdeburg was still Catholic at the time of the

Peace of Passau. His Imperial Majesty wishes to restore to the Holy Church her property—such is only proper."

Willigis looked at His Excellency with undisguised amazement. How can His Excellency speak of "proper" here? he thought. Magdeburg is not a Free Imperial City, so that our sovereign would be the Catholic archbishop! Doesn't His Excellency know that this archbishop would then be able to use the principle of *cuius regio, eius religio* against us? He then saw that His Excellency was well aware of this; for he looked into the honest face of old Tilly, who could neither disguise nor conceal his own pious Catholic wishes—indeed, to him they were what the war was all about! So there they stood facing each other, two taciturn men who each understood the other, and two honest men who had each recognized the other as such. And suddenly the young Low Saxon felt as though he had reached the edge of an unseen abyss and could now go no further. Shaken, he called out: "The Magdeburg City Council have been willing to work with His Imperial Majesty, but His Imperial Majesty is not willing to work with Magdeburg! His Imperial Majesty doesn't understand his Protestant Estates—His Imperial Majesty understands only his Catholic Estates!" He looked at His Excellency like a plaintive deer finding itself entangled in a hunter's snare.

His Excellency had laid eyes on many people in his long life, and the soldiery were fond of saying: "Like our Father in heaven, Father Tilly knows every man's thoughts from afar." His Excellency saw that the heart of this Low Saxon revolted not with the defiance of rebellious Magdeburg but with a pain that was both deep and loyal; at the same time it was also an utterly hopeless and inescapable pain, and it touched His Excellency's old, honest heart ever so strangely. No, what it touched was the old, ever-victorious sword at his side; he thought he could hear it bouncing and clinking with joy. For the sword was so eager for another victory, as was its wont—but it could scarcely hope to achieve victory, having half the world as enemies! His Excellency glanced again at his charts and maps, and for a moment it seemed to him as though it were not the young Magdeburger who spoke but the generalissimo within him, with the sudden desire to separate himself from His Catholic Excellency and issue the only command that could now be issued if he hoped to save the Empire in this hour of utmost peril. In his sober military mind, His Excellency thought: Yes, together we could drive the Swede out of the Empire and sweep the borders clean! But then, as though he were reining in with his sinewy fist a strange, young horse that was trying to run off with him (how did he ever get on it in the first place?), he reminded himself: Surely now it's more than a matter of simply driving the Swede out of the Empire! His Imperial Majesty cannot renounce the Edict—His Imperial Majesty is waging war for the restoration of the Holy Faith, after all! Then His Imperial Majesty will lose the war, the generalissimo within him answered; His Imperial Majesty can be victorious only if he recognizes who his enemy is. His Excellency recalled his recent experience at Regensburg. The cunning diplomats had probably fancied that an old general understood only his soldier's craft and nothing more. But when an old general hears that the prince-electors are preparing to reduce the size of the emperor's army while the enemy is already on Imperial soil, then he can see what's really going on: an army must never be reduced in size; it must always be expanded. Yes, His Excellency had seen through the treachery at Regensburg! In his mind's eye he suddenly saw before him once more the small golden box that the French ambassador had passed around at his table like an amulet. The round box had been decorated with the portrait of a great cardinal, dressed in the scarlet of the Holy Catholic Church; behind the narrow, wraithlike face—it became almost dangerously pointed near the chin—His Excellency had recognized the city of La Rochelle, where Cardinal Richelieu had put down the Huguenot heresy. His Excellency remembered thinking he could actually hear the godly Catholic cannons thundering against the heretic towers. But when he looked down at the image again, listening reverently, he suddenly noticed that the scarlet of the great French Eminence had grown paler and paler, such that he could no longer recognize the Scarlet Eminence of the Holy Catholic Church at all; instead, he perceived the éminence grise in his Capuchin habit: the scheming face he now saw was that of Père Joseph, sly and crafty in matters temporal, whom Cardinal Richelieu had sent to Regensburg in order to strengthen the backbones of the prince-electors against His Imperial Majesty and encourage them to carry through with the reduction of the Imperial army. And now in the background, where the vanquished Huguenot city of La Rochelle had just been, there suddenly appeared rebellious Magdeburg, to whose aid Catholic France now sought to hasten under the auspices of a heretic king. And thus for a moment His Excellency Tilly felt as though he could hear hell laughing at him all the way from Regensburg. For the war had changed at Regensburg—and now His Catholic Excellency had to change. He again pulled back on the reins of the strange, young horse before thinking to himself: Have I, in fighting these heretics, myself been touched by heresy, such that I believe it possible to save the Empire apart from the Holy Catholic Faith, as though these might command two separate courses of action? No, the Empire and the Holy Catholic Faith are in fact one! Turning to Willigis, he said firmly, but without acrimony: "Herr Ahlemann, if the Magdeburg City Council truly wish to remain part of the Empire, then they must once again submit themselves to the emperor's authority. They must chasten the people and the clergy, expel the administrator and Falkenberg from the city, and accept the Edict, or I will have to force them to do so. His Imperial Majesty has entrusted me with executing his will, and His Imperial Majesty commands my obedience, as he does yours!" His Excellency waved his dismissal.

Willigis did not notice this gesture, nor did he leave. Stunned and bewildered, he said: "But we cannot possibly accept the Edict! If His Imperial Majesty does not renounce the Edict, then no Protestant can be loyal to the Empire!"

His Excellency kept silent, for that was precisely the trouble, that Protestants could not be loyal to the Empire! Meanwhile, Willigis continued: "For then they would be beholden to two separate commands; it would mean having to decide between the Empire and the Faith! Then the zealot pastors would be right—then we would have to become rebels; then His Imperial Majesty himself would be driving us into the arms of the Swede ..." Utterly terrified (for now his mission on behalf of his dear native city was surely on the brink of failure), he continued: "And then His Excellency would have to go through with the execution; there would be no point in postponing it, for we should then have no choice but to remain rebels! His Excellency will postpone the execution, however—for there cannot be two separate commands!"

His Excellency looked on, perplexed. It was his very own plight, seen from the other side, that this tall, childlike fellow was expressing with such frankness: either the

Empire or the Faith. His Excellency had the distinct impression that he and this young heretic were entangled together in the same impenetrable thicket.

Suddenly Willigis spoke, sounding like someone desperately trying to escape from an excruciating nightmare: "No, it is not possible for faith to command one thing and the Empire to command another; for indeed a faith that drives one to rebellion is not faith at all, is it? Surely faith cannot rely on subversion and foreign kings—faith cannot rely on anything but God alone!"

His Excellency again kept silent; for the faith that this young heretic spoke of was, after all, an errant faith; it could not rely on God, it could not possibly have God's protection—such a faith led inevitably to rebellion! To rely on God alone, that was something that only the Holy Catholic Faith could presume to do—His Excellency suddenly felt a sense of unexpected danger.

Then, as though he were happily reading His Catholic Excellency's thoughts, the young heretic said: "Could not Your Excellency ask His Imperial Majesty to drop the Edict and likewise put his faith in the hands of God alone?"

His Excellency literally recoiled—this tall, childlike fellow had seized the reins of the strange horse that had been trying to run off with him the whole time! He gave Willigis a cool glance. Willigis stood there with his honest, loyal face, looking like someone with whom he had just managed to escape an impenetrable thicket—it was impossible to look at him without feeling well disposed toward him. And suddenly, the Catholic Excellency and the generalissimo, after having remained separate from each other the whole time, were united as one, becoming old Father Tilly once again—more short-tempered than the other two, but also kinder. "Herr Ahlemann," he said, "our conversation is over. You yourself have done all you could, and you have served His Imperial Majesty well—that will have to suffice for now. I thank you for your report. You shall be my guest at dinner this evening and are welcome to stay the night."

Then His Excellency beckoned to the young priest, who was still standing like a sentry at the window, to escort Willigis out.

Now alone, His Excellency began to pace up and down the room, his long strides revealing just how stiff his old knees had become. His Excellency walked as though the storm outside had blown a foot of invisible snow into the chamber and he was now obliged to fight his way through it; for while he had dismissed the young Magdeburger, his own distress had remained.

A valet came in and brought him the old Spanish courtly garb His Excellency had worn years before at the prince-elector's table in Munich; apparently this garment was to suffice for as long as His Excellency lived. The valet announced that the officers' banquet would begin in half an hour and His Excellency would need to change. But when this was done and the valet had moved the armchair back into place so that His Excellency might rest for a moment—sitting upright, as old soldiers in the field are accustomed to resting—he discontentedly pushed the armchair aside and began to pace up and down the room once more, as though he had to reach a certain destination before dinner began. For the banquet could last a long time; the officers never knew how to bring such occasions to an end, so he had to anticipate sitting at the table all night until it was time to attend the council of war in the morning. Like all old men of a sober disposition, His Excellency was both temperate and able to hold his drink, but his generals—young and ambitious gentlemen who longed for victories to call their own—did let the wine go to their heads on occasion. Thus, His Excellency had to know exactly what he wanted; he had to have already held a council of war before they held their council of war.

There was now no one in the room with His Excellency save for his victorious old standard emblazoned with the image of the Blessed Virgin Mary, known among the soldiery as the Madonna of Victory. The image showed her standing above her famous Chapel of Grace at Altötting, where His Catholic Excellency had recently visited her from Regensburg to seek her blessing for the coming war. A gaping hole opened in the blue silk beside the Most Blessed Virgin's face, where the flag had been pierced by a ball at Wimpfen. And at her feet another hole yawned, acquired at the battle near Lutter am Barenberge; this one was so big that it looked as though the Most Blessed Virgin had walked out over an abyss that day. And then there was a third hole right at the top of her head, which the flag had received at Stadtlohn; for some time during that battle, it had seemed as though the sky above the Most Blessed Virgin might collapse on her. The Most Blessed Virgin herself, however, had always remained unscathed by the enemy; she smiled down on the generalissimo as gently and as unconcernedly as if there had never been any bullets whizzing past her head.

The generalissimo looked from one bullet hole to another: as many holes as the flag bore, that many times had he achieved victory over the enemy. Every victory in his life had also been a victory for the Most Blessed Virgin—that was the tender secret of all those terrible, bloody battles; that was the war-glory of His Catholic Excellency before God, the only glory that still mattered to him. For what was the vain war-glory of the world to one who had already put behind him seventy years and more? But this glory before God was something with which His Catholic Excellency could one day adorn himself in his silent tomb, and above, in eternity. His Excellency lowered the standard toward himself in order to kiss the blue silk. But now, when he bent his face over it—his old, solitary soldier's face, tender and almost coy, like the face of a young page bending over to kiss the hand of the empress—he suddenly recoiled in dismay, for there a fourth hole gaped open once more. Had he not had it carefully patched years ago? For this hole, unlike the other bullet holes, did not come from the enemy but had been inflicted on the flag by the Catholics themselves, in the first battle of this great war at the White Mountain near Prague. In the thick smoke and the fury of battle, the Bavarian cavalry of Colonel Kratz had failed to recognize their own colors. The hole was only a very small one, but it went right through the Blessed Virgin's heart; after the battle, the cornet who had carried the standard had solemnly sworn to the pious soldiery that he had seen the blood of the Blessed Virgin flowing from the hole.

His Excellency looked at the small wound with consternation: How could it have opened up again? There hadn't been a battle since he'd last laid his eyes on his standard—there had only been the Diet of the prince-electors at Regensburg and the silent, undecided battle between His Catholic Excellency and the Imperial generalissimo; that battle was still underway, and it would soon need to be decided. Like the Bavarian cavalrymen at the White Mountain near Prague, His Catholic Excellency felt as though he could suddenly no longer recognize his own colors. Mary was the banner of religious war, after all; Mary was the Vanquisher of Heresy!

If I do not acquiesce to the changing nature of this war, His Excellency thought to himself, then I will be unable to protect the borders of the Empire, and I will have to live out my days as a defeated commander—and I've never lost a single battle in all my life! But if I do acquiesce, then I shall no longer find happiness in my commander's baton, for then my life will have lost its purpose and meaning. His Excellency resumed walking up and down the chamber, but by now the storm outside had blown even more invisible snow into the room. It seemed to gather in a great pile at his feet, so high he could never hope to step over it; he was much too old and gray, his Spanish courtly garb and his knees much too stiff. He again thought to himself: Surely I cannot counsel that the Holy Church be deprived of that which belongs to her! How could I, at my age of more than seventy years, make peace with the heretics? How could I suggest that His Imperial Majesty have patience with those same heretics and suspend the Edict? I cannot do such a thing! Indeed, I would much sooner return my commander's baton to His Imperial Majesty—let someone other than me, someone younger than I, figure out how to deal with this ambiguous age! But since the Duke of Friedland's fall from grace, His Imperial Majesty has no one else but me ... His Excellency stopped pacing and thought of his impetuous generals Pappenheim and Mansfeld, who were constantly fighting over command: in their hands the cause of His Imperial Majesty would scarcely be served, and discord would once again prevail in the German lands. His Catholic Excellency now truly felt as though he could go neither forward nor backward. But go forward he must. In his heart, he thought: His Imperial Majesty has no one else but me—surely I cannot abandon His Imperial Majesty in his hour of utmost need! I cannot abandon the borders of the Empire! I must remain at my post and persevere. I cannot insist on waging a war of religion when I've been placed in a war for the

Empire! Heaven has permitted the nature of this war to change, and what do I know of the purposes of heaven? At bottom, all I know is that I am a soldier, and a soldier must obey the *ratio belli*.[3] The generalissimo turned toward his old personal standard; he had won a real victory over His Catholic Excellency, who now felt as though, like the Bavarian cavalrymen at the White Mountain near Prague, he'd shot his own flag and the Blessed Virgin was no longer the Madonna of Victory but the Madonna with the Sword-Pierced Heart. The generalissimo looked up at her, as if to ask whether she would ever forgive him for having wounded and abandoned her. In his great distress, he found it strangely moving that she continued to gaze down at him as gently and as lovingly as before: she truly looked as though she had pronounced her Fiat on the sword in her breast, as she had once done at the angel's salutation. The generalissimo closed his old eyes again, as if in pain. But then all of a sudden he thought he heard the voice of the Blessed Virgin—as clearly as he'd heard the voice of the young heretic earlier. "But you have not abandoned me," she said, "you have found me!" He lifted his head, confused: Did Mary not want a war of religion? Would she rather endure the pain of religious division instead? He'd plunged the sword into her heart, he thought, yet now he found himself unable to find her wound from the White Mountain near Prague, and he suddenly felt as though he'd misunderstood the Blessed Virgin his entire life. For Mary did not triumph with sword in hand, Mary triumphed with the sword in her heart; she achieved victory through the suffering love of her Divine Son! And it was precisely this victory that His Catholic Excellency had been prepared to withhold

[3] Science of war; i.e., war operates according to its own set of rules.

from her. The generalissimo lifted his head once more, listening. But at that moment the priest, who had escorted out the young Magdeburger, returned.

The figure of the young priest in the room now took on the appearance of His Excellency's shadow once more: slender and dark, intensely reserved; there was but a slight flickering in the low-burning flame in his face, the result of his encounter with the Protestant—His Excellency knew that much about his young priest. The latter reported that he had managed to find accommodation for the guest in the overcrowded town: Marshal von Pappenheim, whom they had happened upon, had directed one of his adjutants to share his quarters with him—the marshal seemed to think quite highly of this young man from Magdeburg. And he really was a splendid fellow, he added, full of goodwill and even now thoroughly attuned to the great order of things—the only thing he lacked was the Catholic name. The dim flame in the face of the young priest flickered once more—or was it the flame of the young Order[4] itself that met His Excellency's gaze? His Excellency turned away suddenly, as if something hurt his old eyes—and he usually quite liked to warm himself at the fire of the young Order! "Yes," he said plainly, "it is a pity that such a good man cannot be helped, Father." How strange it was to hear the old, gray Excellency call him "Father"!

The young priest was taken aback: there was a tone in His Excellency's voice that he did not recognize, and if anyone knew His Catholic Excellency, it was he—he was his faithful shadow, after all! And what did he mean, the man could not be helped? They were just about to help him, were they not? Tentatively, he agreed that it was

[4] The Jesuits, founded in 1540.

indeed a pity, but added that the war of religion was now about to resume, and after the war was over there would be no more misery for these good people.

His Excellency started pacing the room again. "The war of religion is not about to resume, Father," he said curtly. "Rather, it is over—from now on there will be only war."

The young priest pricked up his ears: Was this His Catholic Excellency saying such a thing? The pride and martial glory of his own Order, the onetime student of Liège College, the man who was basically an armored Jesuit with a commander's baton? Or had His Excellency grown too old for the weight of his office? In that case he would need someone to help him sustain what precious strength he still possessed—and that's what he was here for! The young priest looked at the old man with almost tender affection: it always filled him with awe, even intimidated him somewhat, that he had been called to serve at the side of the celebrated commander. His Catholic Excellency was much more devout than he—that he knew quite well. But perhaps it was for this very reason that he needed the young priest's help: for all things on earth, even religious devotion, had their own dangers and temptations.

He said, again tentatively: "If the war of religion is over, then that would mean the defeat of the as-yet-undefeated generalissimo Tilly, and with him, the singular hope of Catholic Christendom—that's not possible!"

His Excellency, his lower lip protruding slightly—for he was not fond of compliments—said in reply: "There is no singular hope for Catholic Christendom anymore, Father."

Now the young priest knew at last—after all, he'd been His Excellency's shadow at Regensburg too. To himself, he thought: Old, watchful soldiers are like faithful sentries at their posts—they can hear the grass grow! They should never have allowed His Excellency to go to Regensburg;

generals belong in the field! Then, rather adroitly, he said: "His Excellency is taking certain matters of high politics all too seriously. Even with the Holy Father in Rome, there is a distinction between the Vicar of Christ and the sovereign ruler of the Papal States. Cardinal Richelieu and Richelieu the minister are, so to speak, two different people, whereby one may very well stand behind His Imperial Majesty's course of war on behalf of the Catholic Church, and the other, beholden to His Majesty the king of France, would naturally have to issue a different command—" He stopped abruptly, for he had indeed just spoken of two separate commands, just as the young heretic had earlier. Was this a mere coincidence, or was it the dawn of a new era, for both sides? In that case the French ambassador at Regensburg who'd passed around the image of the great cardinal at his table had been passing around the future, and enclosed in that small round box was the fate of the coming centuries! He threw a quick glance at His Excellency—perhaps the old man realized this as well?

His Excellency had now stopped pacing and was again poring over the maps at his worktable. "It will be of little use, Father," he said dryly, "if Cardinal Richelieu prays for the victory of Imperial arms while Minister Richelieu is subsidizing the Swede. The only thing that will help now is if from now on we, too, act as though there is no longer a single Catholic Christendom—we cannot strike at the enemy without and the enemy within at the same time."

The priest thought to himself: His Excellency would use all his strength against the enemy without—and how does he intend to defeat the rebellion? He waited. His Excellency was now looking through his maps in silence. The young priest heard nothing but the dark rumbling of the storm at the window and the soft rustling of the charts in His Excellency's hands. He immediately recalled the wager the officers had made with one another that morning: if the looming storm outside came through, then they would elect to storm Magdeburg at tomorrow's council of war. For a moment he thought the dark rumbling outside would surely blow in the glass panes and snatch away His Excellency's maps! Meanwhile, His Excellency had found what he was looking for: the map of Magdeburg.

The young priest now fixed his gaze downward; the tension on his clever, passionate face was almost imperceptible, as though hidden beneath a veil, his own person entirely submerged, and all his strength, all his senses detached from himself and focused entirely on the other. As he always did when he knew he must stand at His Excellency's side, he inwardly expressed his devotion in the words of Saint Ignatius: "Take, Lord, and receive, my entire will ..." Meanwhile, His Excellency had conscientiously folded up the plan of the city and laid it on a side table—it looked almost as though he were putting aside a chapter of the war. Finally, he spoke, coming straight to the point: "You shall travel to Vienna shortly, Father. See if you can encourage Father Lamormaini, as confessor to His Imperial Majesty, to advise that the Edict be postponed another forty years or so, as His Grace the prince-elector of Bavaria recently suggested, in order to forestall a general rebellion."

So this is the future, the young priest thought in his heart: If two separate commands come down, then one of them has to give way. He now saw exactly what old Tilly saw, only much more keenly and much further: the powers that would emerge victorious from this war would be not the forces of Holy Religion but the secular powers to whom they'd been commended; these had suddenly emerged from under the banner of religious conflict like the face of Père Joseph appearing beneath the cardinal's scarlet, and now all of a sudden they faced another foe, one that was far more dangerous than the petty threat of these pious Protestants. To himself, he said: It's as if I can see, off in the distance, the world about to break apart for the second time! Remaining calm, as though he were trying quickly but carefully to descend a dark staircase that plunged down into the dread depths, he continued: So shall it indeed come to pass—the secular powers have set off on their own path, and they will continue along it. Where hitherto the precept has been that all earthly things are to be sacrificed before the rights of Holy Religion, going forward the principle shall be that the rights of Holy Religion are to be sacrificed before all earthly things—it will be these rights that will be surrendered always and everywhere first of all! Where yesterday there had been a holy power to restrain the naked powers of the world, tomorrow there will be only those naked powers, with nothing more to restrain them—who indeed could restrain them, if Holy Religion is no longer able to do so? The nations will turn on one another like the ravenous beasts of the forest, and Holy Religion will stand by and watch, her hands bound. She will be locked up in the narrow confines of the church walls, or in the quiet chambers of the heart, and perhaps one day there will be an attempt to drive her out of these places as well—for to know the world is to know that without power, nothing can survive in it. Eventually there will be nothing on earth more embattled and more imperiled than Holy Religion! Indeed, there might even come a day when the Christian nations reprise the role of the wicked Jews who betrayed the Divine Savior for thirty pieces of silver! Then everything that was done to Christ might well in turn be done to His Bride, the Holy Church—then there will be no scarlet for her anymore but the scarlet of her Lord before Pontius Pilate! He faltered for a moment, for he was suddenly faced with the prospect of martyrdom. But it was not the kind of martyrdom that the priest himself and the fiery soul of his young Order longed for from time to time: martyrdom for the sake of Holy Religion, for the sake of her supreme triumph. Rather, what he saw was the martyrdom of Holy Religion herself—she would be the *Agnus Dei*, subject to the naked power of the world, like Christ Himself! Did the suffering that redeemed the world include the suffering of Religion herself? Did the crown to be worn by the Bride of Christ include the Crown of Thorns? Did the final fight of the young Order include giving up the fight? Take, Lord, and receive, my entire will—Thou hast given me this will; to Thee, O Lord, I return it ... He paused once more, for it was not his will that was at stake here but Holy Religion; what was at stake was the victory of the Church! Quickly and resolutely, he continued: For ourselves, martyrdom; for the Holy Church, never—to the Bride of Christ be the triumph of Christ and all glory! And indeed, they could still fight back; that was what the Edict was for—it must never be allowed to fall. In the great struggle that loomed ahead, the Holy Church would have to be united once more, and that could happen only if her fortresses and sally ports, her abbeys and monasteries, were restored to her! And now old Tilly needed to be brought back to safety—indeed, he was in danger of becoming the first victim of these naked powers:

Who would have thought that His Catholic Excellency would take such a dangerous path?

His Excellency, still pacing back and forth, now stepped right up to his old personal standard. The young priest's gaze lingered on the banner. He suddenly felt a great sense of helplessness, for His Excellency was such an old and pious man; he had no right to drop his genteel reserve before him, he could not possibly rebuke him—he could only win back His Catholic Excellency through His Catholic Excellency himself. The standard would help him! True, the standard was bound to His Excellency by some great mystery: something quite delicate, something sacred. Ordinarily he would not dare speak of it—His Excellency never did. But now it was necessary. He began with a prefatory remark: His Excellency no doubt shared his pain and his concern regarding the Edict . . .

His Excellency stopped pacing. In his face there suddenly appeared Father Tilly, who looked at the young priest exactly as he looked at his wounded soldiery when he went to visit them after a battle to squeeze their hands with fatherly affection and afford them the faithful, valiant, taciturn comfort of an old soldier. The young priest suddenly felt even more helpless; the dim flame in his face turned inward, and it was as though he were seeing his own father again after many years—indeed, it was he who had first taught him Saint Ignatius' words of surrender: "Take, Lord, and receive, my entire will." Why, he had almost forgotten for a moment that he was there to serve at His Excellency's side; and precisely because His Excellency was such an old and pious man, he had no idea of the abyss into which he was about to deliver the Holy Church!

With resolute conviction, he said: "I shall leave for Vienna shortly—His Excellency may wish to confer once more with his venerable and illustrious banner before entrusting me with his final orders for Father Lamormaini."

His Excellency abruptly stuck out his lower lip and turned around, his face once more inscrutable: "I have already conferred with my *ratio belli*"—it sounded as though the generalissimo, with military terseness, meant to dismiss his suggestion about the standard. Yet it was clear that in His Excellency's mind, his *ratio belli* meant the standard itself! As the young priest waited, the dark rumbling at the window penetrated into the chamber once more—the storm seemed to be struggling furiously against some as-yet-unseen resistance, its energies already half-spent.

The old can no longer communicate their religious experiences, the young priest thought to himself; that is what makes it so difficult to support them when they need it: while their silence ought to be accepted with reverence, we should nevertheless offer them support as well. Instinctively, he took a step forward. His Excellency took one as well. The distance between them remained the same—did His Excellency mean to escape his faithful shadow? He now felt as though, in defending the Edict, he was simultaneously defending both the temporal and the eternal salvation of old Tilly.

"If His Excellency has conferred with his *ratio belli*," he said, though visibly reluctant, "then he has conferred with the Blessed Virgin on his illustrious standard—the Madonna of Victory will hardly have advised His Excellency to abandon the Edict." He fell silent, for His Excellency had stopped pacing again and was now looking at him. The loneliness in his old eyes frightened the young priest: His Excellency truly looked as though he, in his piety and devotion, were all alone in the world. Had His Excellency indeed slipped away from him? Had he been left behind? Had the old, icy-gray, stiff-kneed Excellency, at seventy years of age, managed to elude his own shadow? Indeed, it was as though he looked at him from the insurmountable distance of an entirely different world or age; and once more, the young priest felt that he was seeing the future—this time his own, for the sword of religious war that His Excellency was returning to its sheath was, after all, the sword of his young Order! As His Excellency's gaze fell upon him, he felt himself acquiescing to an oppressively silent, faithful defenselessness before God that at the same time meant a tremendous resistance against himself: all at once he could imagine Generalissimo Tilly passing him up without batting an eyelid and proceeding to Vienna on his own so that he might push for the postponement of the Edict there himself.

He nearly leapt backward when His Excellency opened his mouth. His words were terse, though exceedingly polite—such was his every interaction with the ordained priest, after all:

The officers would soon arrive to escort him to the banquet—if it should please the good father, he might let him know tomorrow morning whether he was inclined to undertake this matter with Father Lamormaini or not.

The young priest now turned silently. He placed himself at His Excellency's disposal. Why had he not done so right away? Why had he not spared His Excellency this trouble?

Surely he owed him as much, on account of his age and his piety! Why had he been so fixated on coming to an agreement with him, when he needed only to come to an agreement with Father Lamormaini? Father Lamormaini was discreet; he could safely be entrusted with this dangerous task on behalf of His Excellency. He would not betray His Catholic Excellency or the Edict any more than he himself would! Together with Father Lamormaini, he would fight for both, without causing a stir or making any noise—quietly, but victoriously; for ultimately it was not really necessary to fight at all; he needed only to refrain from doing what old Tilly was asking him to do; all he needed to do was not to stop the stone once it was rolling. And the stone was rolling indeed, for the Edict was no longer located at the Imperial chancelleries in Vienna but was already out there on the wind, so to speak—whirling about in the perpetually looming storm, upon which the officers had wagered that morning. The young priest suddenly recalled how earlier he had come upon the impetuous counts Pappenheim and Mansfeld arguing with each other about the future of "Marienburg", the name, it had been decided in Vienna, that Magdeburg was to be called after the execution of the Edict. Now, however, the officers really were approaching to escort His Excellency to the banquet.

The two counts were still quite red in the face from quarreling when the generalissimo entered, for each hoped the supreme command at Magdeburg would be theirs: the Count of Mansfeld because His Imperial Majesty had already appointed him governor of the city; the Count of Pappenheim in order to redress the crushing defeat he had suffered there in '29.

They sat down to the banquet in the Wedding House's great hall, festooned with flags that had been present at the victories of His Excellency Tilly, their pointed tips now decked with large wreaths. Wreaths also hung before His Excellency's place at the table and over the back of his chair; between them sat the old bachelor himself, who remarked—half-amusedly, half-gruffly—that they must have thought that with him staying there at the famous Wedding House of Hamelin, they had to decorate his place at the table as they would for a bridegroom.

The officers had greeted his entry with loud acclamations, but after the first glass to His Imperial Majesty's good health had been emptied, they sat at the table in silence; for it was now time for the officers to make a speech in celebration of His Excellency, the honor of which Marshal von Pappenheim had wrested away from his comrade Mansfeld that morning. Thus, there in the silence of anticipation, the roar of the onrushing storm could once again be heard outside; it now came in very brief, violent blasts, as though it were trying to find a place to force its way through. Whenever the storm stopped for a moment to catch its breath, Marshal von Pappenheim's spurs could be heard from under the table—he was evidently unable to sit still even for a moment, though he seemed to have forgotten all about the speech. This was no doubt due to the great deal of intelligence he'd again received from Magdeburg—God only knew who kept bringing it to his adjutant!

The adjutants were seated at their own table to the side of the senior officers' table. Willigis Ahlemann had also found his place at the table, alongside Captain Bomgarten, the cavalry captain whose quarters he was sharing; he would not let Willigis out of his sight for a moment. The adjutants drank eagerly to Willigis' health, each one more polite toward him than the other, for the cavalry captain had let it be known that it was the lord marshal's wish that they make a good impression on this guest. They all understood why: this Herr Ahlemann was, so to speak, the rara avis among the gentlemen of Magdeburg; he could be of some use to the Imperial army in the actions ahead, as he was well acquainted with the terrain around the city and its fortifications.

Captain Bomgarten had already had a bit to drink and was growing bolder: "Surely the good sir wishes to join us, does he not?" he asked.

His forthright question startled Willigis; from his place at the table he had a constant view of the bellicose face of Count Pappenheim, which had troubled him so much earlier, as though he saw in it his own future.

Meanwhile, the cavalry captain, encouraged by Willigis' silence, pressed on: The way things were going in Magdeburg now, he was unlikely to have a place there anymore, given his convictions. Perhaps he would not be displeased to learn that the lord marshal had said that anyone who was so loyal to the Empire that he would cast the Swedish ambassador down the stairs could be a Lutheran if he wanted to, and he would welcome him with open arms. What if he were to decide to stay, right here and right now?

The adjutants shouted "Bravo!" and raised their glasses. Willigis looked at Count Pappenheim once more. He now experienced such a longing for his dear bride that he felt the urge to get up from the table straightaway and ride off to Magdeburg. He politely told the cavalry captain that he was honored by the lord marshal's high opinion of him and that he greatly appreciated the comradeship of the officers but that he'd left behind in Magdeburg a dear bride; they'd belonged to each other since childhood—she was like his second self, and he could not part with her.

"Such sentiments are foreign to us," the cavalry captain replied. "We have no second self; nor do we have any need for one. It would only make us weak and listless. We take our women as we take cities—by force—and after that we move on! At heart we're all lifelong bachelors like our generalissimo—that man has probably never looked at a woman seriously in his life, save for the one that graces his standard."

"Bravo!" the adjutants shouted once more. Willigis glanced over at His Excellency, sitting there in his old Spanish courtly garb, stiff and gray despite indulging merrily in the wine, the loneliness of his seventy years evident in his eyes—he really did look like a genuine lifelong bachelor. And yet he did not seem so foreign to Willigis as the others—he could well imagine His Excellency having a second self as he did. Was this on account of the reverence with which he venerated that idolatrous image on his standard? That was indeed most peculiar. The adjutants were now raising their glasses to the war. But then the gentlemen at the other table waved for silence; all eyes were turned toward Count Pappenheim—was it finally time for him to give his speech?

Count Pappenheim sat to the right of His Excellency—he had wrested his place at the table from Count Mansfeld as well. "You see," Captain Bomgarten said quietly to Willigis, "it's all about power around here, in matters both great and small; here, every man must be a hammer if he does not wish to become an anvil. And truly, it's a good thing to be a hammer!"

Meanwhile, His Excellency was listening politely to Count Pappenheim but saying little in reply—he looked almost as though he would have preferred to end the conversation. At His Excellency's left sat Count Mansfeld, languid and sullen, peering at his adversary with hatred from under his heavy eyelids. Thus the two rivals faced off against each other: one like the image of a daring cavalryman who seeks to leap over every obstacle, the other like a heavy harquebusier waiting in ambush to blast his enemies with chunks of lead.

Suddenly the cavalry captain, not taking his eyes off the other table, said furtively to Willigis: "If the good sir would pay attention now, he will see how tomorrow morning's council of war will go. Over there we have an explosive clash of spirits: the lord marshal can no longer wait to see who will be given supreme command at Magdeburg. His Excellency himself, so we all think, will have to lead the main body of our forces against the Swede."

Now both tables fell completely silent. Willigis thought that it was as quiet as the Rathaus in Magdeburg right before a ruling came down; even the storm outside held its breath for a moment.

The high, clear voice of the marshal could be heard speaking to the generalissimo: "If Your Excellency will allow me just five thousand additional men, I give my word that when I am given supreme command, I shall storm the city and take it by force!"

His Excellency recoiled slightly: "God forbid," he said dismissively, "that we should be compelled to storm this highly significant place; to leave it in ruins would be to do His Imperial Majesty a great disservice!"

Willigis breathed a sigh of relief: this was indeed the decision he had requested of His Excellency earlier; His Excellency did not wish to take his beloved native city by storm but was apparently still willing to be patient with her! He turned again to the cavalry captain.

Meanwhile, the marshal's spurs were performing a veritable war march under the table. He continued, more urgently: "Surely Your Excellency does not intend to subjugate Magdeburg with a mere blockade! Your Excellency will be unable to achieve anything with these arch-rebels in that way—they will never allow the Edict to be imposed on them except by force! Your Excellency must use every means available to fight this war, and only by imposing the Edict can we eradicate the root causes of the same—this war will end only when His Imperial Majesty's Empire is united once more!"

His Excellency made a motion as though one of his old war wounds suddenly pained him. But now Count Mansfeld began to speak—the execution of the Edict was meant to be his entry ticket; he had hoped that he might thereby impress His Excellency and establish his claim to supreme command. Count Mansfeld had only recently returned to the bosom of the Catholic Church, so naturally he felt the need to prove his devotion. Like a vicious mastiff suddenly turning up in the hall, he growled: "Does my comrade Count Pappenheim intend to override the wishes of His Imperial Majesty with his swift maneuvering as well?

The return of the Magdeburg heretics to the bosom of the Holy Church is a matter for the Imperial governor—"

The marshal's voice interjected, a note higher than usual: Everyone knew it was possible to solicit a governorship in Vienna with pious talk, but this was a matter of who could best make his proposal at the point of the sword! The cavalierish music of his spurs clinked and jangled like an entire regiment jumping into the saddle somewhere.

"Is my comrade thinking of the proposal he made in '29?" Mansfeld spitefully shot back. "I was always under the impression that the Lady of Magdeburg turned him down on that occasion, did she not?" The vicious mastiff sunk his teeth in.

The marshal's clinking and jangling grew more intense—the horses of the distant cavalry squadron seemed to be bolting. Turned him down? No one had ever dared do such a thing! He'd never failed to get into any chamber he sought to enter, even if, as at Wolfenbüttel, he had to divert an entire stream first, or if, in the case of His Imperial Majesty's hereditary lands, that chamber was all of Upper Austria!

Mansfeld snidely remarked: "My noble comrade Pappenheim has a superb understanding of his own merits—or was that the speech he prepared for His Excellency, the one we've all been waiting to hear for hours now?"

The marshal turned crimson—he had truly forgotten all about the speech! He reached for his glass; at the same moment the storm outside smashed a hail of roof tiles against the shutters. The marshal, like everyone else in the hall, turned to look.

Mansfeld, who never let go once he had gotten hold of someone: "I suppose that rather than drinking to His Excellency, my noble comrade now means to drink to his brother the storm?"

On the marshal's forehead appeared the infamous red mark in which his nurse was said to have recognized two crossed swords when he was a baby. He was furious: "Indeed, I drink to my brother out there, I drink to Herr Storm, for he's on his way to Magdeburg!" At that moment there was a howling in the fireplace like the long, drawn-out wail of a desperate woman.

Mansfeld now went for the other man's throat: "That's not the storm that my noble comrade takes for his brother; it's just the wretched Wind Bride[5] trying to elude him again, as she did in '29!"

Pappenheim, raising his glass, mad with wine and rage: "Well then, here's to the tempestuous Wind Bride, that Herr Storm may soon overpower her; here's to the prickly bride of Magdeburg!" He turned toward His Excellency: "May we soon accompany our glorious generalissimo from this Wedding House, that he may dance the dance of honor! That we may form a circle around the lovely bride and take turns dancing with her until she is out of breath! That we may light our torches and escort her to her wedding night! That we may lay her in the proper bridal bed that His Imperial Majesty has decreed for her—to this I raise my glass and drink to her noble bridegroom: I drink to the next victory of our invincible generalissimo Tilly! I drink to the Wedding of Magdeburg!"

"Here, here!" the officers shouted, leaping up from their seats to knock glasses with the generalissimo, who had risen from his seat and stood there in his stiff Spanish courtly garb, his old, austere bachelor's face looking out from under the bridegroom's wreath that Pappenheim had placed atop his head. He was no longer amused but incensed, for his two generals appeared to be fighting a

[5] *Windsbraut* is both a name for a tempest and a spirit in Germanic folklore.

duel between themselves! Once the cheers finally died down, he spoke, in his sober voice: "And I drink to my valiant marshal, the Count of Pappenheim; I drink to his patience! I drink to concord between my noble generals! I drink to discipline and obedience among the glorious combined forces of League and Empire!"

"Here, here!" the officers shouted once more. But Mansfeld, after knocking glasses with His Excellency like all the others, then raised his glass to the marshal: "To the patience of my comrade Pappenheim!" At that moment the storm crashed against the building as though it were trying to batter down the walls. His Catholic Excellency made the sign of the cross in front of everyone.

"And I, comrade," shouted Pappenheim, "drink to the end of all patience! I hereby vow by my honor as a gentleman that I will take this defiant maiden Magdeburg, even if her house, like the city of Stralsund, be bound to heaven with chains![6] I will bring it down and reduce it to dust, so help me God in heaven!" He threw his glass into the air—there followed a great crash and tinkling as if he'd shattered all the windows in the hall at once, for no single glass could have made such a sound! And at that very moment the lights on the table flickered and went out, the tablecloth blew upward, the glasses fell over—for the storm really had thrown open the windows and now swept through the hall. Suddenly, it was as though they were out in the open in the middle of the night and could hear, out in the pitch black, the pitiful wailing of the Wind Bride, and the hue and cry of the frenzied army that pursued her. Then there was dead silence.

The servants now entered carrying lanterns, revealing His Excellency Tilly kneeling beside his chair, his hands

[6] Pappenheim is echoing the boast made by the Duke of Friedland before taking Stralsund in 1628.

folded in prayer like the stone effigy of a pious old knight. The officers stood by sheepishly, some making the sign of the cross, others thinking that the moment for prayer was already past. Meanwhile, the servants were trying to reset the table so that the banquet might continue. But His Excellency did not wish to continue; he arose from his stiff knees and bade good night. Then, fixing his gaze on the two counts: "The council of war will convene at six o'clock in the morning. I expect that the gentlemen will be sober by then."

The streets of Hamelin were a scene of desolation as Willigis prepared to ride home the following morning; roof tiles and shattered chimneys littered the ground. But outside the gates, the storm had wreaked even more havoc: the trees along the road, which just yesterday had been full of golden leaves, now jutted out of the roadside ditches, shorn of leaves and branches, and the highest treetops of the forest lay dashed to the ground. In the fields, the tempest had burrowed deep trenches, throwing up beside them what appeared to be earthworks, as though someone had been trying to erect fortifications. In the villages, the houses had their roofs blown off and their windows blasted out. Shattered fences blocked the road, and distraught livestock wandered about like beasts in the wild. In front of one house, Willigis saw an old man sprawled out on the ground, his skull crushed by debris from the crest of the roof; other houses had collapsed entirely, their homeless inhabitants rummaging through the rubble for their possessions. And the closer Willigis got to the archbishopric, the worse things became: one might have thought he was following in the wake of a ghostly swarm of soldiery—usually the only places that looked like this were those that had witnessed the savage fury of war. He thought of the officers at the banquet in Hamelin who'd wagered on the storm, and how the fiery young marshal had greeted it with jubilation, as though it were the coming war itself. What sad creatures this wild and unruly soldiery are, he thought in his heart, even if they consider such a life to be the jolliest thing in the world. What kind of a life was it to spend day and night intent on smashing everything to bits in one's own country? It's just as well that His Excellency holds his council of war with his standard and not with his generals; now I'll be able to bring comforting news to my native city when I ride back to my dear bride.

He reached the halfway point, where he had changed horses on the ride out and left his own horse behind. Now, sitting on his gray once more, he could scarcely wait to see Erdmuth again. "Old Gray," he said, patting the horse on the neck, "my dear bride always said you had hooves of silver, but today I need them to have wings!" But the gray did not have winged hooves, and the roads were churned up by the storm—Willigis made only slow progress. In his heart, he thought: I shall think about my dear bride, and how she's waited for me so loyally and patiently these past several days even though she knew nothing of what I was doing—perhaps then I will find it less difficult to be patient myself. But he did not find it less difficult to be patient; in fact, he became more and more impatient the more he thought of Erdmuth. He thought he might barely survive the last leg of the journey. Again, he thought in his heart: I never knew before how difficult a thing patience is! What my dear bride must have gone through when I left her there in the great cathedral and sent her no word all day; only now do I realize what I was demanding of her! He considered whether he should commend Erdmuth for her patience and thank her. But he dared not do that—it might offend her and make her think that he was not entirely certain of her patience. No, I will not say anything to her, he said to himself; I will only pull her close and kiss her, and that alone will tell her everything! Imagining all this, however, made him feel all the more as if he could not reach the end of his journey soon enough.

The early autumn night had already set in by the time Willigis finally reached the gates of Magdeburg. He found them locked for the night. The guard who appeared at the tower window in response to Willigis' pounding made no move to open it, but shouted down curtly and unkindly in reply to Willigis' bewildered questioning that things in Magdeburg were different now, not like before; they had their reasons for locking the gates, and certain people would no longer be let in at all.

But, Willigis retorted, not letting in a weary citizen of Magdeburg who showed up in the evening knocking at the gate—that was something new.

Of course it was new, the guard replied, but everything in Magdeburg was new these days. When had Willigis left the city, anyway? "If I recall," he continued pompously, "it was on the same glorious night that my companions and I had the honor of admitting Colonel von Falkenberg into the city—that's right, we were the first ones to see him: it was through this very gate that the savior and liberator of Magdeburg entered! And if you still don't know what I mean, then you were away for quite a long while indeed, though you may think it was but a short time yourself! I very much fear that you will not be able to find your way around here at all anymore!"

Willigis, suppressing his anger, responded by requesting that the guard kindly refrain from giving speeches and open the door to him, as was his duty. To which the guard replied, didn't he already say that some people would no longer be allowed in? Imperial-minded traitors who rode out to Johann Ahlemann in Wolmirstedt each day would have no place in Magdeburg from now on. Thereupon the guard slammed the window shut.

Willigis now stood before the locked gate in the cold, dark autumn night—he stood on the same spot where Colonel von Falkenberg had stood and been refused entry by the same guard. But he did not know that, and neither did the guard. Everything will be cleared up in the morning, he told himself, though it does seem that I will have to spend the night here outside the gate. Right now, however, it's important for me to remember the patience of my dear bride! Though I do wish I could let her know at least, so that she doesn't have to spend another night worrying. He sat down on the wooden bench in front of the gate and thought about what he should do.

After a while he heard a noise behind him, and when he turned—the late moon was out at last—he perceived, through a small doorway that had opened up in one of the larger doors of the city gate, the face of an elderly woman. She handed him a mug of warm beer and whispered that she was very sorry to see him out there in the cold night, but that her husband had already explained to him how things stood here—they both had to be very careful. The woman seemed familiar to Willigis; he thanked her and asked her where they'd met before. She replied that it had been at the Plögen house, where she used to look after his maiden bride years ago when she was a little girl, and she had sometimes been told to look after the little master bridegroom as well when he came to visit.

Willigis remembered now. "Oh yes," he said, "you would always tell me the old stories of the Plögen maidens of the past: about fair Engelke, who had a counterfeit bridegroom appear at her wedding, and the maid Itze, who said: 'Pride makes all things possible.' But I never wanted to believe those stories—I wanted to believe only the beautiful words above the front door: 'Love is strong as death'—I always had you read them to me too!" Then he asked whether the gatekeeper's wife might be so kind as to look after the grown-up bridegroom as she once looked after the little one. Could she deliver a message for him? He would really like to let his dear bride know that he was back before it got too late.

The woman hesitated. "Sir," she finally said, looking at Willigis almost with pity, "please, forget about this message! Better you should ride away at once; it's not good for an Ahlemann to be sitting here at the gate; people here in Magdeburg are like vicious dogs now, attacking anyone who won't run with the pack." Now Willigis did grow concerned—he hadn't taken the puffed-up gatekeeper seriously, but surely this quiet woman spoke the truth. He asked whether it was really true, then, that there were no Imperials left in Magdeburg. Oh no, the woman replied with a faint smile, there were still just as many Imperials as before, but these were the very ones who now, out of fear, were behaving the most like Swedes and persecuting those who were actually of the same mind as they were; one had to be much warier of them than of those who really were on the side of the Swedes.

Willigis looked at the woman in astonishment. "I don't understand," he said. "Surely one cannot act as though he were of a different mind than he truly is?" The woman remained silent, seeming troubled. Suddenly his bright eyes darkened from the pupils outward, like craters spewing black lava over a pale landscape: "Those scoundrels!" he rumbled, as though from deep within a mountain. "Those cowardly, shameless liars! The one time that their opinions would have counted for something, and they deny them!" Then he thought to himself:

So Captain Bomgarten was right after all—there really is no place for me in my native city anymore! Well, he said to the woman, he would ride away again, then, but now she would have to deliver another message. She must go and tell his bride to come herself; he would not move from this spot without her. The woman made an apprehensive face; it looked almost as though she were trying to come up with an excuse to avoid this task. Finally, she said that Willigis was not yet married to Erdmuth; it wouldn't be proper for her just to go off with him like that. But now Willigis interjected: If they were going to bar him from entering the city, then they would have to let his bride leave: they were not two but one, destined for each other by their parents even as children, as good as married for some time now; for the will of parents regarding their children was the will of God. Surely no one in Magdeburg would presume to dispute the rights of parents over their children and contradict the will of God—that would undermine the very foundations of mankind! At last, he said that if the woman did not go and get his bride, he would remain sitting right there before the gate, even if he had to wait a thousand days! It was no use arguing, then, the woman replied, though visibly troubled; she would go, for he had to get away from this gate as quickly as possible! And now, might God protect him until she returned.

She closed the little door, and Willigis sat back down on the bench. In his heart, he said: Now they've shut me out of my dear native city as though I were an outlaw! All I wanted to do was to save my native city the best way I knew how, and if I really did go about it wrong—though I did not—then surely they must allow that my intentions were good. What sort of a government is it that can no longer distinguish the good intentions of its subjects from those which are evil? Such a regime should not be permitted to govern at all! But now one such regime governs in Magdeburg, and I must bid farewell to my dear native city.

He looked out into the quiet countryside of his native land. There it spread before the city gate, the gentle landscape stretching far into the distance, almost without a straight line in sight; one might think there was nothing special about it all, and yet it was the loveliest landscape on earth! Willigis had known this even as a little boy, but the landscape out here had never seemed so beautiful to him as it did this evening! He could not even make it out exactly, blurring and shimmering as it did in the indistinct light of the waning moon, as though it lay not before his eyes at all but before his heart. Magdeburg is my home, he said to himself; a man cannot just say farewell to his home as one does a foreign country! What are the ruling gentlemen of the city thinking? Do they have such little love for their homeland that they are willing to see another separated from her? Then they contradict the will of God yet again, for it is He who ordained that I should belong to Magdeburg! He turned around and looked at the city; like the countryside, it, too, lay spread out, as it were, before his heart only: with his heart he looked through the thick walls and towers and into all the familiar streets and alleys that had been his playground when he was a little boy. He saw the magnificent Rathaus, where his fathers had sat with honor in the city government, and on the market square he heard the song of the great clock that rang out the hour of birth and death for every child of Magdeburg. He stepped over the threshold of his dear childhood home, where his cradle had stood and where his own children's cradle would one day stand, and the pain he felt in his heart was so great that he thought one might sooner pull up the great linden trees of his childhood home with all their ancient roots than separate him from Magdeburg! But with this thought still on his mind, he saw before him the Plögen house, rising so steeply and gracefully toward the sky, above its front door the passage from the great Song from which it took its name. And now he was suddenly overcome with the urge to sing the High Song[7] himself amid the pain of his parting; for indeed, it was from the door of this house that his dear bride would follow him into exile! Truly, love is strong as death, he said to himself.[8] The gentlemen of the Council mean to drive me from my home, but I will take my home with me! Magdeburg is the faithful maid; but if my dear bride comes with me, then what am I to mourn? Like Emperor Otto, I will lay my head in the lap of a faithful maid; she will be my Queen Edith, my Magdeburg!

In the meantime, however, one quarter hour after the other had passed. Willigis had not heard the striking of the clock tower at first, but he began to notice it now, realizing that the gatekeeper's wife should have returned long ago. Perhaps Erdmuth had already retired for the evening, he said to himself; perhaps she had to get out of bed and get dressed when the woman came. I have no right to reproach her for not being here yet. I'm the last one who should be reproaching anyone—I kept Erdmuth waiting much longer than this, after all! What am I doing counting the quarter hours at all? Meanwhile, however, the clock in the tower was already striking once again. Of course, Willigis continued, it's also possible that Erdmuth will need to pack a few things first—after all, a woman can't just get on a horse straightaway as a man

[7] The Song of Solomon.

[8] Song 8:6.

can. A woman's always got to have so many little things at hand: combs and smelling bottles and who knows what else! And perhaps Erdmuth also had to bring a change of clothes with her—after all, a woman can never wear the same clothes for very long as a man can. He looked down at his old buff coat, which he had not taken off for days. No, he continued again, I've no right to be concerned about the time she's taking; I've got no way of judging what a woman needs to take with her in such situations—why, that would be like Erdmuth trying to judge whether I had to leave her in the cathedral the other day to go to Wolmirstedt! The clock struck another quarter hour. Or maybe, thought Willigis, Erdmuth had to order the maidservants to do this or that before she left—after all, a woman can't just up and quit her household without taking care of some things first. I've got no right to judge there either; again, that would be like Erdmuth trying to judge whether I had to go to Wolmirstedt and Hamelin! He waited. Now the clock tower struck a full hour—the second since the gatekeeper's wife had left him. But it's also possible, Willigis continued anew, that Erdmuth was impatient to see me herself! Or maybe she didn't go to bed because she was up waiting for me the whole time—or maybe she was afraid for me, since everyone here has turned against me! Or maybe she didn't take the time to pack her things or speak with the servants at all—maybe she came running to me right away, as fast as she could, to come and fling open the gate. He turned and looked at the gate, as if he expected Erdmuth, in all her beauty, to emerge from it at any moment. It would not have taken much to convince him to spread his arms and embrace the old, weather-worn city gate. Just then the little door opened and the gatekeeper's wife appeared—she was alone.

"Where is my bride?" Willigis asked, nearly shouting. "Why aren't you letting her out to see me?" The woman, looking sad, said nothing—as if she were searching for the right words. "Is Erdmuth ill?" he stammered. "Or could you not find her? Did you not go to the House of the High Song?"

"Sir," the woman said—her voice sounded gentle, as if she were comforting a sick man—"your bride is not at the House of the High Song; she's at the Rathaus."

Evidently misunderstanding her, Willigis replied: "All right, then, she's at the Rathaus; but what's she doing there, and at this hour?" Then, suddenly alarmed, for the woman's face bespoke nothing good: "Did they order her to come, or drag her in? Do they mean to harm her? Do they mean to lock her up because she's my bride?"

The good woman's eyes began to tear up. "Oh, sir," she said, "no, no harm at all will come to your bride; they're having a celebration at the Rathaus for Falkenberg."

Willigis looked fixedly at the woman: "A celebration for Falkenberg? But what has that got to do with my bride? Didn't you tell her I was waiting for her at the gate?"

The tears were now running freely down the woman's face. "Sir," she groaned, "you must abandon the idea of taking your bride with you: she isn't coming! She has put on her prettiest dress for the celebration; indeed, I believe it is her wedding dress."

"She's not coming?" Willigis cried, apparently having heard only the first part. "So then she is being forcibly detained! Why didn't you tell me this at once?"

The good woman threw her hands up to her face. "Please don't make me answer, sir," she sobbed, "for it rends my heart to look at you so; do you still not believe the stories of the fair Engelke and the maid Itze? It's the same with your bride as it is with the whole city of Magdeburg—the only one who holds sway here now is Falkenberg!"

There was dead silence for a moment; then the good woman cried out in horror, for suddenly the tall, sturdy man grabbed her by both shoulders, pushed her aside like a small child, and raced past her through the open door and into the city.

The windows of the Rathaus' great banquet hall were brightly lit as they would be for the great formal balls of the leading families, but outside there was no sign of solemn formality to be seen; in the streets and alleyways, the triumphing city of Magdeburg was once again singing her old *Trutzlied*, that it would be better to die than not send pope and emperor packing. They had indeed sent the pope and emperor packing once and for all, but no one would have to die for it now: with the arrival of the valiant colonel von Falkenberg, the vanguard of the Swedish army was practically in the city already. Now the doubtful gentlemen of the Council could no longer say: "Magdeburg must be on her guard, for Tilly is at Hamelin and Halberstedt"; now what they said was: "His Royal Majesty of Sweden is at Magdeburg, and Tilly had better beware, lest we give him a send-off quite different from the one we gave Friedland and Pappenheim in '29!" The councillors still looked strangely doubtful, though; they were evidently unable to grasp the magnitude of the event. One almost got the impression they'd invited the musicians and the pretty ladies to the Rathaus only so that they might, with music and dancing, relieve themselves of having to answer to the Swedish commander. But he was there today to speak to the city of Magdeburg on behalf of His Royal Majesty of Sweden—so of course they had to express their gratitude with a festive welcome celebration.

"And because His Royal Majesty of Sweden has heard," the imperious voice of Colonel von Falkenberg concluded, "that this illustrious city of Magdeburg bears in her coat of arms a virginal maiden, and indeed considers herself to be such a maiden, His Royal Majesty of Sweden has adopted as his own the manner of speaking used here in this illustrious city of Magdeburg, and hereby informs her that on this day, as august potentates are wont to do, he wishes to by procuration extend his hand in marriage to the Magdeburg Virgin. Therefore, may this illustrious, prudent, and glorious maiden, whose pride has not thus far yielded to any of her suitors, confidently place her wreath in the hands of His Royal Majesty's procurator in attendance, henceforth rendering to him loyalty, allegiance, and obedience in all things, as though he were His Royal Majesty himself. In turn, His Royal Majesty, in the person of his procurator, pledges his royal word and vows by his royal honor and the glory of his royal arms to the same Magdeburg Virgin to come and, instead of her maiden's wreath, place upon her head a crown!"

Colonel von Falkenberg fell silent, the gentlemen of the Council likewise; the crowd, which was piling up outside the door, rejoiced, and it seemed as though the fair, blond waters of the Elbe, which had so recently overtopped its banks at this spot, would surge into the hall once more. The musicians, meanwhile, struck up the dance music.

Suddenly a voice cried out: "Where is the fair Virgin of Magdeburg, anyway? She led the royal procurator into the city; let her bring him the wreath of the city as well—we want to dance the dance of honor with the Magdeburg Virgin!"

By that time, Willigis had reached the Rathaus. No one paid him any mind—they were all occupied with their own celebrating and cheering. He made his way unnoticed up the stairs to the banquet hall, at the entrance of which the crowd now stood like a solid wall. Willigis broke through it heedlessly—his pushes and shoves were hardly felt by anyone, it seemed, for in the middle of the hall, where everyone was staring, there was something happening! It was—now Willigis was standing in the front row—it was . . . no, it couldn't be that, surely his eyes deceived him! The woman at the gate had spoken of a celebration for Falkenberg, yet what he saw before him now actually looked like his own wedding celebration! For those were the solemn bars of the dance of honor that the musicians were playing, that was his bride whirling in the middle of the hall, that was Erdmuth in her bridal gown, just as he'd seen her in his mind's eye the whole ride back from Hamelin: there she was, dancing before his eyes, splendidly and sweetly and somewhat clumsily, just as a bride fully bedecked in her wedding finery dances. Surely Erdmuth couldn't be here dancing in her bridal gown—a pretty young maiden was supposed to wear such a gown only at her wedding, and the dance of honor was supposed to be played for her only then as well! And this was certainly not Erdmuth's wedding—they couldn't be having it without her groom, after all; otherwise that would mean he'd shown up uninvited at his own wedding! No, it had to be just a dream—or perhaps everything he'd experienced before had been a dream: the ride to Hamelin, his apparent exile from his own native city, what the gatekeeper's wife had told him about Erdmuth, and forcing his way through the city gate. Maybe it had all been nothing but a wild nightmare, from which he was just now awakening. So it was Erdmuth's wedding after all, but he was there not as a stranger, not as an uninvited guest, but as the bridegroom, doing only what was expected of him and standing aside as his dear maiden bride danced the dance of honor. She would have to give each and every man in the hall one last turn to dance with her. But the very last turn, that is the bridegroom's turn, never ended—he would take the beautiful bride in his arms and dance with her, but instead of letting her go again he would lead her out of the hall and take her to the bridal chamber, and all the others would have to go before them carrying torches—then she became his forever.

Erdmuth was now being blindfolded—for when the bridegroom's turn came, the fair maiden bride had to seek out her beloved bridegroom from among all the other men while practically blind! She mustn't get it wrong either; if she did, she would have to dance with another man again. But she couldn't get it wrong, for the bridegroom would help her: he'd watch her the whole time, lending her his own eyes, as it were, so that she could pick him out of the crowd—for indeed, love made all things possible!

The men were now forming a circle around Erdmuth; Willigis joined their ranks. There he stood among all the happy, well-groomed men in his shabby, weather-beaten buff coat, his boots splattered up to the shafts with excrement and mud, the hair on his temples matted with the sweat of hard riding, his youthful face sunken and unkempt from exertion and anxiety, not noticing that those around him were staring at him like a ghost (for he himself was looking only at his bride). But nobody could admit to himself that he recognized him; each one thought—just as Willigis had thought a few moments before—that he must be dreaming. For if the exiled Willigis Ahlemann had really dared enter the hall, then surely the crowd at the door would now be rushing in like the fair, blond waters of the Elbe coming to swallow him up. But the crowd was still quite calm (like Willigis, their eyes were fixed on the bride), so it couldn't be Willigis Ahlemann.

Erdmuth was now blindfolded, and the music began to play once more. It's the bridegroom's turn now, time for me to help Erdmuth, thought Willigis—love makes all things possible!

As he watched, however, it was as though Erdmuth had no one helping her—Willigis saw how she kept moving to the wrong side, and he began to doubt whether love was capable of anything at all. He started to pull at the chain[9]—it looked as though he, not Erdmuth, was the one meant to be looking for someone; his neighbors could scarcely hold on to him. Suddenly the musicians began to play hurriedly, as though the solemn bars of the dance of honor were running away from someone; but the people were still quite calm—only Erdmuth seemed to grow uncertain. She suddenly stopped and began to move the blindfold back and forth a bit, as though it were too tight (as pretty brides often did when they wanted to cheat a bit in the last round). At that moment, Willigis yanked the chain around so violently that he came to a stop right in front of Erdmuth. "Love makes all things possible!" he shouted at the top of his lungs. She gave a start and lifted the blindfold in alarm—he looked into her eyes and froze, for the eyes that stared at him coldly and dismissively from beneath the raised blindfold did not say in reply: Yes, love makes all things possible. Rather, what they said quite clearly was: Pride makes all things possible! And then—the musicians were suddenly playing madly, wrongly—she turned with a curt, childishly willful movement—she could now obviously see clearly—to the other side. There

[9] I.e., the chain of men that has formed around Erdmuth.

stood a man whom Willigis had never seen before, yet he recognized him right away—a man whom he would not allow to leave this place alive. He walked toward him, fists clenched.

Suddenly the hall was pierced by the loud shrieking of female voices—the musicians stopped playing, as though frozen in horror. From the door there came a dull roaring sound as the fair, blond waters of the Elbe prepared to rush into the hall—the crowd had now recognized Willigis Ahlemann! At that moment Willigis felt a flash of pain in his forehead, as if it came from a cut or a blow, and he did not know whether the flush of red that suddenly colored everything before his eyes was his own blood or that of the other man—had he already struck down his hated enemy? At once he lost sight of the man, and instead he saw leaning over him (had he fallen to the ground himself?) the slender, clever, and at that moment utterly impenetrable face of Otto Guericke as it suddenly emerged from the red haze and appeared before his eyes like the high rampart of the city of Magdeburg. And now Guericke looked as though he was about to strike him over the head with his rapier once more. "Traitor!" Willigis shouted, but the city constables were already seizing him.

When he came to himself again—his wound appeared well dressed, but it hurt—he found himself lying in a dark room that he was sure must be the jail, though it evidently had a very large window; for from his berth he had a clear view of the Rathaus' banquet hall, where they were still dancing, though the candles had by now burned down low, the little flames glowing eerie and indistinct like will-o'-the-wisps. Just then, Erdmuth floated by, nestled longingly in the arms of Falkenberg—so he hadn't succeeded in slaying him after all! But when he looked closer, he saw that it wasn't Erdmuth and Falkenberg at all but the fair Engelke and her counterfeit bridegroom. And as the couple whirled past a second time, it was no longer the fair Engelke and her counterfeit bridegroom either; instead, it was Lady Adventure, and the counterfeit bridegroom looked like His Royal Majesty of Sweden himself! Lady Adventure, however, was the spitting image of the Magdeburg Virgin as she looked in the city's coat of arms—though she'd lost her handsome wreath of German rue while dancing with His Swedish Majesty. And now she looked like one of the foolish virgins from the Bride's Portal at the great cathedral, who'd suddenly entered the hall as well! Yet they were behaving as merrily as if they were the wise virgins, and they all danced with the pastors—even pious Herr Bake had taken one in his arms, though he was clearly unfamiliar with this dance and kept sauntering around in the wrong direction, as though he actually meant to go somewhere else entirely—just like the proud gentlemen of the Council: they had indeed deigned to dance with the people, but now all of a sudden it was the people who danced with them! And thus a swirl of mismatched couples danced round and round the banquet hall—except the maid Itze had not found a man to dance with and was obliged to dance with a broom instead—she was a witch, after all. She stopped in front of Willigis, looked at him just as Erdmuth had done earlier, and said: "You might suppose I'm dancing with a broom, but really I'm dancing alone—I dance with my pride! And with whom do you dance?"

"I, too, am dancing alone," shouted Willigis. "I dance with my wrath!" And all of a sudden he was there among the dancers, and just as Itze had her broom, Willigis held in his hands a sword; this pleased him so much that he began to dance with it, pressing it savagely and tenderly against his wrath, as one presses a bride close to one's heart.

Then the last lights in the hall went out, and it became so dark that it seemed as if they were dancing toward an abyss—Erdmuth in the lead, with the whole world, as it were, plunging in after her, like at the Fall of Eve. There was a loud crack, as though the earth were ripping open and swallowing them all up. And then it was over.

When Otto Guericke opened the small portal in the city wall a few nights later, he told Willigis—who was no longer seeing people dancing, as his fever had passed—that he was truly sorry he'd had to inflict a minor wound on him, but otherwise it would have been impossible to get him out of the hall alive; surely the crowd would not have been satisfied unless they saw blood, and doubtless the same could be said for Willigis himself! And if he wanted to call his rescuer a traitor again as they parted, then he—Otto Guericke—would have to bear it. He was afraid no longer of words but of other things entirely. For it was certainly difficult to be exiled, like Willigis, from one's beloved native city, but it was much more difficult yet to be an exile *within* one's beloved native city, having to look on in silence at all the foolishness that went on, as though one were no longer even there! And he—Guericke—could well understand if Willigis wanted to pass judgment on the Council for being so weak, but Willigis did not yet understand what it was like to *be* this weak Council, and to have to endure as though one were a strong Council, silently accepting, endorsing, and sharing responsibility for all the injustice and all the ignorance (though one could certainly never justify it), just so that one might be around to help at the very last moment when the mischief of the pastors and the people of this city finally came to an end. But whether this should be difficult or easy, whether one thereby gained honor and glory or ended up being branded a traitor, the only thing that mattered now was to protect their beloved home from the worst that might befall her; and, in their concern for this, he and Willigis were surely of one mind still. And so, he implored him, please remain kindly disposed toward his native city despite everything, and when he went to Johann Ahlemann in Wolmirstedt—and indeed, that was where he would have to go—don't be like him and sit down with the Imperials to bemoan and chastise the rebellious city, but instead put in a good word for her, or at least remain silent and have patience; for one day all those who'd gone astray and been cast out would return home again, and he, too—Willigis—would yet regain his place and see his beloved home once more.

Otto Guericke said all these things calmly and knowledgeably, almost jokingly even, as he had spoken to his little cousin Anna—for when dealing with the distraught and resentful, one had to act as one did with women or children. And Willigis was distraught and resentful: he wasn't responding at all! In his heart, however, Willigis was saying: What does Guericke mean by concern for one's beloved home, anyway? I no longer have a home, and the only thing I ought to be concerned with now is striking this Falkenberg down—even if it means seeing the whole city of Magdeburg reduced to rubble! Why should I care about Magdeburg from now on? And how can Guericke say that I will regain my rightful place one day, when everything has been turned on its head and nothing is in its place anymore! How can he be so sure that I will ride to Johann Ahlemann in Wolmirstedt? No, I will ride to Hamelin, for that is the place where I belong in this upside-down world! Like the officers there, I have no bride now, and everything I thought about a second self was but a figment of my imagination! For there was but one woman on earth for me, and she is gone; so from now on there are no women at all: in the whole world there are none but men and soldiery!

The devastation wrought by the storm was still visible in the fields and villages as Willigis rode back to Hamelin, but he now took a strange pleasure in it. It seemed as though the ghostly army that had forged ahead of him the other day was now leading him back, and he was following it through the night into the middle of the war. Yes, he said to himself, this is how the world ought to look today; it's only reasonable, it cannot be otherwise! Many more fields should be trampled here, and many more houses should collapse! And if they then pull the dead and the wounded out of the ruins, their fate, too, will have been well deserved. For when everything that is created for patience and for meekness and for obedience leaps out of its proper order, when no one is willing to wait any longer, to show humility, and even to tolerate injustice at times, then all that remain are the proud, the defiant, the domineering—and if such is the case, then this world is bound to collapse, and truly, it deserves nothing more! The bride is no longer prepared to wait on the bridegroom, and the city is no longer prepared to wait on His Imperial Majesty; the people are no longer willing to wait on the Council, the pastors are no longer willing to wait on God—what else is there to do, then, but smash it all to bits in anger? And that's what I intend to do now! Yes, he continued, I want to see great culverins spewing fire, I want to hear the harsh roar of field pieces and siege guns; that would make me happy. I want to join the raucous chorus of the soldiery, which I once found so repugnant. I want to raise a glass to the arrival of the war in Magdeburg along with the officers at Hamelin, and like Marshal von Pappenheim, drink to my brother the Storm. I want to hear drums; I want to hear trumpets sounding the attack. Then, in the distance, he really did hear the sound of drums and trumpets, as though the invisible soldiery in whose wake he followed now came toward him. He looked around. There, through the wispy veils of mist that hung everywhere in what was now the light of early dawn, he could make out the glow of nearby watch fires, as though the invisible soldiery advancing in his direction were preparing to break camp for the day. He rode faster. The drum rolls were getting close; it was as though they were driving the columns of fog before them. Willigis heard voices singing the song that had greeted him outside the generalissimo's house as the flags filed in:

The old and prickly maid the chance
The Emp'ror did deny to dance;
She dances with his men tonight,
Oh, how it serves the proud girl right!

The invisible soldiery now burst out of the fog: Willigis made out a cavalry troop, at whose head rode Captain Bomgarten and some of the other officers from his table in Hamelin. "Hear, hear!" and "Hurrah!" they shouted when they saw him. The cavalry captain dashed out to meet him: "You've come back to us, Herr Ahlemann," he cried. "I can see it in your face, and truly, you've come at just the right time! His Excellency has taken the main body of the army and marched on the Swede, leaving us with only a small blockade force for Magdeburg, under the joint command of the lord marshal and Count Mansfeld. But we've intercepted letters from His Swedish Majesty that have allowed the marshal to learn their entire war plan. His Swedish Majesty intends not to give battle to His Excellency on the Oder but to draw him there and pull him to and fro till he's got him in checkmate! And the lord marshal says that if that is really what the Swede intends to do, then there is no other recourse for His Excellency but to force him into battle—that is, to fall back on Magdeburg with the entire army. His Swedish Majesty has sworn to aid the city, and he'll have to keep his royal word! The marshal is now making every preparation for the storming of the city, so that we don't lose any time while waiting for His Excellency to return: tomorrow begins the dance of honor with the Virgin of Magdeburg!"

Part III

The Bridal Chamber

Up on the rampart, Colonel von Falkenberg joked with the men about the icy-gray suitor who'd suddenly turned up outside the Magdeburg Virgin's house with the first swallows of the year. He thus described the old generalissimo Tilly, who had just returned from the Oder. He also related to them how His Royal Majesty of Sweden had spent the whole winter drawing old Tilly back and forth across the snow-covered, iced-over marshes of the Oder in a game of hide-and-seek. At no time had old Tilly been able to locate and ensnare His Majesty, the youthful king of Sweden—no doubt he was too stiff in the knees now; he would always show up on the scene after the king was already gone. All this back-and-forth had eventually tired out the old man, it seemed, and he'd decided to return to Magdeburg. Now it was time they gave the suitor a proper welcome: they'd regale him with one love song after another from their heavy guns and cartauns![1]

It was quite odd to see Colonel von Falkenberg joking like this—it did not befit his unreadable, unwavering countenance—but the men on the rampart certainly appreciated it; their own hearts had nearly faltered at the sight of the large retinue that old Lord Tilly had brought with him to the gates of the city as he prepared to call on the Magdeburg Virgin and extol her with song. And the retinue continued to grow, arriving from all ends of the Empire, so many that it was impossible to count them all! From Erfurt came galloping the League cavalry, and from Wolfenbüttel Pappenheim had the entire arsenal brought in—from the

[1] A cartaun (or kartouwe) is a type of heavy artillery used in the sixteenth and seventeenth centuries.

city's ramparts they could see the great mortars and the terrible augers for digging sap trenches and throwing up earthworks. And they were supposed to have employed three thousand peasants for the digging! And then from the Weser came thundering the harquebusiers and their dreadful artillery—each of their great pieces so heavy that the stout horses nearly collapsed under the weight; they, too, would have a part to play in Lord Tilly's love song! People in Magdeburg had thought that when March came, the little children would be able to go and pick violets and cowslips outside the city gates again, yet now the Imperials were out there digging trench upon trench in the soft, willing spring soil, coming closer and closer to the city. It would be a long time before little children picked violets down there again! And if one stood up on the rampart by night—as every able-bodied man of Magdeburg now did, because Colonel von Falkenberg did not permit anyone to escape his duty—then he would see the great wreath of campfires surrounding the city, one light right upon the other, and not a single dark spot between them where even a mouse could slip by unnoticed. No longer did it look as if the dance of honor were being played for the Magdeburg Virgin; now it looked like the dance of the torches that would escort her to the bridal bed!

But out there beyond this garland of lights, far off in the distance, there was surely another torchlight procession making its way here; surely His Royal Majesty of Sweden would now be making a forced march and coming to the aid of his bride—he'd already given her his hand in marriage by proxy and pledged his royal word that he would never again allow her to be dragged into the wrong bridal bed!

No, there was no need for people in the city to be alarmed, no matter how importunate old Lord Tilly became outside the gates. The Magdeburg Virgin had more than enough experience fending off troublesome suitors while waiting for the right one to arrive. And the right one was now on his way! It was not for nothing that the pastors took to their pulpits each day and with burning zeal preached the good news of His Royal Majesty's imminent arrival. And hadn't they also heard that Colonel von Falkenberg had already visited some of the grandest residences on the New Market, seeking accommodations for His Royal Majesty? There could hardly be any doubt that the king himself would soon be announcing his arrival at a certain day and at a certain hour—indeed, as if by some miracle of God, letters were still making their way unsinged through the wreath of campfires. Then of course there was also talk about how one of the men of the city had been standing nearby the other day when a breathless courier came up on the rampart to deliver the most recent missive from His Royal Majesty of Sweden to Colonel von Falkenberg. The colonel had immediately grown curiously stiff and stone-like, and when they later asked him whether His Royal Majesty was at last announcing his arrival, they were met with a curt, imperious rejoinder as to whether His Royal Majesty's word was enough for the people of Magdeburg or not. Colonel von Falkenberg was supposed to have looked terribly unreadable and unwavering as he said this, as though what he really wished to say was: "Whether His Royal Majesty comes or whether he comes not, it should make no difference to you people! You stand here or you fall here for the rights of conscience and for German liberty, and whether you live or you die does not matter in the slightest!" Yet it did matter to them whether they lived or died—they all had wives and children, after all, and in a city as lovely and cheerful as Magdeburg, who indeed wanted to die? Surely Colonel von Falkenberg knew this as well—so then what did he mean by his cagey response?

Had there been bad news? Was His Royal Majesty delaying yet again? Just what on earth did that letter say? So wondered the men on the ramparts, but no one answered them—indeed, they were no longer free to speak their minds as they had been before when they wanted to know something. Colonel von Falkenberg was not one to be trifled with; he demanded subordination and silence.

There was nothing else they could do but wait until their relief came—then on the way back home from the rampart, pay a visit to the Plögen house; for, as everybody knew, when it came to the maid Erdmuth, Falkenberg kept no secrets from her. And she almost certainly kept none from him either—otherwise he would not have been permitted to go in and out of her house as he pleased; for it was not really the custom in Magdeburg for strange gentlemen to go in and out of the houses of respectable daughters of the city. But that probably wasn't something they should be discussing either—Falkenberg would brook no idle chatter: they were to concern themselves with manfully doing their duty and nothing more. No, it was surely better for them to keep their mouths shut; and if that was something people in Magdeburg had never really learned to do, they'd learned their lesson now!

And so they went to see the maid Erdmuth. But arriving at the Plögen house, they saw the stable boy standing right outside holding the horse of Colonel von Falkenberg, who had dismounted and gone into the house; thus, they did not dare enter.

Erdmuth stood before the door, behind which Colonel von Falkenberg awaited her; in the distance the guns were roaring. She felt as though she could hardly raise the handle—but not because of the roaring of the guns, which she scarcely even noticed: What was the siege of Magdeburg to her, anyway? She hardly thought about it at all. She thought only of Falkenberg: every time he visited, he made her heart pound and took her breath away; in his presence she could scarcely control herself. What she felt during Colonel von Falkenberg's visits was more powerful than anything she had ever experienced, but at the same time it was always as though it were not happening in reality at all. He filled every drop of her blood and every fiber of her life, and yet it always seemed as though the ground were disappearing from under her feet. It felt like that time in Itze's chamber, when everything had been so magically transformed, and it was as if she'd been transported to an entirely new, enchanted world, from which she thought she might fall out again at any moment. It was such a wonderful sensation that it could not possibly be real; it was like a powerful force that snatched her up, only to drop her again—above all, it always made her feel as though she were loved and desired and yet scorned at the same time. And it could not be otherwise, but that Colonel von Falkenberg loved her and desired her—why else had fate led him to Magdeburg? Anything else would have made no sense at all; surely it had to mean something that he'd come upon her in the dark night, at the very moment she was about to leave Willigis. And then when she'd brought him the wreath of the city of Magdeburg, that couldn't possibly have been about Magdeburg alone—no, that, too, had mostly been about her. And Colonel von Falkenberg made it quite clear to her too—he was always bowing to her as if she were the queen of Sweden, after all. And how reverently he kissed her hand—no one else had ever done that; the small-minded townsfolk of Magdeburg had no understanding of such things. And he also gave her such a prominent position in the city by coming to visit her all the time—indeed, it was said that he never asked after any other woman! No, with Falkenberg she did not stand in the corner as she did as Willigis Ahlemann's bride; he would not humiliate her and keep her waiting as Willigis had—he was too much a gentleman for that. And this would be all the more evident when the king came to Magdeburg: for now Colonel von Falkenberg had to govern and defend the city on his behalf, but after the king arrived, he would be free for her. Then he would say the words he'd spoken that night at the Rathaus, this time to her: "When His Royal Majesty arrives, he will instead of her maiden's wreath place upon her head a crown!" Yes, when the king arrived, Colonel von Falkenberg would take her before the altar, and then she would truly be a proud and resplendent bride. His Royal Majesty of Sweden himself would dance the dance of honor with her and lead the torchlight procession to the bridal chamber.

Falkenberg stood in the neat burgher's parlor, his noble face just as unreadable and unwavering as it had been on the rampart when he'd read the letter from His Royal Majesty of Sweden, which he now read again in his mind. The windows were open: on the other side of the alley, the white blossoms of a pear tree were spilling over the wall, and whenever the distant guns fell silent for a moment, the sweet song of starlings could be heard.

Falkenberg was impatiently striking his riding crop against his high riding boots, for this little, lovestruck burgher's daughter was making him wait once more. Perhaps she was still preening herself for him—that would be just like her. She would no doubt get dressed up even for the end of the world; she was doing so even now, in fact, for as far as Magdeburg was concerned, the world was indeed about to end. He thought about the letter: His Royal Majesty has chosen to follow the *ratio belli* and is thus marching not to the succor of Magdeburg but to Frankfurt and Landsberg, whence he might threaten His Imperial Majesty from his own hereditary lands in Silesia.[2] Thus we will also follow the *ratio belli* here in Magdeburg—it is to our death that we will march. Our role in His Majesty's war plan is to pull Tilly away from the Oder and to hold him here until His Royal Majesty has broken through to Silesia; and indeed, that is what we intend to do—we will defend ourselves to the last man, even if the entire city is reduced to rubble and ashes! The important thing now is to make sure these little shopkeepers keep up their courage and hope so that nobody goes to Tilly behind my back.

He looked out the window, but not at the blossoming pear tree—which he did not see any more than Erdmuth heard the guns. Rather, he looked down at the alley: there were still people standing down there who'd come to the Plögen house to inquire about the arrival of the king, and if people were standing around and chatting idly anywhere in Magdeburg these days, one had to be careful. At that moment, Erdmuth walked in.

He gave her a reverent bow as though he were greeting the queen of Sweden. That always seemed to please her so much—he knew he must never neglect to do it if there was something he wanted from her. But then he immediately asked whether those people down in the street had come to ask her about the king again. Yes, she thought so, she replied, somewhat disappointed—for he had never greeted her so curtly before; he'd even forgotten to kiss her hand! But she also felt flattered that he'd once again

[2] Frankfurt refers to Frankfurt an der Oder, on modern-day Germany's border with Poland, rather than the much more well-known Frankfurt am Main in the west of Germany. Landsberg is Landsberg an der Warthe, the modern-day Polish city of Gorzów Wielkopolski. Capturing these cities would open the way to Silesia and thus to the lands of the Bohemian Crown.

reminded her of the important position she held here—for who else could people in Magdeburg look to, to tell them when the king was coming?

Quite matter-of-factly, he remarked that this was an excellent opportunity, since she could now give the people an answer right away. He'd been looking everywhere seeking accommodations for His Majesty, and her house, he said, was one of the loveliest homes on the square—might she perhaps be up to the task of receiving such a distinguished guest?

Her face lit up, for when the king came to Magdeburg, the bride would wear the crown! And that he should stay with her, that was the sign—how subtle Colonel von Falkenberg was in communicating this to her! No, she could no longer be in any doubt about her happiness when he had so honored her before the whole world.

Oh yes, yes, she said, she would gladly do so; she would gladly do anything, if only His Royal Majesty would come to Magdeburg. She was ready to give him a tour of the whole house, so that he might advise her on the apportionment of the rooms.

He looked at her with satisfaction, but also with astonishment, for she had never struck him as genuinely concerned with the king's arrival. As far as he could tell, she gave no thought at all to the fate of the city; he always thought it poor and petty of her that she was only ever concerned with her own person—indeed, she didn't even seem to notice the crack of the guns.

Meanwhile, in the distance, another heavy ball came crashing down, this time somewhat closer than before: every object in the room shook violently, but the maiden stood there without wavering or flinching, radiant as the white pear tree outside the window. Now, that made an impression on the soldier in him. He said, with a fleeting smile: "Why, the fair maiden is as undaunted as a bullet-proof harquebusier—does she no longer yearn to live?" But no sooner had he said this than he fell silent, taken aback; for the young maiden's eyes gazed at him like life itself yearning to be lived; indeed, they longed downright feverishly for life! And now, all at once, the guns were silent for him as well, as though retreating before an entirely different enemy who suddenly sought to attack him—and for whom he had been least prepared. Indeed, back on the night of his arrival, there on that lonely, unfamiliar street, this maiden had cast her spell on him; and when she'd begun to glow with such curious alacrity, she'd seemed almost desirable to him, as though within her the Magdeburg Virgin burned with flames of longing for her savior. But after seeing her and speaking to her by day, it became clear that she was just as common and ordinary as everyone else here. Indeed, he again saw within her the celebrated Magdeburg Virgin, only now in an entirely different sense; for in essence this city was itself but an arrogant, self-absorbed, little burgher's daughter, who did not burn with zeal for her great cause but, once things got serious, thought only of her own safety and salvation. But now this maiden suddenly glowed once more; now all of a sudden she was as alluring and desirable as she had been that night—no, as desirable as life itself to one who faces death! Was the city once again trying to show herself to him in the form of this maiden, was she trying to hide behind this girl, was it through her that the life of Magdeburg was to be wrested from his hands?

Quite troubled, he spoke: "Is the fair maiden so happy about the king's imminent arrival, then? Why, the fair maiden is glowing like a bride on her wedding day!"

She lit up even more, and he realized he'd caught her in her thoughts. He said to himself: She truly thinks that I will lead her to the altar, when in fact I'm leading her to her grave! What a curious misunderstanding indeed—how close life and death are, close enough to embrace each other! Everything here will soon be rubble and ashes; why should this maiden not be my life now, if I am already to be her death? He did not take his eyes off her face.

She had now begun to give him a tour of the house and was leading him from room to room, her splendidly voluptuous figure curiously buoyant, just as it had been on the night of his arrival—it was as though she led him through her native city for the second time, but this time through its innermost chambers. The house was filled with the dainty little things that belonged to the world of woman: spinning wheel and spinner's weasel[3] and sewing kit and flowerpots at the windows, and under a bench he saw a pair of the maiden's little shoes. It was all so delicate and so trifling, yet it seemed so dangerous all of a sudden—far more dangerous to him than the enemy's great instruments of war. Those, he felt, were much easier for him to deal with than these little, meaningless things. And nowhere did it smell of gunpowder either; everything in the house smelled faintly of dried rose petals and lavender—just as the dresses and gowns of young maidens always smelled. One of these—he touched it in passing—lay over a chair, where she'd probably taken it off earlier, when she'd gotten dressed up for him. All of a sudden her ensemble did not seem so ridiculous to him anymore either. Something sweet, something heavy, something yearning seemed to cling all over him, confusing his senses and confounding his thoughts, as though without warning his fate were slipping out of his own hands and into the hands of this

[3] A spoked wheel with gears onto which yarn is transferred from the spinning wheel and is automatically measured to the desired length (usually a skein).

fair maiden—suddenly he could no longer imagine all this turning to rubble and ashes!

Meanwhile, the maiden and her splendidly voluptuous figure continued to lead him up stairwells and over landings, from room to room; each one was cozier and more inviting than the last, and everything was kept so neat and tidy, and the maiden looked so comely in every room—and she seemed to know it herself too. Still beaming with pride, she suggested this or that idea for when the king arrived—it was almost embarrassing to him how seriously she took it, as though he were now caught in his own stratagem, like some enchanted web. This room, she said, was where the king should dine, and that room was where his worktable for all the big maps and war plans would go, and there across the hall was where his adjutants would stay. Indeed, she eventually began to open chests and cupboards in order to show him their contents: This was the silver centerpiece that belonged to her aunt Regula; it would go on the table when the king arrived. And over there was the chest that belonged to her aunt Engelke containing the choicest tableware, which had never been used before—she would set it out for the king. And here were the polished glasses from her aunt Itze's trousseau; no one had ever put these to their lips either—in these she would serve the king muscat wine. It was as though with every piece she showed him, she offered him her hand and said: Take it! For surely when she said "When the king arrives," what that meant for her was: "When Colonel von Falkenberg leads me to the altar"—that much he understood now.

This truly is a curious misunderstanding, he again said to himself; I yearn for one last drink from the cup of life before it's shattered to pieces, and she's showing me treasures as though she means them for our children and our children's children! He couldn't help but grin at how attached this little burgher's daughter was to her possessions, yet he was captivated by the womanly pride with which she kept raising her lovely, full arms and the almost tender affection with which she took out her treasures and placed them back again in the well-guarded, solemn orderliness of old chests and cupboards standing steadfastly in their places as if they meant to stand there for eternity—just like the old chests and cupboards that belonged to his mother back home in Herstelle, for they, too, had always seemed as if they held themselves to be the actual foundation of things. It was as though his homeless mind had unexpectedly brushed up against the great, silent, assured order of multiple generations, like the wings of a roving bird touching the mirror of a still pond. He suddenly found himself imagining that he was back in Herstelle in Westphalia, sinking his roots into his native soil, as if here, a woman gave him life for the second time—or as if death approached him in a hitherto unknown form. It was as though all of a sudden, the gravity of affairs dropped out of the world of great conflicts and ideas and came to rest here in these most intimate chambers where man and woman kiss, where little children are born and old people die, and where people call out to God from the torment or the jubilation of their lives—without a thought for the rights of the person or the liberty of the Estates. He said to himself: It really does seem as if the whole city is trying to hide behind this fair maiden—why, it's like in those Papist images in which all take refuge under the mantle of Mary! All of a sudden he felt no longer that fierce desire for one last drink of life but an oddly gentle sense of defenselessness before it—he looked at the maiden as though she were really a Papist image, capable of making him fall to his knees before he was even aware of it. But he had to guard himself against such a thing! Abruptly, he announced that it was time the fair maiden granted him leave, that he might return to the rampart—duty called, and he had already been away for far too long.

She looked somewhat abashed—just a moment ago, she'd felt quite sure of him, yet now he was slipping away again. Were the accommodations for His Royal Majesty not to his liking? she asked dejectedly. But by then he had fully resumed his role as commander of the city, doing the things that needed to be done. He responded, with a deep bow and a kiss on her hand, that she need only concern herself with preparing her home for His Majesty's arrival; he would return at the proper time and inspect everything.

The sound of carpets being beaten and floors being swept now filled the Plögen house from morning to evening; all the windows stood wide open; the floorboards were scrubbed white, the furniture immaculately polished. The precious glassware was carefully washed and the silver tableware shined; counts were taken of the place settings and the fine bedding linens; the maidservants hung a wreath over the front door—just as when Erdmuth was to be the bride of Willigis Ahlemann. And it appeared not to matter that the great guns continued to roar in the distance or that the cannons continued to pound at the gates of the city; no, that seemed to make no difference whatsoever to the occupants of the Plögen house. It was a true testament to the absolute certainty of their conviction that His Royal Majesty of Sweden was fully on his way, and this indeed restored people's hope and courage. The girls who attended the Plögen maid might have cried out like everyone else and rushed into the cellar covering their eyes or their ears whenever there was an especially terrible flash or a loud bang, but the Plögen maid herself looked on as merrily as if she were listening to the singing of the starlings and the blackbirds—she didn't seem to notice the terrible firing of the guns any more than the blossoming pear tree beneath her window did—so eventually people began to think they must be hearing things.

And they would soon turn out to be right; for one day all of a sudden the guns really were silent. And where had all the regiments disappeared to overnight, where was Lord Tilly and his large retinue now? Why, it looked as if he'd taken the Magdeburg Virgin's rebuff and left—it looked as though the only army left out there was the small blockade force under Counts Pappenheim and Mansfeld, like over the winter! It was an absolute miracle: Lord Tilly had been forced to withdraw, and the only one who could have possibly brought it about was His Royal Majesty of Sweden. There was nothing more to do now but run to the home of the fair Plögen maid, to see the distinguished guest alight there; but there was no need to ask now—now people were shouting it to one another throughout the whole city: "His Royal Majesty is approaching at full force! Tilly has fled, and Pappenheim and Mansfeld are covering his retreat!" Thus, every street and alley of triumphant Magdeburg rang out once more with the city's old *Trutzlied*, singing the song of resistance with the exuberant joy of newly bestowed life: "Though soul and body perish ..."

Colonel von Falkenberg was making his solitary rounds on the rampart—he always made his rounds alone. In the city, the bells were ringing for Easter; the pastors were up in their pulpits preaching the gospel of His Royal Majesty of Sweden to the resurrected city of Magdeburg. Colonel von Falkenberg, however, could not listen to the sermon, for he did not believe in the resurrection of Magdeburg, and his understanding of the gospel that the pastors preached was quite different from theirs.

To himself, he said: His Royal Majesty has marched on Frankfurt and Landsberg so that he might threaten His Imperial Majesty in Vienna from his own hereditary lands in Silesia, and if Tilly has withdrawn from here, it can only be because he still hopes to save Frankfurt and Landsberg and block the route to Vienna. But Frankfurt and Landsberg can no longer be saved, and that means Tilly will have to return to Magdeburg a second time. His Royal Majesty used us to draw Tilly away from the Oder, and now Tilly will attempt to use us to draw His Royal Majesty away from Silesia—we must prepare ourselves for the storm! For only if we are at our last can Tilly hope to force His Royal Majesty to quit Silesia and come to our succor. But His Royal Majesty, God willing, will not allow Tilly to force his hand and cause him to abandon his grand plans—for what is one city, what are a few thousand lives, compared to the safeguarding of conscience and of German liberty!

He removed his helmet, as if to pray: Let His Royal Majesty come, or let him not come—myself he shall always find prepared to live or to die, as the cause demands. God grant only that the people of Magdeburg do not realize where we are headed too soon! He placed his helmet back on his head and, holding his hand over his eyes, looked out over the other side to see whether Lord Tilly's returning Imperial army might perhaps already be visible in the distance.

Some distance away, he spotted Otto Guericke standing on the rampart, alone like himself, his hand over his eyes, peering into the distance; and then he, too, turned around and started coming toward him.

This made Colonel von Falkenberg uncomfortable, as he rather disliked Otto Guericke; he could not get a clear idea of the man, even though Guericke's face was an open book. The other gentlemen of the Council he could tell were secretly reluctant; their griping and grumbling were clearly evident behind their expressionless faces. They sat on their big sacks of money like geese sitting on their eggs, each thaler[4] that the siege cost having to be painstakingly extracted from them—presumably this was their final, impotent act of resistance. Guericke, on the other hand, always showed himself to be ready and obliging—no trace of resistance could ever be detected in him; one never knew with that fellow!

By now Guericke had reached the colonel and in his calm, friendly voice said: "Has the colonel heard the great news just brought in by the courier? His Royal Majesty stormed Frankfurt and took it on Palm Sunday, and it seems Landsberg, too, is about to fall!"

Colonel von Falkenberg could not turn pale—never in his life had he understood it; but he suddenly recalled the festively decorated Plögen house and all the people crowding around it, hoping to get a glimpse of His Royal Majesty alighting there this very day.

Meanwhile, Guericke continued unselfconsciously: His Royal Majesty had won such a great victory, and they couldn't even announce it in Magdeburg! For he agreed with the good colonel, of course, that the people should be left to think that His Swedish Majesty was marching on Magdeburg; above all, they had to ensure that the people's courage didn't falter when Tilly returned now—he was almost certainly in agreement with the good colonel on that point too. By the way, had he noticed the troop movements off in the distance as well?

Colonel von Falkenberg could not turn red—he was no better at turning red than he was at turning pale. And why should he, anyway? It was his duty to stand and fight

[4] A silver coin issued by German states in the fifteenth to nineteenth centuries.

with every means at his disposal—of course it had been necessary to deceive the people in this situation. But the fact that this Guericke fellow had found out about it and then presumed to mention it to him—that was dangerous. He said, coldly—for when someone thought one's guard was down, that was the time to strike back: Even if Tilly returned, they could withstand it; Magdeburg was not as poorly defended as it had been when he'd arrived. He'd fashioned the city's rough soldiery into an excellent fighting force, devoted to him like a faithful dog, and he also had the people firmly under his control—they would not refuse him obedience, as they once had the Council. A company always said: "As we are paid, so also shall we fight," and thus he had seen to it that the troops were now paid better. A people, on the other hand, always said: "He who can truly command us, him we shall also obey."

Guericke understood that Falkenberg was threatening him with the troops and the people. Yes, he said obligingly, the good colonel had indeed trained an excellent fighting force and had the people firmly under his control—if he understood correctly, the colonel planned to use both to make his last stand here. For indeed, it would now have to come down to that; otherwise Tilly would scarcely be able to force His Swedish Majesty to keep his royal word to the city—and that was what Tilly would now have to try to do in order to divert the enemy from Silesia. He and the colonel were surely of the same mind on this matter as well, he wagered.

Falkenberg replied—for when someone thought one's guard was down yet again (and surely that was what Guericke thought in bringing up the royal word), it was all the more necessary to strike back: Not only had he produced a dependable populace and a capable fighting force, but he'd also put the fortifications in order—surely, as chief engineer of the city's defensive works, Guericke would know best of all in what miserable condition they'd been. The new outworks which he'd built bore their defiant names—"Trutz-Kaiser", "Trutz-Tilly", and "Trutz-Pappenheim"—with good reason: just let the enemy try to storm them!

Guericke was now on familiar ground, for he was well acquainted with the new outworks and the guns of the enemy. He spoke, even more calmly than before: "So an accord with Tilly is entirely out of the question, then—again, assuming I've understood the good colonel correctly. The only thing for us to do now is to keep Tilly away from His Royal Majesty for as long as we can—without any hope of succor."

Guericke wants to make peace, Falkenberg thought to himself, and he most likely has the whole Council behind him. It's just what I've always expected these shopkeepers and peddlers to do when things got really serious! And that is why it's necessary to strike hard at the first opportunity. Yes, he said trenchantly, Guericke had indeed understood him correctly; anyone who even spoke of an accord he would have hanged, and he would also hang anyone who doubted the king's promise of succor, without respect to rank or standing, starting at the top! The great cause which they'd been given the opportunity to serve here deserved nothing less. Let no one imagine that he might save himself at the cost of this universal endeavor! When Tilly stormed the city, they would know how to fight him off, that was nothing; but as for the storm that would be unleashed here inside the city if they did not keep calm—he did not advise anyone to conjure up such a thing if he knew what was good for him! Guericke shook Falkenberg's hand: Now, now, surely it wouldn't come to that—after all, no one had said anything about an accord until now. It sounded almost like a joke, as though Guericke were speaking to his little cousin Anna—for one had to deal with the possessed as one dealt with women and children; that Falkenberg was a man possessed was something he'd long suspected, but now he had the proof in his hands.

When he came down from the rampart a few hours later, the sound of jubilant shouting echoed throughout the city: There must have been a great battle! Tilly must have been dealt a devastating blow, for the entire Imperial army was surging back, and they appeared to be on the run—clearly His Royal Majesty of Sweden was hot on their heels!

The following day, the fleeing army began to fire on the city once more.

Almost at once, curious rumors began to spring up in Magdeburg: During Holy Communion at the great cathedral, all the lights on the altar had suddenly gone out—the same thing that had happened in the plague year, before many, many people had perished. And on the old market square in front of the Rathaus, the stones had begun to sweat blood—sympathetic women had brought cloths to wipe them off, and Trina Klaas, who was usually quite good at stopping a bleed, had spoken some words over the stones, but the poor stones just would not stop bleeding. And then there were also rumors that the city's powder supplies were dwindling at an alarming rate, as though the city's arsenal was infested with mice and rats that fed on gunpowder—it wouldn't be long before the big guns up on the ramparts screamed and roared out of sheer hunger. They even learned, though it had happened several months prior, that the administrator had gone to the great cathedral and broken open the tomb of Emperor Otto in search of gold and treasure to ensure they would have enough powder when the enemy came! But the most troublesome thing of all was the peculiar crackling and creaking that could be heard in every house, the same sound that was heard in the Rathaus before they'd entered into the accord with Sweden. Many times a night, people would rouse themselves from sleep and clamber up to the attic to see whether one of the enemy's missiles had struck and caught fire. All these rumors were the direct result of the terrible bombardment inflicted on the people of Magdeburg by old Lord Tilly, causing them to become quite confused in the head: who'd have thought it possible that a defeated army would still have the audacity and the strength to fire on them with such terrific violence? Did old Tilly have no fear that the victorious Royal Majesty of Sweden, who must at this point be hard on his heels, would utterly destroy his army? Did old Tilly think he still had a chance of snatching the youthful Royal Majesty's fair bride away from him? It was high time they gave him a proper send-off once and for all! So why, then, had Falkenberg raised no objection when Lord Tilly took possession of the new outworks? Why did he allow savage Pappenheim to capture the magnificent Zollschanze redoubt, and even the "Trutz-Kaiser" works up on the Mühlberg? Indeed, it appeared as though *they* were the ones who were losing ground! And why had Colonel von Falkenberg given up the proud bridge that spanned the Elbe and the Isle of Virgins that lay between its banks? Was it merely a stratagem to lull old Lord Tilly into a false sense of security so that His Royal Majesty of Sweden could destroy him all the more easily? Or was the now-unbridled Pappenheim indulging in a reckless attempt to harass and intimidate the detested Virgin once more before having to withdraw again, like in '29? Because it was indeed intimidating to see him drawing closer and closer to the suburb of Neustadt;

and Mansfeld, too, had already advanced right up to the fortifications at Sudenburg—as though they were the iron arms of Lord Tilly spreading out to embrace them from both sides at once. And all the while his terrible artillery continued to regale the city with its furious love songs that roared and rumbled over one another until it sounded as if Magdeburg were beset by seven thunderstorms at the same time. But how was it that an icy-gray suitor continued to woo her with such impetuosity? And now it seemed he was preparing to force open the door to the royal bride's chamber—suddenly all the guns converged on the tower at the High Gate, as though they meant to blast open a breach. Unless His Royal Majesty of Sweden came now, there would be no resisting him.

But as often as they asked Colonel von Falkenberg why His Majesty continued to delay—and such was their fear that they were able to summon the courage to question him—they received the same curt, imperious reply he'd given before Tilly's withdrawal: He would teach the people of Magdeburg to doubt the royal word of His Swedish Majesty! Shouldn't they be singing their old, stalwart song of resistance with even greater gusto—that they would rather die than submit to the emperor and the pope? But strangely enough, no one felt like singing the old *Trutzlied* anymore—not even Colonel von Falkenberg could make them do it.

On the morning when the High Gate tower collapsed, Dr. Bake was holding a field service in the shelters built into the rampart. Bake had entered into the midst of the world, as it were, and now took his stand with preaching just as the pugnacious townsfolk took theirs with arms, striding ever forward at the head of the rebelling, triumphing city of Magdeburg. When the great thundering sound of the collapsing tower rumbled through the air—Bake was just repeating the incendiary words that Dr. Gilbert impressed upon his heart daily (he was now more pleased with him than he had been before)—he was suddenly unable to continue speaking, as though the swirling dust from the shattered masonry had stifled his voice. His pious schoolmaster's face turned color, and the only words he could get past his lips were those of the anxious prayer of Peter as he sank in the waves: "Lord, save us: we perish!"[5] And as he turned his terrified gaze toward the scene of the disaster, he suddenly recalled the Gospel about the destruction of Jerusalem; he had completely forgotten about it for months in favor of the gospel of His Royal Majesty of Sweden, and now it was as though he could actually hear, from within himself, the words of the Lord Christ: "If thou hadst known, in this thy day, the things which belong unto thy peace!"[6] Finding himself unable to resume his sermon, he instead hurriedly descended from the rampart.

There once again, as on that fateful morning, the fair city of Magdeburg lay at his feet, rising up from the banks of the broad, billowy Elbe, still magnificently rolling along like a great highway of destiny; but now in command of it was no longer the proud Virgin of Magdeburg but the two proxies of her fearsome suitor—it was under the command of Lords Pappenheim and Mansfeld, and in the silver mirror offered by its waves, the maiden beheld the iron face of Lord Tilly. For no longer was her towering home encircled by the dense, thorny maiden's wreath bristling with bulwarks and bastions; around it now lay a torn and tattered wreath, its entire length marked by the ruins of spires

[5] Mt 8:25. Bake appears to be mixing up this passage (in which the Lord calms a storm while out at sea with the disciples) with the story in Matthew 14 in which Peter attempts to walk on water.

[6] Paraphrase of Lk 19:42.

and battlements broken off from the walls like the prongs of a shattered crown. And inside the Virgin's fortress, it was no longer a bustling and cheerful scene but one where every heart trembled and quaked. Where had the gaily leaping gables gone—who had toppled the jaunty bricks from their heights? And why was the honey-brown of the mighty half timbers covered with so much soot and smoke? What were all those dark, ugly holes gaping over doors and cornices? The festive garland of emblems and images that festooned the lovely homes and courts and gave them their names was hardly recognizable anymore—as though every house had suddenly become nameless. Was the darkness of obliteration and oblivion already upon them? Was the city, decked in these shadows, being transformed into a ghastly wedding chamber? Bake shuddered. The enemy guns were silent for a moment, as though catching their breath after the effort of destroying the High Gate—the streets were as quiet as a tomb. In the still silence, Bake felt that he could hear every stone in his path calling out to him: "If thou hadst known the things which belong unto thy peace!" He could not help but think that today he had preached the gospel of His Royal Majesty of Sweden to this city for the last time.

At that moment his gaze fell upon the beautiful wreath of green rosemary above the front door of the Plögen house, past which he was just now walking. The wreath hung there as resplendently, as solemnly, and as confidently as if it were the very same wreath that Bake had seen there on that fateful day, back when the Plögen maid was preparing to marry Willigis Ahlemann and the whole city had seemed to him like a proud, radiant bride. True, if one looked at it right, the wreath was already somewhat withered, just like the wreath of the fair Plögen maid—who, thanks to Colonel von Falkenberg, was now the talk of the town. Bake felt a twinge in his heart. He really did not like to walk past the Plögen house, because even if the maid Erdmuth's bridegroom had run off to join the Imperial Papists, a virtuous maiden still could not just go and find herself a counterfeit bridegroom—it was against all Christian discipline and morals! And that she was so convinced that His Royal Majesty of Sweden, when he arrived, would stay not with the high-ranking gentlemen of the City Council but at her house—whence the wreath hanging there—why, that was downright ridiculous! She was completely ruining her reputation with such nonsense. Bake had long felt himself obligated to make an earnest effort to approach young Erdmuth regarding this matter; he was, after all, her shepherd and pastor. Yet he had never had the time for it; he'd had to go up on the rampart and into the pulpit each day to preach the gospel of His Royal Majesty of Sweden and enflame the people to utmost resistance. And this resistance, as he'd been given to understand, even included the irksome rosemary wreath that hung above the door of the Plögen house; it included the maid Erdmuth receiving visits from Colonel von Falkenberg and always being able to tell the people what she'd learned from him: the king was expected to arrive on a certain day and at a certain hour. The people drew comfort from this, he was given to understand; it gave them a sense of courage and confidence that could not be taken away from them. So Bake kept finding himself having to turn a blind eye and somehow appease his restless conscience, because it was the struggle for the freedom of pure doctrine that was at stake. But now that this struggle was coming to an end, he could no longer quell his conscience. It now burst forth with such force that he felt it necessary to admonish not only young Erdmuth but himself as well; after all, he felt that he was partly to blame for all her outrageous behavior since her maiden's eve: he'd gone there intending to exhort her to patience and meekness and had ended up letting his own sermon elude him, so to speak. Bake suddenly recoiled, as though he realized his thoughts were going in the wrong direction—he knew himself, after all, and knew he had a habit of ending up in different places than he actually meant to be. But perhaps he'd started off on the wrong foot to begin with; it certainly seemed possible—Bake was also familiar with how easily dismayed his soul could be, and the collapse of the tower had made him fearful. Things were ultimately not as bad as he'd thought—indeed, the guns were now silent; perhaps the valiant townsfolk had driven back the enemy. Yes, surely it had been the cunning devil playing a trick on him once again, hoping to break the resistance of the protesting city of Magdeburg—but no one had ever been able to break protesting Magdeburg; Magdeburg had always come out on top. No, Magdeburg was not yet at her last—there was no need for anyone to prepare for death.

As he was thinking this, he heard a small, sweet voice quietly singing the beautiful hymn of mortality:

In the midst of life
We are in death.
Of whom may we
Seek for succor,
But of Thee, O Lord![7]

He now stood before his own house; the door was still open, as required by city ordinance due to the bombardment—people on the street needed to be able to flee into the homes on short notice. The singing sounded rather sad and somewhat fearful, yet still quite heartfelt and trusting,

[7] From the Latin hymn *Media vita in morte sumus*. An English translation appears in the Book of Common Prayer. The German version would have been a well-known Lutheran hymn.

like a soul preparing itself for its final hour, to fall willingly and confidently into the hands of God.[8] Bake stopped on the threshold of the door, looking as pale and distraught as he had when the tower collapsed—and indeed, that was how he felt too. For the voice he heard singing was that of his dear wife—but why would she be singing that hymn about death? His wife had always been so cheerful and fearless, after all. Just what was she doing frightening him like that, after he'd just managed to compose himself and find his bearings? "In the midst of life we are in death" was supposed to be sung only at a funeral service!

Reluctantly, Bake stepped into the hallway of his home. There stood his dear wife with her back turned to the door, for she had not heard him coming; their four young children clung to her skirt, just as they had done on that fateful day—their little faces could again be seen peeping out from all the folds of her dress. Like before, the fifth was not yet visible; Frau Bake still bore it beneath her heart. But as she turned around to greet her husband, he was clearly reminded of how soon she would be holding the babe in her arms. Bake was overcome by a strange, painful feeling, such that all displeasure, and likewise all resistance, suddenly fell away from him, and he felt nothing other than concern for his dear wife: how would she fare bringing this fifth child into the world amid the constant crashing of those terrible guns? Thus he again felt he heard the voice of the Lord Christ from the Gospel about the destruction of Jerusalem, this time the words "And woe unto them that are with child, and to them that give suck in those days!"[9] He now understood only too well

[8] Possibly an oblique reference to Heb 10:31: "It is a fearful thing to fall into the hands of the living God."

[9] Mt 24:19.

why his wife had just been singing "In the midst of life we are in death."

Seeing Bake enter, she immediately stopped singing and presented him her little, girlish face for a kiss. It lay nestled in the white platter of her ruff, looking as kindly and sweet and bride-like as if the terrible firing of the guns that had raged all morning were but one part in the song of their marriage and their lives together. And now the four young children, evidently quite excited by the sound of the guns, joined in as well, clapping their hands and shouting: "Boom, boom! And again—boom, boom!" as Frau Bake had taught them to do right at the beginning of the siege before they had time to become frightened in the first place.

Bake's eyes suddenly welled up with bright tears. He felt that all the resistance, all the opposition, all the protesting and rebelling and triumphing that he constantly preached up on the rampart was an altogether pitiful, almost faithless gallantry compared to the courage and fortitude that his dear wife had shown before him and their four young children this whole time. He put both arms around her and said, almost sobbing: "God protect you, my love, God protect you and our fifth little one! Alas, my love, let us surrender to God's will, for it is He alone who determines the fate of His precious Word! From now on we will rely on Him alone, we will be mindful of that which belongs unto our peace!" It felt very good to say this; it was as though a severe, vicious cramp in his innermost being had been thereby released, and everything was now wondrously clear, quiet, confident, and certain, whatever might come to pass—and as his head lowered to his wife's heart, he felt that his soul now rested in God's hands. He did not even notice the thudding hoofbeats coming from the street outside.

Colonel von Falkenberg halted his steed in front of the parsonage; the four young children rushed to the door to admire the black beauty. Coming up behind them, Bake and his wife gazed not at the spirited horse but silently and anxiously at the colonel. Why were all the children around here so shy, he asked in an ungracious tone; was it because of all the cannon fire?

Frau Bake replied sheepishly—for it was well known that all the children in Magdeburg were curiously shy around Colonel von Falkenberg: Oh no, the guns didn't bother her little ones at all—indeed, they quite liked hearing them. Then, turning to the children, for she felt sorry for the colonel that the children disliked him: Come now, she told them, put on a happy face, for it was thanks to this good gentleman that they always got to hear the guns go "boom". And perhaps their father would hold them up so that they might shake hands with the good colonel up on his horse—such a courtesy as he might well expect of them. And then they would surely wish to ask him when the king would arrive, for she knew how much they were looking forward to it.

Meanwhile, all four children resolutely put their hands behind their backs, and when a single, solitary shot rang out in the distance, they began to weep bitterly and buried their little heads in their mother's skirt, such that every one of their little faces was hidden from view. It was as though they had realized for the first time what the firing of the guns actually meant. Frau Bake stroked their hair comfortingly, and asked—again somewhat sheepishly—whether the good colonel would please excuse the poor children; but then all of a sudden a look of great astonishment came over her little, girlish face, for the colonel was looking at them with such timidity that it seemed the young children made him even more anxious than he made them. This touched her heart so strangely; she felt like removing the helmet from his head and comfortingly stroking his hair as if he were one of the poor, terrified children. She quickly led the children into the house so that the sight of them would no longer upset him.

The colonel now turned to Bake. It had come to his attention, he said, that the good pastor had broken off his sermon on the rampart this morning when the tower at the High Gate collapsed. The people had been quite discouraged by this, he continued, and right at the moment when they needed something to bolster their resistance too. Such a thing must never happen again! Bake would have to make up for this poor impression before the day was done, and the afternoon sermon would be his opportunity to do so.

It annoyed Bake that the colonel interfered with his sermons. He recalled how recently, Dr. Gilbert had railed about how Falkenberg, just like the obdurate city authorities, did not know his place in relation to the ecclesiastical ministry. Flushed, but firmly, he said that he had planned not to preach this afternoon but to attend to the most pressing pastoral needs of his congregation. Then, screwing up his courage—for when the fearful Bake grew bold, he always overshot his mark—he remarked that he thought he might call on the maid Erdmuth Plögen; it was time to do away with that irksome wreath above her door, and he felt that there were some other things that needed to be set right as well, things that endangered the reputation of an honorable Christian maiden.

All of a sudden, Colonel von Falkenberg's black stallion began to rear and dance, and Bake clumsily jumped aside. The colonel used his spurs. Then, curtly, he said that there was no need for the good pastor to concern himself with the Plögen maid; he would see to her himself. There was thus nothing to prevent the good pastor from preaching this afternoon.

Bake stubbornly replied that he intended to follow his conscience.

The black horse again began to dance, causing sparks to fly from its hooves—this time Bake's hasty escape almost landed him in the gutter. When the horse at last stood still, the colonel said, coldly: "I am quite happy to see pastors follow their conscience; for it is I who determine the conscience of pastors now, and if anyone dares dispute that, I will have him hanged—the good pastor can thus take the pulpit without worrying about his conscience!" Then he rode away.

Bake stood there as if thunderstruck. Falkenberg is always claiming to be fighting for freedom of conscience, he muttered to himself; that's the reason we let him into Magdeburg in the first place! Yet now it seems that all we've done is betray our own freedom of conscience! Surely, the master of our conscience is the holy and all-knowing God—so how, then, are we to account for the fact that Falkenberg is permitted to say that he is the master of our conscience? Indeed, we cannot account for such a thing—should we find ourselves before the judgment seat of God, we could expect nothing other than eternal damnation. Bake blanched, as though he unexpectedly found himself gazing into an abyss that he'd been unaware he was approaching—or perhaps he had been aware? Again, he suddenly thought he heard the words from the Gospel about the destruction of Jerusalem, as he had earlier when the High Gate tower collapsed; but now it was the tower of a high gate within his own soul that seemed about to collapse, opening the way to the judgment seat of God, and henceforth in his conscience—as in the city of Jerusalem—not one stone would be left upon another. But then he heard his name, and when he lifted his eyes—he could hardly bring himself to do so—he saw Dr. Gilbert rushing up the street. Still some distance away, he called out to Bake: The High Gate tower had not, as they'd feared in the initial shock, fallen into the city moat to serve as a bridge and a breach for the Imperials; but by the manifest grace of God it had leaned in the wrong direction, smashing to pieces the enemy's own tunnels and trenchworks! And so the tower of the high gate in Bake's soul likewise fell to the wrong side, and in place of the destroyed Jerusalem before the judgment seat of God he saw triumphant Magdeburg once more.

Meanwhile, Colonel von Falkenberg was riding to the Plögen house; he could not allow the wavering Bake to beat him there—these pigheaded pastors simply would not obey any man, even when the knife was at their throats! Colonel von Falkenberg quite resented Dr. Bake for forcing him to ride to the Plögen house, and at this particular moment too: he could still see the little, girlish face of the pastor's young wife and hear the sobs of her four children—the fifth was quite obviously on the way as well. And how she'd admonished the children to put on a happy face for him, because he was the one behind the cannon fire! And then how she'd wanted them to ask him when the king would arrive, that was the most troublesome thing of all, for there had actually been a moment there when he'd felt as though his king had abandoned and betrayed him. I've long since learned to deal with the men of this city, he said to himself, but when it comes to the women, there will be no managing them when things get really bad here, and the children even less so. The women know this too: that little pastor's wife actually looked at me as though she would have loved nothing more than to wrap me in her apron like the little children hiding beneath it. Oh, how the men of Magdeburg would love that—then they could deal with Tilly without fear or shame! No, he continued, a man in my situation can do no better than to steer clear of women, and that is what I have done all my life! He thought angrily of Bake, because of whom he now had to ride to the Plögen house, where it had once seemed to him as though all life in the city sought refuge in one woman, and he'd almost been swept along himself. So he had to be on his guard—he looked with unease at the blossoming pear tree, which stood there still, snow-white as a luminous bride, in the middle of the bombarded stronghold.

Erdmuth had decorated her house from top to bottom, and every morning she put on her finest dress; His Royal Majesty could be expected at any hour, and she had to be ready to receive him. To be sure, the wreath over her front door and the flower bouquets in the rooms were by now beginning to wilt; Erdmuth's festive gown was somewhat wrinkled from constant wear, and she herself looked a bit tense, her mouth drawn taut like a pouting child; for before her stood the maid Ilsabe Fricken. Ilsabe had not shown her face at the Plögen house for many weeks, though it would have taken her but two small hops across the street—surely this was due to pale envy over Colonel von Falkenberg, whose doting admiration everyone seemed to begrudge her—it wasn't like any of her other friends ever came by anymore either! That was quite all right with her, however: the girls of Magdeburg no longer fit into her new life; it was clear they were far too mundane and small-minded, and on top of that, there was something about being in their presence that always made her feel insecure. Yet Erdmuth had no reason to feel insecure anymore: ever since Colonel von Falkenberg had decreed that His Royal Majesty of Sweden was to stay at her home, she couldn't possibly doubt her happiness any longer. Haughtily, she eyed Ilsabe: she was making the same pointed expression as on the night of her maiden's eve and saying in her shrill voice that she'd heard that the Council no longer believed that His Royal Majesty of Sweden was coming to Magdeburg at all; that Falkenberg had merely talked the people into believing that he would, and Erdmuth had genuinely believed it—so what did she think when she looked at her decorated house now? And as she spoke, Ilsabe looked as though she could scarcely wait for the look on Erdmuth's face to turn to one of horror.

It did not make the least bit of difference to her what the Council believed, Erdmuth replied. She would know much better than they whether His Royal Majesty of Sweden was coming or not—the whole town came to call on her because Colonel von Falkenberg was in and out of there on a daily basis, so she always got the latest and most reliable news.

Ilsabe gave a look that immediately made Erdmuth's cheeks turn red; she continued: That chatty Agnete Brauns was telling everyone in town that Falkenberg's time here was nearly up, that Magdeburg could hold out no longer; she'd heard from her father, the burgomaster, that Johann Ahlemann sought to mediate between Lord Tilly and the city—so what did she think about Herr von Falkenberg coming in and out of her house on a daily basis now?

Erdmuth replied that she was not the least bit concerned with what that chatty Agnete Brauns said—indeed, it was utterly beneath her, and she wished she hadn't heard it at all. And Agnete Brauns could thank the Lord in heaven for that too; for Colonel von Falkenberg, who held everything here in the palm of his hand, she held in hers.

Ilsabe gave another look that made Erdmuth's forehead turn red: Even with all the cannon fire, old Frau Spitznase still clearly heard what people whispered in Magdeburg, and her granddaughters claimed that a number of prisoners were saying that Willigis was in the Imperial camp, and that he swore every day that when the city fell, he would be the first to ride in and strike Falkenberg down—so it looked as if Erdmuth could expect to see her former bridegroom again soon. What did she think about that?

At the name Willigis Ahlemann, Erdmuth became white as a sheet, and Ilsabe thought that now she would finally get what she wanted. However, she did not get what she wanted, for Erdmuth jumped up and ran out the door—right into the arms of Colonel von Falkenberg, who was standing outside. Ilsabe immediately disappeared, as quickly as if she'd been swallowed up by the earth.

Colonel von Falkenberg looked surprised: How was it that the maiden was rushing out to meet him? He was accustomed to being made to wait while she dressed herself up, and now it was almost as though she'd been waiting for him—she was already dressed up too! Did she put on her finest clothes every day now, so that she might be well dressed for the end of the world? For she must have realized that it was fast approaching: her burgherly sense of peace and security seemed to have completely fallen away all of a sudden!

With a deep bow, he said that he'd come to inspect the quarters for His Royal Majesty, as she'd recently promised him she would arrange. Today, however, the fair maiden did not look as bold and confident as a bulletproof harquebusier anymore—had the cannon fire grown too much for her after all?

She again drew her mouth taut like a child about to cry: Of course not, she said, she was glad the guns were firing—at least they were still putting up a fight; she feared only the moment when they stopped. The maid Ilsabe Fricken had come by and told her that the city could not hold out for much longer and the Council was hoping to negotiate a capitulation through Johann Ahlemann. And that if the city capitulated, then her former bridegroom would return, and he would put her completely and utterly to shame! She could never survive that—it would be the death of her; Colonel von Falkenberg could not do such a thing to her—he could not allow the city to surrender!

Colonel von Falkenberg did not bat an eyelid: he was not surprised to hear about the negotiations with Johann Ahlemann; he'd long suspected that the Council might do such a thing.

But the maiden did surprise him. It really is quite strange, he said to himself: I've avoided her because I thought she might be able to wrest the life of the city from me, and now she's wringing her hands and pleading with me to put up a resistance—because she fears her former bridegroom. One cannot help but laugh: the combined forces of League and Empire are out there preparing to storm her native city, and she's worried that she herself will be put to shame!

With a hint of scorn, he asked why she cared about what these little people thought. The Council, after all, no longer had a say in any of this—it was up to him alone. He would certainly not capitulate—of that she could be sure. He would sooner see everything here fall to rubble and ashes—he paused, for he'd recently found himself unable to imagine everything here falling to rubble and ashes with this fair maiden at his side; that was precisely why he'd avoided her! And now, all of a sudden he could imagine it again: at once, all the gravity slipped from her hands and back into his, and he was once again the sole master of affairs—he, and he alone! He felt a disappointing sense of liberation.

Meanwhile, she kept pressing him, still not reassured: So, he would truly never do that to her, would never capitulate?

Now, however, he really had to struggle to keep himself from laughing: she saw the capitulation of this venerable and renowned stronghold of Luther as something that was done or not done to *her*. He told her that no, he would not do that to her; he would wait for succor to arrive.

But now her concerns turned in another direction: Ilsabe Fricken had also said that His Royal Majesty wasn't coming to relieve them at all, and if His Royal Majesty didn't come, then the city would ultimately have to capitulate, and her former bridegroom would return and put her to shame after all! She suddenly became fearful: "When *is* His Royal Majesty of Sweden supposed to arrive, anyway?"

He furrowed his brow slightly, for she'd asked that terrible question that everyone here kept asking him. At once he imagined he saw Bake's four weeping children again, and the lovingly protective gestures of that little, girlish pastor's wife. Would he have to put up a fight after all? He looked at the maiden standing there before him, all dressed up in her unseasonable finery, her face still pale at the thought of her former bridegroom, that preposterous question of whether she would be put to shame still on her lips. No, he said to himself, this maiden demands from me not the life of the city but herself and her own haughty pride. No one shall take refuge in her; she cannot offer anyone protection—she cannot even defend herself. He again felt that strangely disappointing sense of liberation from knowing that he, and he alone, was the sole master of affairs!

He said: "Why, the fair maiden has decorated her entire home for His Royal Majesty—how, then, can she doubt that His Majesty will come? And I do recall that the fair maiden was hoping there would be a wedding too ..."

She immediately began to glow again, for it sounded as if he was about to ask for her hand! And if Colonel von Falkenberg asked for her hand, then he could not possibly capitulate—he would have to defend her to the last against her former bridegroom. Now, at last, she felt secure.

Sensing what she was thinking, he said to himself: So here again we have a misunderstanding; she thinks she holds everything in her hands, while everything is slipping out of her hands!

He now followed her from room to room as on his previous visit; everything was as it had been then, and yet quite different: the pear tree at the window was positively bursting forth with blossoms—but this was its final splendor; tomorrow they would fall. And every room smelled even more strongly of rose petals and lavender—the maiden had likely brought out fresh stores to drown out the smell of gunpowder, which today was palpable. And spinner's wheel and spinner's weasel and sewing kit, all the delicate things that belonged to the life of a woman, were still there too, as were the maiden's little shoes; but they no longer seemed a match for the great instruments out on the ramparts; instead, they appeared genuinely fragile, almost, indeed, as if they were broken already. It was as though, beneath this outwardly secure, inviolable order of multiple generations, there lurked a trembling fear of some hidden disorder. Even the heavy, old chests and cupboards no longer seemed so steadfast to the colonel, as though they, like those of his mother back home in Herstelle, held themselves to be the foundation of things; instead, it was as though they were suddenly aware that there were no foundations anymore. It seemed to him as if there was not a single thing in the house that stood firmly in place—just like the maiden herself: Was it because of her crumpled finery, or was it the blond strand that had come loose from her hair? Or was it the way she feared her former bridegroom?

Though she led him through her home with the same confident air of self-assured splendor as before, this time it felt not as if she were leading him through the innermost chambers of her native city but as if he were following a woman fleeing from something.

They had now reached the room where she'd planned to lay the table at which the king would dine. Today there was no need for her to open the chests and cupboards to show him her trousseau: the table was already decked out with her aunt Engelke's choicest tableware; her aunt Regula's silver centerpiece stood resplendent in the middle; and her aunt Itze's polished Bohemian glassware shone and sparkled. Everything was all ready to receive a king—or to celebrate a wedding, for of course the maiden understood "when the king arrived" to mean "when Colonel von Falkenberg took her as his wife". However, the king was not coming; what was coming was the storm of the Imperials, and everything that shone and sparkled here was already destined to fall into their clutches—as was the maiden herself. Why not take her away then, before it happened? But today he did not feel that oddly gentle sense of defenselessness in the face of life; instead, he felt contempt for life, from which he might wrest one final thrill, precisely because he despised it—he felt no longer disappointment but only the liberation of knowing that he, and he alone, was the sole master of affairs!

He spoke abruptly: "So, here the royal table is laid, here the fair maiden will serve the king muscat wine, and over there—I suppose that is where His Majesty will lay his head?"

She grew somewhat abashed, for she had not planned to show him the room which he now approached: the one which, ever since her maiden's eve, contained the bridal bed and the bridal chest that Frau Bake had prepared for her. Erdmuth had not been in that room since then, nor did she have any desire to enter it—that was where she would have stood trembling before Willigis!

Noticing her hesitation, he looked at her carefully: "Why does that door remain closed?" he asked. "Is that the fair maiden's own bedchamber?"

No, she replied hastily, that room was to be the king's bedchamber, but she still had to prepare it properly; it was locked, and she didn't have the key at hand.

He fixed his gaze on her. Suddenly, almost imperiously—for he knew nothing of how to woo a woman; indeed, he'd never bothered to try—he said: "Why does the fair maiden wish to wait until the king arrives before she marries? She could be married today if she so desired, could she not?"

She turned red all over, but perhaps she'd misunderstood him—he was such a genteel cavalier, after all, and entirely in her hands. In her embarrassment, she nearly burst out in reply: "Because I very much wish to dance with His Royal Majesty at my wedding, because I want my wedding to be grand and magnificent!"

To himself, he said: If she waits for the king, she'll have a grand wedding indeed—the entire Holy Roman Empire will escort her to the bridal bed! He reached for the handle; it gave way: "Why, it seems the room is not locked after all," he said.

There stood the bridal bed, still piled as high and wide as it had been on that day when Erdmuth, slipping out of Itze's chamber, had glimpsed it through the open door: the pillow covers white as pear blossoms, the silk sheets delicately turned down, the bedposts wound with garlands of withered rosemary; beside it, the carefully packed bridal chest lay open, the little linens for her future children and the two death shrouds visible at the top. It was as though time had stood still here, or as though something silently awaited its time. It was getting dark inside the room, and at the same time there was a kind of paralyzing glare: Erdmuth thought she could make out a figure of some sort—was that Willigis? Then, right against her ear, she heard the words: "What would the fair maiden say, were someone to ask her for her love?" The voice suddenly grew rough and trembling: "Someone who might soon be destined to die?"

She wrenched her eyes open in confusion and said, her voice aflutter: "What did the good sir say about death? Why, that sounds horrible!" Silently, he placed his arm around her and drew her deeper into the bedchamber—right toward the mysterious figure, she realized; it wasn't Willigis! Suddenly, her voice helpless with dread, she uttered: "But someone who is destined to die should not ask me for my love; for then I would be left defenseless—"

The very next moment she threw herself into his arms as if fearing for her life—and her terror collapsed under the weight of his kisses.

But then, from Saint John's Tower, came the sounding of the guard's horn.

When Colonel von Falkenberg emerged from the front door of the Plögen house, he found his black horse tied up, and the little stable boy who was supposed to be holding him was nowhere to be seen. And as he looked around and noticed the crowd some distance away now rolling in his direction, the colonel realized that it was not on account of the enemy that the guard in Saint John's Tower had blown his horn but because the fair, blond waters of the Elbe were once more topping their banks. He suddenly remembered something an old corporal had recently said to him up on the rampart: that unless the lord colonel was "hard-frozen",[10] as they say among the soldiery, then he might wish to refrain from always going out all alone to make his rounds, else there might come a day when the lord colonel did not return. No one in Magdeburg knew who would fire the last shot, he'd said, but there was no doubt that the last shot would soon be fired; they were rapidly running out of powder, and there were quite a few who wouldn't have learned to shoot without powder and weren't going to learn now either. Colonel von Falkenberg had retorted that the last shot would never be fired by those who knew how to die. Then he'd gone off to make his rounds, all alone, as always. Thus he now stood motionless in the doorway, facing the approaching crowd with cold indifference: they were coming straight from the Rathaus, where he was sure an accord was being negotiated with Johann Ahlemann behind his back. And now, perhaps, the last shot really would be fired; for they were just about to run out of powder—he'd already had to borrow mortars from the apothecary to grind saltpeter.

He said to himself: Now we'll see who gets the last shot. I, for one, know how to die—so I suppose the shot will go to the Rathaus.

He crossed his arms over his chest. Then he saw his little stable boy rushing up breathlessly; would the lord colonel please forgive him, he stammered guiltily; he'd only gone away for a moment to see what was going on in the market square. People were gathering there from the suburbs of Neustadt and Sudenburg, which, of course, the lord colonel had ordered evacuated and burned down to prevent the enemy from entrenching themselves there. Then, anxiously:

[10] A reference to a common superstition of the period, that someone could be made invulnerable to ordinary weapons by means of dark magic.

"I think my lord colonel had better mount his horse and ride away fast!" he suggested, pointing his master toward the stirrups. But the colonel did not mount his horse and ride away; instead, he looked at the crowd, unmoved: it truly was rushing toward him as though the broad, blond life-stream of Magdeburg itself had been unleashed—Colonel von Falkenberg suddenly had the impression that he saw a mass of sinking, drowning souls, utterly defenseless despite their savage ferocity; they appeared to be raising their arms threateningly against him, but in reality they were sinking beneath the waves, begging only for pity. But Colonel von Falkenberg no longer had any pity; he was the sole master of affairs—he, and he alone! By now they had spotted him and were shouting at him: He was a liar; he'd deceived them! The king was still nowhere to be seen, and they couldn't wait for him any longer! Their homes had been burned down; where did he expect them to go if they no longer had a place to stay or a roof over their heads? The whole city reeked of tinder and smoke; where did he expect them to go next—into the Elbe? All at once the shouting stopped, for now Colonel von Falkenberg held the crowd under the spell of his gaze—the stream of drowning souls backed up and stood still.

The colonel eyed those in the front ranks from top to bottom. "So, you want to move into the Elbe, then?" he said calmly. "Is that all you have to say to me?"

A dull murmur went through the crowd, until finally one voice, at once menacing and wavering, spoke up: "We're not going to move into the Elbe, and there's no need for us to move into the Elbe either; Lord Tilly wants the fair city of Magdeburg alive. And so we think it might be best if Colonel von Falkenberg went into the Elbe first." The speaker pointed his musket at him, but he did not pull the trigger.

"Why don't you shoot?" shouted the colonel. "Is the target not close enough for you? Are you that bad a shot?" He took a step forward. The crowd was now backing away—only the man pointing the musket remained in place.

"Come on, then! Why haven't you fired yet, you cowardly knave?" shouted the colonel. "Answer me!"

The man with the musket began to shudder, and the rifle came down, as though someone had knocked it out of his hand. "I can't," he said in a low voice. "The colonel is *hard-frozen*." The crowd went stiff.

Suddenly a woman's voice wailed from the backmost ranks: "But then we are bound to die—oh, how the thought horrifies us!"

"If you do not wish to die," said the colonel, "then you must defend yourselves! And if you are terrified of death, then you must turn against those who wish to deliver you to the fate you so fear: your Council is negotiating with the traitor Ahlemann; what sort of an accord do you think they're concocting? You say Tilly wants the city alive—well, you're in for a surprise! As far as Tilly is concerned, you are rebels and heretics; do you really believe he's going to spare you? To him the Magdeburg Virgin is a harlot, just good enough to hand over to his wild soldiery—and from them only the royal arm will save you. And now may your Virgin choose for herself whether it's to Tilly or to His Royal Majesty that she opens her bridal chamber!" The colonel beckoned to his distraught stable boy to hold the stirrup for him. Without haste, he swung himself into the saddle and calmly set off for the Rathaus. The crowd followed him.

The little stable boy turned to look at them: "Now my lord colonel has got them all behind him again," he said, in awe. "They'll want to go to the Rathaus and get hold of Johann Ahlemann's messenger—I bet they'll run him right out of town." With a boastful swagger on his still-pale boyish face, he said: "They're so terribly afraid of the Imperials, aren't they!"

Johann Ahlemann's messenger, whom the people of Magdeburg had run out of town in disgrace, had been summoned to the Imperial headquarters for questioning. His Excellency had also received a courier who'd come from the north in a great hurry, and now he was awaiting Generals Pappenheim and Mansfeld for a council of war.

The two counts met each other outside on the road that passed through the village. Their faces were bright red, as always when they saw each other, though today it was not out of anger; rather, they were somewhat embarrassed at having felt compelled to make peace with each other so that, together, they might oblige His Excellency to give the order to storm Magdeburg—it could not be put off any longer! They had fired their guns day and night so that His Swedish Majesty might hear their thundering as far away as the gates of Silesia and give up his march on Vienna. And he had indeed heard it: based on sure intelligence, he was advancing on Magdeburg at full force, so that, at the final hour, he might honor his royal word.

For once, His Excellency Tilly had managed to impose his will on him, but now he needed to see it through to the end! His Excellency, however, had grown so old that it seemed he was no longer capable of making up his mind—just what was His Excellency waiting for?

The young marshal was the first to speak: "Surely my comrade Mansfeld would never in his wildest dreams have imagined I would be so eager to see him again, but by God, I could scarcely wait! I'm pleased to see that my noble comrade has made it here!" The music of his spurs clinked and jangled resplendently, as though the marshal were clearing his own hurdles with a brilliant mounted leap; he extended his right hand in a chivalrous gesture to his likewise mounted rival.

The other man sat heavily in the saddle, sweating from the hard ride on his high-legged nag. He had not seen Pappenheim since they had left Hamelin, communicating with him through his adjutants only as often as their joint operations required, and then hesitantly, as he was loath to offer the other any support—a sentiment which he now regretted.

Stiffly, but politely, he apologized for having kept his noble comrade waiting; he'd ridden as fast as he could, for of course he knew that there was no time to lose, and indeed he hoped that he was not already too late!

The marshal gave a carefree laugh: His noble comrade had no cause to worry; the only one who would be here too late was His Swedish Majesty. He was looking forward to it too, for he planned to greet him with the sound of his own fanfares! He'd instructed his trumpeters to practice the "March of the Finnish Cavalry",[11] which the regiments of Conti and Savelli had picked up during the Pomeranian campaign.[12] He also wanted to play something Swedish for the people of Magdeburg: it was to the tune of this march that he intended to make his triumphant entry!

The thought of the marshal entering the city made Mansfeld uneasy. He hastily reminded the marshal that he was Imperial governor of Marienburg (as Magdeburg was meant to be called in the future).

The marshal laughed: Let Mansfeld be governor, then; that didn't matter to him now, as long as the governor was willing to support him today! He'd make sure the lord governor got his entry into the city too, he added cheerfully.

[11] One of the oldest still-used military tunes in the world. It is closely associated with the Swedish monarch.

[12] Italian field marshals Torquato Conti and Federico di Savelli led Imperial troops against Protestant armies in Pomerania, on the Baltic Coast, in 1628.

Now, on the side of the city where he held command, everything was ready for the assault, and if anything was still lacking on his noble comrade's side, it really made no difference—once his men were in the city, they would open the gates to his comrade's men from the inside. And that his own men would make it in, his comrade could rest assured—he wouldn't forget the oath he'd made at the banquet in Hamelin. In his bright elation at the prospect of battle, the marshal gave not a moment's thought to the quarrel that had occasioned this oath; Mansfeld, however, did remember. His face doggedly grim, he said, evasively yet politely, that as governor of Marienburg, he was prepared to support his noble comrade when they spoke with His Excellency.

Having dismounted, they now entered the generalissimo's headquarters. In the hallway, they were met by His Excellency's "shadow". Pappenheim walked up to him, accompanied by music of his brightly jangling spurs—perhaps they might recruit a confederate to their cause: Would the reverend father be attending the council of war today? Today they would discuss the happy business of storming the ancient stronghold of heresy! Mansfeld obsequiously flung open the door for the priest, who replied reservedly: "Does the lord marshal refer to the rebel city of Magdeburg? Surely that is a concern for the generals only." He stepped briskly past the generalissimo's door, the once-flickering flame in his face now completely dim.

The two counts looked at him in amazement: What on earth had happened? The priest had always been inseparable from His Excellency—was His Excellency now without a shadow?

His Excellency appeared to have changed over the past few months. His hair had grown paler and thinner—he looked as though he stood all alone in some leafless forest, bathed in autumnal light from all sides, as it were. It was thus immediately apparent, not only from his stiff knees but also from the look on his otherwise fresh face, that His Excellency counted no longer fifty but seventy years. This was no doubt attributable to the youthful war-glory of the Swede, which had drawn the aged war-glory of His Catholic Excellency back and forth from a distance all winter long, such that it now rustled and quivered like a withered old wreath; it was no doubt attributable to the fruitless campaign on the Oder, to the failed relief of Frankfurt and Landsberg. It was true that His Excellency had not been defeated in open battle, but His Swedish Majesty had imposed his will on him even without a battle, forcing His Excellency to return yet again to Magdeburg. And now that His Excellency was finally dictating his will to His Swedish Majesty, having pulled him away from Silesia, he was still unable to act according to his will, and His Swedish Majesty dictated his own to His Excellency all the more! It was as though he was being taught the meaning of the Bible passage: "When thou wast young, thou girdest thyself, and walkedst whither thou wouldest: but when thou shalt be old, thou shalt stretch forth thy hands, and another shall gird thee, and carry thee whither thou wouldest not."[13] And this was not a good passage for a commander to have to learn; even if he, as a Christian, should wish to learn it, as generalissimo he should never be willing to allow another to carry him "whither he would not"! His Excellency did not want to strike at the enemy within—he wanted to strike with all his might against the enemy of the Empire. He had thought he might defeat the rebellion without recourse to the sword—but he had

[13] Jn 21:18.

failed in that as well. This His Excellency simply did not understand, for his plan had been the correct one—he saw that with his clear, sober commander's eyes, but also with his pious, Catholic eyes; the Most Blessed Virgin herself had approved of the plan, and she was prepared to endure the pain of religious division, for she wished to triumph with the sword in her heart and not with the sword in her hand. But now they'd placed the sword back in her hand once more—His Excellency had suffered defeat in Vienna just as decisively as on the Oder and in Silesia; for the Edict would not be dropped. He'd discerned it on the face of his young priest immediately upon his return. Truly, His Excellency was without a shadow; he was indeed all alone with his standard. And now they would both have to go whither they would not. This, too, His Excellency did not understand—was the Most Blessed Virgin not powerful enough to triumph, then, as she always had before? Was she just as defeated as he was in his old age—was she not the Madonna of Victory? Only the standard itself could answer such questions. But His Excellency had not had time to consult with his standard for weeks now, for one operation immediately followed the other, and His Excellency could only kiss the blue silk in silence. Nor was there any time now either, for his two generals had arrived for the council of war.

His Excellency looked at Counts Pappenheim and Mansfeld disconcertedly—truly, there was no need for anyone to tell him: he already knew that he had to order the storming of Magdeburg now; they could not run the risk of becoming caught between the approaching Swedes and the city, after all—they would be crushed! Curtly, he said that he'd already prepared the ultimatum for the City Council of Magdeburg; it was to go out today.

The marshal's spurs twitched impatiently, but grave Mansfeld was becoming restless as well; His Excellency was about to offer the city the door of mercy yet again—this was exactly what they'd hoped to prevent with their urgent appeal, and now that the Swede was approaching, they had no time to lose.

The marshal spoke up, his somewhat too-high voice bright and clear as a bugle call—he took the lead, with Mansfeld, as though firing a heavy gun, interjecting only periodically to remind them that he was Imperial governor: "Your Excellency continues to show mercy, but according to certain intelligence, His Swedish Majesty is already negotiating passage through Saxony. The elector is embittered over the Edict—Your Excellency cannot trust him an inch—for all intents and purposes, the king is already here!"

His Excellency replied that he already did not trust the elector of Saxony an inch; that was precisely why he'd recommended that the Edict be delayed, after all—but the elector was also a timid man, and he had not yet allowed the Swede passage; there was still enough time to offer the city the door of mercy one last time.

The two counts looked at each other: Was His Excellency still not willing to adjust to the rapid movements of the youthful Swedish Majesty? That was the same mistake he'd made in Pomerania! His Excellency really had grown very old, it seemed.

"But the city has already refused our peace accord!" shouted the marshal. "Johann Ahlemann's messenger returned with a clear refusal, and that was with no succor in sight! If Magdeburg now learns that the king really is approaching, they will turn down Your Excellency even more firmly—in their arrogance, they simply will not see that it is precisely this succor that impels us to storm the city! What does Your Excellency actually have to say to the city? What does Your Excellency have to offer those traitors but naked subjugation? If it were possible for Your Excellency to grant the Great Lady the status of Free Imperial City or remit the Edict, then perhaps there might be some hope ..."

His Excellency—again recalling the failed endeavor in Vienna—replied that he wished to tell the city exactly what the good marshal had just said: that it was precisely the approach of succor from the king that would bring about their doom.

"They will not accept such a thing from Your Excellency," insisted the marshal, "and even if they were to accept it, Falkenberg will talk them out of it—that one will surely never capitulate; that one will have his way, consequences be damned!"

Indeed, that one is very much like my gallant marshal, His Excellency thought to himself. Then, aloud, he explained that it was precisely for this reason that they had to try twice as hard to reach an accord; those who would have their way regardless of the consequences are never the ones who bear the brunt of those consequences.

The two counts looked at each other again. The marshal spoke: "Your Excellency is being merciful yet again, but perhaps those who have to bear the consequences should be made to bear them. It would serve Magdeburg right: let them experience where their defiance leads them for once! Truly, Your Excellency must demonstrate his power to these rebels; Your Excellency will never get through to them otherwise." Then Mansfeld interjected that it was also a great opportunity to demonstrate the power of the Imperial army to those in rebellion against the Church, which would make it easier to execute the Edict in the future.

His Excellency did not respond to this last remark. "Are my noble generals sure that it is not we to whom the army will demonstrate its power when we let them loose in the city?" he said. "Surely the gentlemen will be aware that according to the articles of war, if the soldiery storm a city, they are entitled to plunder it."

Hesitantly, the two counts said that they would vouch for their own regiments.

And what about the other regiments? replied His Excellency; would they likewise vouch for the Croats and the Spaniards, who considered this a foreign country? And then they might also consider for a moment the dissolute regiments of Conti and Savelli, who'd greeted the Swede's approach in Pomerania by setting fire to their own positions!

The counts were now silent. Finally the marshal spoke: His Excellency needed to think about the conquest of the city, not its plundering; the soldiery wanted only what was their due. They were already beginning to suffer shortages out here in the exhausted countryside, but the city should still be flowing with enough milk and honey for seven kingdoms. Yet His Excellency only ever showed concern for the rebels!

With firm resolve, His Excellency reminded them that he was concerned with taking the strategic position intact, and his good generals were concerned with their victories—but in ruins there were only lost strategic positions, and no victories. His Excellency made as though to dismiss them, arising slowly, which was all his stiff knees would allow. The two counts recalled the Oder campaign, which they had missed out on.

The marshal, now quite desperate, pushed ahead one last time, his words as though dancing on the bright edge of a sword blade: "Excellency, it is better to have a heap of ruins in our possession than a fortress in the hands of the Swede; better to see the wreath pried from the hands of the bride than to see her left to another—there is no time left to coax her! Believe me, Your Excellency, prickly maids such as this have got to be taken by force!"

His Excellency now made an overtly dismissive gesture. In an irritated tone, he remarked on the good marshal's penchant for bringing up weddings when discussing military operations; the good marshal could do as he pleased, but he was too old for such things himself. Then, his lower lip sullenly protruding: "If my noble generals can no longer stand behind the ultimatum, then it will simply be issued without their support. The trumpeter will ride under my own personal standard: I will give the people of Magdeburg twenty-four hours' time, after which the assault will begin; my noble generals shall see to all the preparations. Thank you, gentlemen."

His Excellency had now dismissed them unequivocally. The marshal, however, raised his voice in protest one more time; with an undertone that was almost rebellious, he asked whether this meant they would call off the successful bombardment that was currently underway until the trumpeter returned and give Magdeburg a chance to catch their breath.

His Excellency was now quivering with rage. He raised his voice: "All batteries will continue to fire without ceasing!"

In the antechamber, the two counts ran into Willigis. He told them that he had been summoned by His Excellency, but for what reason, he did not know. The marshal was somewhat displeased at this, for he did not like having to do without Willigis Ahlemann for any length of time. The man had come to be his right hand: he knew the terrain around Magdeburg and the fortifications of the city like no one else, and he was as wholeheartedly committed to the siege as the marshal himself. Like the marshal, he thought of naught else but siege trenches and gun batteries; in Willigis' heart, the whole world really was as it had been at Hamelin: there were none but men and soldiery—and it was written all over his face.

His Excellency looked at him, unsettled; he felt that he could hardly recognize Willigis Ahlemann anymore. This was no longer the tall, childlike, trusting fellow that had touched his heart so strangely, full of goodwill and attuned to the order of things; no, the individual who stood before him now was a wild, reckless swashbuckler! He looked like a man who did not care about death or the devil; indeed, the expression on his face was almost like that of Marshal von Pappenheim when even the generalissimo himself could scarcely rein him in! What could possibly have happened? His Excellency thought to himself: What has happened, of course, is nothing other than this fratricidal war being fought among the German people—this is what a man looks like when he's spent six months fighting against his own native city, and how could he look otherwise? His Excellency proceeded to the matter he wished to discuss: "Herr Ahlemann," he said, "back in Hamelin you asked me to grant your native city a stay of execution; I have not forgotten your request. You have since become an Imperial officer, but you are still a son of Magdeburg, and that is what I need at this time. You know the situation your native city finds itself in. You will ride there with my trumpeter and my personal standard, and there you will announce the final stay of execution. You will deliver my ultimatum and persuade your fellow citizens that if they wish to save their lives, then they must accept the ultimatum I give them at this final hour. Will you agree to this?"

For a moment Willigis was silent; then he said, with marked conviction: "If Your Excellency deigns to ask me, then no."

His Excellency looked at him disconcertedly; for his question, of course, had not really been a question—an Imperial generalissimo doesn't ask his officers whether they want to obey his orders, after all! With a tinge of severity: "Does Herr Ahlemann have a compelling military reason for thinking he might not be of use in bringing about the capitulation of his native city?"

Magdeburg was no longer his home, Willigis retorted, and he could not help to bring about the city's capitulation because he hoped to see the city taken by storm—Magdeburg deserved nothing better.

His Excellency looked at him, dumbfounded—this really was no longer the same Ahlemann as before; evidently all that remained of that man was his honesty! But there was clearly something going on here, and His Excellency, always thorough, had to get to the bottom of it at once; for if this young fellow thought as he spoke, then he was indeed not the right messenger. His Excellency became old Father Tilly, short-tempered but kind: "Herr Ahlemann will now unburden his heart and tell me, straightforwardly and without equivocation, how badly things have deteriorated between himself and his native city!"

Willigis complied.

"So you have vowed to yourself, Herr Ahlemann," said His Excellency, "never to set foot in Magdeburg again, unless it be at the head of the Imperial regiments storming the city. You wish to deliver judgment upon Falkenberg, sword in hand, because he took your bride from you; and even if the whole city should perish in the process, that would suit you just fine! And you are still of the opinion, as a soldier and an officer, that your wishes are in agreement with those of His Imperial Majesty, from whom your city has fallen away?"

Willigis gave a simple "Yes."

"And this," His Excellency continued, "is the reason why you became a soldier in the first place: you think that a soldier is a vessel of wrath, that his purpose is to smash everything to pieces—truly, what a fine opinion of a soldier you have!" Yes, Willigis answered frankly, that was what he'd thought; for if everything leapt out of its proper order, then what must come was the end of all order—thus, the sword. Nothing else on earth could accomplish anything now, for all things were indeed out of their proper order.

"But the sword is not the end of all order," replied His Excellency calmly. "Rather, it is itself the ultimate instrument of order—it restores order when all other means have failed. But for this reason it must be kept within its own proper order—a soldier is not a blind destroyer and manslayer! This may well appear to be the case at times, because there are bad soldiers, brutish and beastly soldiers; God knows such men exist"—His Excellency thought with a sigh of the regiments of Conti and Savelli and the savage Croats—"but those men are not true soldiers. A true soldier is a man of discipline and of obedience. He is not free to smash and destroy as he pleases; for he is under the law just as much as anyone else and must account for every idle act of destruction and bloodshed—precisely because he must destroy and shed blood! For in this you are right, Herr Ahlemann: the sword is the only thing on earth that can accomplish anything now; but that also means that it is to the protection or the mercy of the sword that God now means to entrust all living things today. Have you ever considered what great trust God places in the sword?"

Willigis thought he'd misheard—for he'd never heard such a thing from anyone in the Imperial camp; indeed, it knocked the bottom out of everything he'd thought up to now! The mercy of the sword? And the one who'd said it was not someone who knew nothing of soldiers or the sword, but the greatest soldier in the Imperial army, still undefeated in open battle, Generalissimo Tilly himself! How was he to understand this? He replied, confused: "But the sword, Your Excellency, surely the sword cannot exercise mercy, that's not what it is for—"

"Only the sword *can* exercise mercy, Herr Ahlemann," replied His Excellency indifferently. "Or do you perhaps imagine merciful sickles and plowshares? Mercy is the concern of him who has power—mercy is a privilege of the sword, not its foremost and most obvious one, but its finest and its highest: a sword entirely lacking mercy is a fallen sword, a vain sword. The *ratio belli* itself commands mercy—we cannot kill the fruit of victory. His Imperial Majesty needs to have your native city alive." His Excellency thus came back to the mission.

Willigis now looked like a man who was about to have his life's dream shattered and was desperately trying to resist it. "But the city is no longer His Imperial Majesty's city," he said, struggling to compose himself. "The city has fallen away from His Imperial Majesty—it doesn't deserve mercy! Even the Swede has abandoned it to its fate: we know that the king sacrificed it to his war plan from the very beginning, and if he is now prepared to bring it succor, it can only be because he's trying to save his reputation—and he must know as well as we that he thereby endangers the city all the more. Are we to treat the city better than the Swede?"

"Again, you are right," replied His Excellency. "The Swede has sacrificed the city, which is not his own; but His Imperial Majesty will not sacrifice his city, for even if it has fallen away, it remains His Imperial Majesty's city. So, Herr Ahlemann, now I think you understand me at last and are ready for your mission."

Willigis didn't understand anything, nor was he ready. He remained stubbornly silent. His Excellency suddenly raised his eyebrows; now his patience was at an end. It really did seem as though this individual meant to refuse him his obedience as a soldier—it was outrageous, how he looked at him with such effrontery! His Excellency flushed red with indignation all the way up to his forehead. I should discharge him at once, he thought to himself, and I would discharge anyone else that was in his place; yet this man I cannot discharge. His Excellency recalled the invisible snow through which his own obedience as a soldier had compelled him to tread—back in Hamelin, when His Excellency, forsaking the cause of religious war, had decided to give the fallen-away city some leeway. That had been immediately after his conversation with this same individual, who'd touched his heart—no, his sword!—so strangely then. His Excellency felt as though he'd dragged his own soldierly obedience through the invisible snow, toward the Yes of the Most Blessed Virgin on his standard—indeed, she had said to him then: "You have found me." I cannot lead this man back to the right order of faith, he again thought to himself, but he will return to me in the order of soldiers—I can force him to obey. I owe him that much; he is worth that to me.

Now the generalissimo barked at Willigis: "Is Herr Ahlemann aware that at this very moment he is on the verge of becoming a rebel, just like those in his native city? Let him remember that he is an Imperial officer and a soldier; a soldier must obey, no matter how difficult it is for him." Inadvertently, His Excellency uttered the same words that he had once said to himself.

At the word "rebel", Willigis had turned deathly pale; no one had ever called him that before. He clicked his heels together. His Excellency noted this with satisfaction.

Very calmly, as though nothing had happened, he communicated his detailed orders for the ride to Magdeburg.

Willigis sat atop his gray once more; beside him rode the Imperial trumpeter carrying the personal standard of His Excellency Tilly. It was still night when they left Tilly's headquarters; they were to arrive at the gates of the city with the first light of dawn, His Excellency insisted.

It was a hard ride, such as Willigis had never dreamt of when he became a soldier. He would have preferred to turn back. To himself, he said: I made a vow to myself that I would be the first man in the Imperial army to ride into Magdeburg, that I might deliver the judgment they so richly deserve, and now I really will be the first to ride in. I am not permitted to deliver judgment, however, but must instead offer them the emperor's mercy—that is what His Excellency wants. I am to do everything in my power to persuade the rebels in the city to capitulate at this final hour, so that His Excellency can grant them the life of their city, whole and intact. Yet how can I bring myself to do it? I really ought not to think about it at all, or I'll end up a rebel myself—that's what His Excellency called me, and he was right: I was one. His Excellency should have dealt with me much more harshly than he did! I am an Imperial officer, and I must carry out my generalissimo's orders without question; I am a soldier, and I must obey, no matter how difficult it is for me—but God knows this is difficult for me! Willigis cast a timid look at the standard being carried by the trumpeter beside him. He was glad the early morning darkness covered the image on it, for that was still the most troublesome thing of all for him: that he was accompanied by this Papist Madonna. Not on account of the people of Magdeburg—just let them try to curse his flag—he'd be more than happy to help them be silent! However, this Madonna was surely to blame for his having to go to Magdeburg in the first place: she interfered with the *ratio belli* of His Excellency Tilly; it was with her, after all, that he held his secret council of war, and that was why his *ratio belli* differed from that of his generals. Willigis knew from the marshal that they had opposed the ultimatum—as well they should have, for that was war, after all: men and soldiery. What was this Madonna doing out here in the field? Willigis felt that he was becoming insubordinate again. Yes, His Excellency had spoken as though mercy was a privilege of the sword and of power, but that, too, was something he could have gotten only from the Madonna here. I ought not to think about this flag either, he said to himself; the only thing I ought to be thinking about is my duty to obey my generalissimo—none of those other things is of any concern to me.

They were now getting quite close to the city. The trumpeter, who was not very familiar with the area, asked Willigis the way to Saint Ulrich's Gate, for that was where His Excellency had instructed them to announce themselves. If they did not want to get caught in the fire of their own guns, they would need to head directly there.

Willigis had spent the ride up until now immersed in his thoughts, paying no attention to the path they were taking. He now looked at his surroundings. He had not seen the area immediately around the city for quite some time; the marshal always kept him at headquarters, close to his war maps and siege plans. He felt as though he were in a foreign land—indeed, he could not answer the trumpeter right away, even though the sweet May morning was now beginning to awaken. God in heaven, what a scene confronted him! Everything was trampled down and trodden over, riddled with tunnels and trenches; there was not so much as a single living stalk anywhere in sight, only the dead undergrowth of the savage instruments of war! It truly looked as Willigis had once wished it would: that time after the great storm, when, on his way here and filled with wrath, he'd felt he was following the trail of a ghostly swarm of soldiery. Now the traces were no longer ghostly. Willigis felt a strange pain in his heart. Where had the fertile fields gone, where were all the silky green seedlings that shimmered so sweetly at this time of year? Where were the gentle meadows with their golden buttercups and their red and white clover? Where were the silver willow bushes, from whose wood he had so often drawn the sweet notes of the flute when he was a boy? Back when he'd stood at the gates of the city, bidding farewell to his home, it was as though this whole quiet landscape spread out not before his eyes but before his heart only—and there it still lay today, fully intact. Willigis felt the strange pain again. He felt the urge to hurry and slam shut the gates of his heart so that he might be able to bear the scene that lay before his eyes.

Meanwhile, however, the trumpeter was still waiting for an answer—he needed to know where to go. The scene before Willigis' eyes was no help at all: it remained equally foreign and confusing no matter how long he looked at it. If he was going to comply with His Excellency's orders, he would have to turn to the scene in his heart.

They now rode in an arc skirting the city. Their own guns were silent on this side, as had been ordered for the hour of their journey, but on the other side, shot after shot cracked and boomed. Though enveloped, as it were, by a great crescent of roaring and thundering, the city itself was entirely still and soundless, as though awaiting her fate with bated breath—Willigis suddenly recalled the famous prophecy of the scholar Lotichius,[14] so often a

[14] Petrus Lotichius Secundus (1528–1560), who wrote a famous elegy for Magdeburg after the siege of 1550–1551.

subject of ridicule and laughter in Magdeburg; it was as though he were seeing the city as the learned poet had beheld it in a dream one night a hundred years ago and elegized in verse: its walls cracked and crumbling, a beautiful virgin standing atop the battlements, wringing her hands and awaiting her savior.

The trumpeter beside him spoke: it looked as if Magdeburg was out of powder, he said; not a single gun answered from within—well, so much the better for themselves, then! Willigis felt the strange pain again: Where had all the neat little houses of the two stately suburbs gone? All he saw in their place now were sprawling, charred ruins! Where were the famous towers of the city's proud, undaunted gates? Where were the irrepressibly bold, almost blusterous lines of the battlements atop her indomitable walls? They, too, existed only in that place where the tranquil beauty of his native countryside still survived: in his heart. He again felt the urge to slam shut the gates so that he might bear the scene that lay before his eyes. But just then the trumpeter asked whether that badly shattered structure over there was Saint Ulrich's Gate, thus compelling him to consult the scene in his heart once more.

Willigis had prepared himself for the inevitable sneering of the soldiers at the city gate when they saw the flag he had with him; however, they behaved with curious calm. This was likely due to the heavy bombardment of the past few days; they all looked bleary-eyed and exhausted. Only one of them said anything: "Who's this you've brought with you?" he asked, with a fleeting glance at the Madonna. "Don't you know this city belongs to the Magdeburg Virgin?" Willigis replied flippantly that as far as he knew, the city, like the standard beside him, was the emperor's.

They were given an escort to take them to the Rathaus, and they rode into the city. The standard was now brightly illuminated in the morning light, the blue silk shimmering cheerfully, like a patch of sky peeping out from between all the houses that lined the narrow street.

Willigis knew he must not neglect to keep a close eye on the standard now, for he knew the people of Magdeburg. The standard was his responsibility, and despite the early hour, the streets were already a scene of crowded confusion. Large numbers of people had been burned out of their homes in the suburbs; they now sat all over the place with their shattered belongings, weeping and wailing. Against his will, Willigis felt pity for them.

"Look here! It's the Papist Madonna," a young lad shouted, straddling the path in front of the riders. Willigis flushed red with wrath. "This is the personal standard of His Excellency Lord Tilly; will you show some respect?" he screamed at the boy. "Get out of the way, or find out how fast I can come down off this horse and make you!" The lad looked as if to challenge him; he whistled to his right and to his left, but when no one came to his aid, he stalked off. Willigis was again surprised; he'd expected people would flock together to curse the standard once they were inside the city, but they hardly seemed to pay it any mind at all. They were now near Saint Ulrich's Church. The bells were ringing for the service; seeing the churchgoers, Willigis again glanced at the standard. But none concerned themselves with it here either: they stared down at their hymnals in silence, so withdrawn, so somber—Willigis had never seen the people of Magdeburg like this before! Where were the headstrong and impetuous men who'd thrown out the old Council? Where were the cheerful, strapping blond women whom people joked sang their little children to sleep with the old *Trutzlied* against the Interim? Where was their gay and splendid attire; where was their jewelry and their fine adornment? They all wore black, as if they were going to a funeral! Indeed, it looked as though the fair, blond waters of the Elbe had ceased to shimmer and flow as they always had. No longer did people parade about, no longer did anyone laugh, no longer did anyone sing, hardly anyone spoke; though the streets were filled with people, the scene was as still and silent as the guns up on the rampart. Willigis could again not help but think of the prophecy of Lotichius; for truly, everyone here looked like the virgin in the poet's dream-vision—desperately waiting for something!

He was greeted by a soldier from the city's cavalry, which had likewise been made homeless by the conflagration of the suburbs and now filled the streets with men and horses. "What are you doing here, then?" asked Willigis somewhat condescendingly. "We're waiting for the king," answered the soldier, his tone cool and composed. Willigis again felt pity.

Willigis and the trumpeter had been directed to a chamber where they were to wait for the Council to convene. They were also served a hearty meal—the councillors had to show the Imperials, after all, that though they were under siege, they still wanted for nothing here in Magdeburg! The trumpeter made sure to savor everything; he wanted to tell his comrades back at camp about this meal, so that if they did end up storming the city, it would urge them on! Willigis, meanwhile, busied himself with trying to find a place for the standard. In fact, he did not want the trumpeter to notice that he had no appetite. He was now in the Rathaus of his native city, after all, where they had once treated him so wretchedly. Suddenly, it all came back to him: the celebration for Falkenberg and the counterfeit dance of honor they'd played for the Bride Magdeburg and his own bride; and how the Council had exiled him from his native city; and how Guericke had given him a blow to his head because it was the only way to make sure he got out alive! He moved the standard from one corner of the room to the other, under the pretense that everywhere he tried to put it was too dusty, while saying to himself: Now, at long last, I am indeed happy to have this flag with me! I'm here to represent the *ratio belli* of my generalissimo, and now if I become so angry that I do not know what to do, I'll at least be able to look at the standard and pull myself together! Now comes the difficult moment in which I dare not think of anything else except that I am a soldier and that I must obey—what happened to me here before is of no concern to me now.

Willigis Ahlemann again stood in the old, familiar Council Chamber, beside him the trumpeter bearing the personal standard of the generalissimo; here, too, its blue silk shimmered, like a patch of the May sky peeking into the dim room through the tightly shut windows of opaque crown glass. It was even sultrier and more stifling inside the room than on that fateful day; yet at the same time it was frigid, out of the spring sun's warm reach. Indeed, they actually had a fire going in the fireplace—were the proud gentlemen of Magdeburg shivering?

Willigis had just delivered the ultimatum. None of the gentlemen exchanged a word with him; their pride would not allow it. After all, they'd exiled him from their native city, and now he came before them as a conqueror and as messenger of their enemies—perhaps he would even welcome their tribulation as a triumph! Willigis likewise spoke not a word, for outside, the cannons were now roaring and thundering as never before: Generalissimo Tilly was having his ultimatum proclaimed from the mouths of his great cannons, that he might provide support for Willigis here in the city—in a language that no person in Magdeburg could fail to hear or to understand. Thus

Willigis could remain silent for the time being. That was just as well for him, for it would at least allow him to relish the opportunity of having the gentlemen plead with him for Imperial clemency; he did not intend to make it easy for them, for truly they did not deserve it, either for the city or for themselves!

Meanwhile, the ultimatum passed from hand to hand around the hall, no one commenting on it, for again, the gentlemen's pride would not allow it. When the last of them had read it, their reply was curt and constrained: All right, then—they requested that His Excellency provide them with passes for a deputation to the friendly Hanseatic cities[15] so that they might seek advice on how to proceed in this matter. They would let him know their answer in due course. Willigis could tell they were trying to buy time: His Excellency, after all, had said he knew from intelligence reports that the councillors themselves were not awaiting succor from the Swede but wanted to capitulate, and that it was only Falkenberg who prevented them from doing so.

Willigis replied gruffly that they could not seriously expect His Excellency to allow their delegation to the Hanseatic cities to pass; by the time they returned, Magdeburg would long since have fallen.

Remaining cool and composed—for their pride would not allow them to let Willigis see their distress either—they said they would just need to confer with the neighborhood administrators, then.

There was no time for that either, insisted Willigis in the same gruff manner. Did they not hear the cannons outside? They had to decide right here, right now.

[15] The Hanseatic League was a network of German towns and merchant guilds formed to protect trading interests.

They said they would have to confer with Colonel von Falkenberg, then—there was no use for him to continue pressing them.

Willigis turned pale with wrath: he did not ever want to hear that name out of their mouths, and they knew that perfectly well; it wasn't as if they were speaking to one another for the first time.

They did not respond to this but maintained a steadfast and dignified silence, as people from old, aristocratic families often do when faced with a crude display of the conqueror's fist. Willigis realized that he would not be able to get any further with them. But that meant he would not be able to carry out His Excellency's order either; His Excellency, after all, was operating on the assumption that the gentlemen of the Council would place their trust in him. Would he have to plead with them to trust him, then? Then the world would be upside-down indeed! He was here on behalf of the Imperial generalissimo in his capacity as conqueror and judge—no, he did not need to plead with them; it was up to the gentlemen to plead with him. They did not plead, however, instead attesting by their silence to the dignity of misfortune.

The great cannons outside proclaimed His Excellency's ultimatum a second time, the individual blasts drowning one another out in rapid succession—it sounded almost as though the guns were losing their patience. Willigis noticed that the gentlemen seemed to be preparing to bring their session to a close. I cannot bring myself to persuade them, he said to himself, but I've got to try, or else I cannot obey His Excellency's command. He glanced over at the standard. Then, pulling himself together with great difficulty, he asked whether he might take his old place here in the hall—perhaps that would make it easier for them to speak with him. He took his old place. There he sat in his big riding coat, his eyes gazing at them from his wild and unkempt face, his look half-defiant, half-diffident. Watching him, they thought this was yet another attempt to show them the conqueror's fist.

Willigis wiped the sweat from his brow—they still had not responded to him; he knew he would have to make another attempt at persuading them. With another glance at the standard, and again pulling himself together with great difficulty, he spoke: Right now, he said, they would do well to think first of the many small children that lived here in Magdeburg. Just imagine, he urged them, what it would be like to hear their pitiful screaming and crying! What a terrible thing it was to hear innocent little children being killed—it was not something they would ever be able to forget for as long as they lived, once they heard it, and they would surely hear it soon if they did not agree to an accord right now; for the Swede would arrive much too late to rescue them. Willigis again glanced at the standard; even now they uttered not a word in response. And then, he continued, there were still women here in Magdeburg too, and surely their fate would be the most terrible of all, unless they agreed to an accord right now. They would likewise never forget, never overcome the horror of what would happen if the savage Croats got their hands on the poor women here—and the Croats would surely come for the women. That able-bodied men defending themselves should fall in battle was something one had to accept; that was all in the order of war. But that those who could not defend themselves should be sacrificed—that was not in the order of war, that was something they could not allow. Surely they could not deprive little children of their mothers, and indeed, there were still other little children yet to be born—the people of Magdeburg could not act as though there were none but men in the world! Willigis again wiped the sweat from his brow; he looked as if he said all this against his will, and yet at the same time it was as though he was drawing it out from some hidden corner deep within himself.

The gentlemen sat with their heads bowed, but they still did not answer him. Willigis again glanced at the standard. And then, he began again, they also had such beautiful, stately homes here in Magdeburg, inherited from their fathers and destined for their grandchildren. And inside those houses there were heavy chests and cupboards filled with delicate linens, spun by their mothers and their grandmothers, and all the old, handsome furnishings likewise inherited from their fathers—surely they couldn't abandon all that to be pillaged by a foreign soldiery, and the soldiery would surely pillage this place unless they agreed to an accord right now. Then there were some who'd set fire even to their own positions in Pomerania—the gentlemen could not allow the poor women and children to become homeless. He'd just seen for himself what a terrible fate that was: indeed, the streets were filled with people who'd been burned out of their homes in the suburbs—how pitiful a sight it was, how it made one's heart bleed! Willigis did not need to look at the standard anymore; for now he could see the poor people burned out of their homes, and likewise the somber churchgoers at Saint Ulrich's, the women in black dresses—all the still, silent people of Magdeburg! And they were all his dear fellow citizens—they couldn't allow them to be abandoned to the terrible storm of the Imperial army! Still, the gentlemen remained silent—it really did seem that they, like all the others, were intent on waiting for the Swede to arrive. Willigis could again not help but think of the dream-vision of Lotichius.

The cannon fire on the ramparts outside suddenly ceased, as though the guns were giving up their efforts to make the city capitulate. Could this be the calm before the storm already? Willigis jumped up from his chair: Good God in heaven, they had to give him an answer now—he was here not as their enemy but as their fellow citizen and brother! Magdeburg was his native city, after all, and even if they had cast him out, that did not mean that his dear native city was cast out of his heart; at least at this hour, he implored them, they would have to count him as one of their own! And if before he'd treated them somewhat coarsely, he begged them to forgive him and to believe him when he said that he held nothing against them personally and that they could trust him. He needed an answer from them right now, for Magdeburg had absolutely no time remaining, and when he'd left before, Otto Guericke had told him that they would stay here and endure so that they might be around to save the city at the very last moment—so where were they? What were they waiting for?

"Willigis Ahlemann, I am here!" Otto Guericke spoke up. Passing through the middle of the hall, as though descending from the high rampart, he approached Willigis and candidly held out his hand. Then, in a low voice, he suggested that if Willigis would send the trumpeter out of the room, he was sure the gentlemen would give him their answer.

Once Willigis had sent the trumpeter away, they all walked over to him and shook his hand, and now they spoke to him without reserve: What he'd said was true—the heavy weight on their own hearts when they thought about the many women and children here in the poor, good city of Magdeburg was nigh unbearable. And it was also true that they'd always said they would stay here and await the final moment. Yet the final moment for a regiment to hold their ground was really only ever the first moment—after which everything was out of their hands. This was something they'd had to learn back when they'd been overpowered by the people: as long as the Swede tarried, they had hoped to be able to get the people back behind them in considering whether the city might once again submit to the emperor, but they'd been unable to get them back in time! And now the Swede really was on his way to bring them succor—it was too late; His Imperial Majesty could no longer forgive them now—they'd had no other choice but to put their hope in the Swede.

Willigis replied that he'd already told them that the Swede would not arrive in time to save them.

Yes, they said, they were well aware of this danger, but the king of Sweden was doing everything he could to save their city; it all came down to whether the electors of Saxony and Brandenburg let him through in time—surely this would be known in the Imperial camp as well. Suddenly a crackling and a creaking sounded through the room, just as it had on that fateful day (for the cannons were still silent, and there was no other sound but the flickering of the flames in the fireplace).

Willigis spoke: They had to realize that His Excellency Tilly would not wait around for this passage to be granted. Even if the electors of Saxony and Brandenburg granted it this very hour, the Swede would still arrive too late. The approaching succor of the Swede was not their hope, but their doom: His Excellency would now be forced to take the city—at any cost. Suddenly it was as though they once again beheld the great show booth of the war, just as they had on that fateful day; as though painted in the scene, they saw the city of Magdeburg standing on the chessboard of two hostile armies, now utterly checkmated; they now saw, not a gloriously blazing torch beckoning the victor and lighting his path, but the sacrificial flame of this war.

The pile of logs in the fireplace suddenly collapsed—the room turned gray. Willigis saw that the gentlemen now realized the situation they were in—all at once their chins drooped low and long; what a terrible sight it was! Willigis bowed his head and looked at the floor.

At last, a low, raspy voice spoke: "So, we are not the key to everything, with the parties rolling the dice over us; it is we ourselves who have become the die in this war, and now the die shall fall—we have been utterly forsaken."

Willigis, his voice likewise very low, said that it was only the Swede who was forsaking them; the emperor wanted to save them, and he was here to offer them his clemency. The flame in the collapsed logs darted to and fro, as though it did not know whether it was to live or to die. Guericke now asked whether Willigis could tell the gentlemen what the city might expect if they capitulated, for he believed the gentlemen were reluctant to jump in the dark.

Willigis replied that they would at least avoid the horror of an assault. Everything else they would need to negotiate with His Excellency themselves—perhaps one of the gentlemen might accompany him to the Imperial camp? He looked at the two burgomasters: they were still sitting there with their chins drooping, their heads bowed low. Willigis lowered his own head: it was a difficult hour for the proud gentlemen of Magdeburg! The flame in the fireplace flickered and struggled.

At last, the low, raspy voice from before spoke again: Willigis talked of Imperial clemency, but for the Protestant Estates this clemency came with a dark secret: in the end, all it meant was that Magdeburg would be kept alive, but declared a mere provincial town, and they would all be "saved" on Papist terms. The Imperials had already tried to impose the Edict upon them when the city still had power; how did the gentlemen think they would fare if they were obliged to approach His Imperial Majesty in this state of powerlessness?

Willigis started, for once again he had not been thinking about the Edict; however, he knew the men in the Imperial camp—they were already talking about the future Marienburg over there! They won't be able to escape the Edict if they submit to the emperor, he thought to himself, yet they must submit to the emperor; the city cannot be allowed to perish on account of the Edict! Aloud, he said that in the past they had always maintained this was not the sacristy, this was the Rathaus; what concerned them was not what the zealous pastors thought, but the very life and security of the city. They had to abide by the order of authority and submit to those in authority over them.

His Imperial Majesty was the one who did not abide by the order of authority, they replied; they had hoped to separate sacristy and Rathaus while remaining faithful, but today there was no separating them anymore—and they couldn't do more than all the rest of the world could do. Willigis knew, they reminded him, that the old Council had been toppled on account of the Edict and that they themselves had been overridden because of it. The same thing would happen today if they were to surrender the archbishopric. There might have been a time when the people were restless and despondent and ready to capitulate at any cost, but now Falkenberg had managed to get them all behind him: in their hour of utmost need, the protesting, rebelling city of Magdeburg was coming forth once more, not in triumph, but in silence and solemn readiness to face the utmost peril. They could not remain aloof: they had no choice but to join with the people and with Falkenberg, for it was the only way they could ever hope to bring about the capitulation of the city. They could not separate what His Imperial Majesty himself was unable to separate, after all.

Willigis replied that as long as Magdeburg was in rebellion, His Imperial Majesty would never be able to separate the two.

Then, they replied, as long as His Imperial Majesty could not separate them, the rebellion would persist. What a man believed was a matter not for His Imperial Majesty but for God. And if His Imperial Majesty was unable to accept that, if he insisted on using worldly means, violence and oppression of every kind in order to achieve unity in faith and spirit, then His Imperial Majesty was bound to learn that not only would unity in faith and spirit not thereby be achieved but that the body of the country would be torn to bloody shreds in the process. Then there was a chance that Magdeburg the vanquished might yet emerge as Magdeburg the triumphant once more: whether the electors of Saxony and Brandenburg let the Swede through now or not, when Magdeburg was fallen and violated, they would let him through; whether the Swede was too late today or not, he would come then!

The flame in the fireplace suddenly caught a rush of air and blazed high; again it was as though the great show booth of war opened up in the dim room: as though painted in the scene, they beheld the entire horizon as far as the eye could see covered in the glow of flames; they again beheld the city of Magdeburg as the sacrificial flame of this war, igniting everything it touched; they beheld the entire fatherland of the German nation, violently ablaze from the Oder to the Rhine, from the Baltic to Bavaria—they beheld the whole Empire as a future pile of rubble!

I think I've misunderstood His Excellency this whole time, thought Willigis; the task I've been assigned is not what I thought it was at all: this mission isn't about saving the city of Magdeburg—it's about saving the Empire!

The great cannons outside now thundered the ultimatum once more.

Willigis spoke: "So before capitulating, you mean to offer a choice: either the Empire, or the Faith?" Pausing, he wondered to himself: Where have I heard this question before?

They replied that they were not asking anyone to make this choice but that it was the choice being asked of them.

If only I could remember where I've heard this question, Willigis thought, then I would know the answer; what I do know, however, is that it's the wrong question. Aloud, he said: "So you mean to betray the Empire for the sake of the Faith?"

They replied that the Swedish ambassador had once said in this very room that it was no longer possible to betray the Empire, for it had already been betrayed.

Willigis, flatly: "Do you mean to say that His Imperial Majesty himself ..." He shuddered at the words; he could never say such a thing, even in the depths of his own heart!

That was what they were saying, they replied: that a government that oppresses and harasses its subjects on account of their faith is indeed asking them to choose between the Empire and the Faith. It was this that disturbed the peace of the land; it was this that inspired rebellion; it was this that drew the enemy into the country; it was this that constituted— The glow from the fireplace suddenly burst into the middle of the room, as though the whole Council Chamber were ablaze!

Willigis thought to himself: I was under the impression that there was no choice between the Empire and the Faith. Indeed, there cannot be such a choice; if this is the choice His Imperial Majesty asks of us, then no Protestant can remain loyal to the Empire, then I cannot carry out my mission here either, then I must disobey my generalissimo, then I must become a rebel like the people of my native city—for I am a Protestant myself! Then Magdeburg shall perish, then the Empire will fall to pieces! The red glow of the flame now snatched at his hands—Willigis pulled them away. To himself, he continued: Yet I must fulfill my mission—I am a soldier and I must obey, no matter how difficult it is for me. No one should have to choose between the Empire and the Faith, and yet this is the choice that His Imperial Majesty asks of his Protestant Estates each and every day. His Imperial Majesty oppresses and harasses the same for the sake of their faith; thus it is he who disturbs the peace of the land; thus it is he who inspires rebellion; thus it is he who draws the enemy into the country; thus it is His Imperial Majesty himself who commits— The red glow of the flame suddenly struck him in the face. Willigis jumped up from his seat: It was suffocating in this cramped room—did they mind if he opened a window? If only I had the trumpeter back in here with the standard, he thought to himself, then I could look at it and pull myself together as before. He walked over to the window and opened it. Down below, the Imperial horseman still rode straight for the Rathaus, as though it were his own ancient, ancestral possession. Above him hung the May sky of his homeland, delicate and light, as though it were a vast mantle spreading down from the firmament above, enveloping the city and countryside in its loving protection—blue, like the standard, he realized; and suddenly it was as though he were looking at it. He drew a deep breath and returned to his seat. Again pulling himself together with great difficulty, he urged them to think about their beloved fatherland of the German nation, how terribly it would suffer if this cruel war continued to rage across it, how all the fields and meadows would be trampled underfoot, just like those outside the gates. He'd seen it with his own eyes on his way in:

there was not so much as a single living stalk anywhere in sight—they could not allow the entire fatherland of the German nation to look like it did outside Magdeburg! And if His Imperial Majesty himself was endangering the fatherland of the German nation, then it was up to them to save it: they would have to submit, they would have to endure under His Imperial Majesty! He glanced at the open window, where a patch of the familiar May sky hung like the corner of a light mantle—blue, like the standard; he again felt as though he were looking at it. And then, he continued, they should also think of all the fair cities and towns throughout the fatherland of the German nation; he'd seen with his own eyes on entering the city how all the walls and towers here were shot to pieces, and how the two suburbs lay in ashes—they could not allow all the cities in the fatherland of the German nation to look like the city of Magdeburg! And if His Imperial Majesty himself was endangering them, then it was up to them to save them: they would have to submit, they would have to endure under His Imperial Majesty! Willigis wiped the sweat from his brow. Then, with another look at the patch of blue in the window, he continued: And finally, above all, they had to think of the Empire itself, and the state of utter helplessness to which it would descend if the Protestant Estates should break with it! Then the whole Empire would be in the same situation as the city of Magdeburg, surrounded by enemies on all sides; all the other nations were already gathering on its borders, poised to invade just like the Swede! So if His Imperial Majesty himself was endangering the Empire, then it was up to them to save it: they would have to submit, they would have to endure under His Imperial Majesty! Willigis again wiped the sweat from his brow.

Meanwhile, the gentlemen were growing restless; he kept talking past the choice they were faced with: the choice was not "Empire or no Empire" but "either the Empire or the Faith"—if they were to endure under the emperor, they would not be able to save the Faith.

The cannons stopped firing again—Willigis got the impression that the guns outside the gates were holding their breath. My God, he thought to himself, if only I remembered the answer! All I know is that they must endure! He stared at the open window. The flame in the fireplace was smoldering again, as though it could not live but could not die either—for a while, the only sound was the crackling in the walls.

Suddenly Willigis spoke: "But the Swede will not save the Faith either—for how could he save it? After all, the Faith can be saved only by God alone!" Willigis paused; there it was, the answer he'd been searching for but couldn't remember; it had just come from his own lips, just as it had when Willigis and His Excellency Tilly managed to escape the impenetrable thicket together.

Meanwhile, they pointed out that while what he said sounded nice, he had to consider the difficult plight already faced by the Faith in those parts of the country where the Edict was being carried out; what it was like to be driven back with utmost violence and forced to the margins, compelled to keep utterly silent—it would be contrary to all experience of this world to suggest that they could survive in such a situation by trusting in God alone!

Willigis shot back: "But faith is something that *is* contrary to all experience of this world—"

Clearly he's forgotten where he is, they thought to themselves, or else he couldn't say such a thing to us! Then, aloud: Again, what he was saying sounded quite good, but to their knowledge it had never shown itself to be the case.

Willigis now turned red. Do I need to recite the catechism to them right here like a little boy? he thought to himself; even His Excellency has never demanded that of me! He furrowed his brow and fell silent.

At that moment, the thundering of the cannons shook the walls of the Rathaus once again, causing the plaster around the fireplace to fall into the smoldering logs—red sparks showered the Council Chamber like fiery rain. I'd better go ahead and recite the catechism to them after all, Willigis thought to himself; we'll get no further otherwise. He glanced at the blue of the open window. Quietly, with manful reserve, he said that it was shown to be the case when the Lord Christ was crucified, died, and was buried and on the third day rose again—that was what the Christian creed said. He began to stamp out the sparks that landed near his feet. Then, almost defiantly: "You have always insisted that you stand on faith alone—that is what you shall do with the emperor. If you save the Empire, you save the Faith as well!" Meanwhile, the gentlemen looked at him, speechless—they did not understand him at all; they felt only as though he were pulling the ground out from under their feet. Another piece of plaster fell into the fireplace, but it did not throw up any more flames. The cannons were silent. "So, Herr Ahlemann," a hesitant voice said at last, "what you are saying is that the emperor cannot destroy the Faith any more than the Swede can save it; the emperor can only destroy the Empire, and that is what we should be concerned about. But what is the Empire now but a specter from bygone days—no one has seen the Empire here for a hundred years; the only thing that anyone has seen here is the Faith!"

"No one here has seen the Faith," Willigis replied, "but you have seen the Empire. Back when the ambassador called it an old ghost, you still thought the emperor

Otto was going to come back and lay his head in the lap of his maid, entrusting to her once more the glory of his Empire—or have you forgotten all about that? Emperor Otto stands before the door again today." Thus he again pulled the ground out from under their feet; for indeed, not one of them had forgotten the hour of which he spoke! They lowered their heads.

The voice from before spoke again: "Herr Ahlemann, they opened Emperor Otto's tomb in the cathedral to use the gold in there for the fight against Emperor Ferdinand. No longer will the emperor lay his head in the lap of the maid and entrust to her the glory of the Empire." The voice broke, as though in pain—the fight was over.

"No," Willigis replied, "now the maid lays her head in the lap of the emperor and returns to him the glory of the Empire. The city must render to Caesar the things that are Caesar's,[16] for otherwise the Faith will perish; but Caesar must render to God the things that are God's, for otherwise the Empire will perish."

The sunrise over the city of Magdeburg that morning was as gorgeous as on her very first day: she appeared set to reemerge fully unscathed in her virginal glory, so radiantly did the splendor of the new day crown her high roofs and towers, and so tenderly did the early morning mist veil the streets below in its sweet haze. Within the city, it was as quiet as in times of peace. The guns had been silent since the previous day; in the houses there stirred neither man nor beast: no doubt the poor, good people of Magdeburg were dreamlessly sleeping off the exhaustion of nights spent in anxious wakefulness. Not a single drum sounded from the ramparts.

[16] Paraphrase of Mk 12:17.

Willigis had wanted to ride with the dawn, but Otto Guericke, who was supposed to bring him the city's letter of surrender and accompany him to the Imperial camp, had still not appeared. Willigis could not understand what was taking so long, for everything had been agreed upon in detail at the conclusion of yesterday's Council session. He began to grow impatient; the period of respite that His Excellency had granted the city would be over shortly, yet he could not return without the letter of surrender from the Council.

The trumpeter, who'd been leading the saddled horses back and forth in front of the inn for some time, now insisted that they leave at once—they didn't want to be caught in the storm of the Imperial troops! He'd heard they were planning to take Magdeburg by surprise early in the morning, as they did Maastricht. Willigis knew that this was so. He said that he nevertheless hoped they would wait for them to return. They couldn't be sure of that, the trumpeter said apprehensively: a temporary respite was a temporary respite, and the appointed time was the appointed time. The whole city had gone home to rest, and there was something terribly ominous about the silence of the guns. Willigis began to grow nervous; good God, didn't the gentlemen at the Rathaus notice how much of a hurry they were in? At last, however, he saw Guericke coming toward him—he was not equipped for a ride.

"We've got to go! We've got to go!" he shouted to him. Guericke asked Willigis if he would please come back to the Rathaus; Falkenberg had come down from the rampart in the early morning, just as the gentlemen had finished writing the letter. He'd been talking to them for hours and would not permit them to sign it.

"But they have to sign it this instant!" cried Willigis, beside himself.

Guericke was taken aback; never had he seen the other man so anxious! He said that the Council were no longer accustomed to governing on their own; the one in charge here was Falkenberg. The gentlemen needed Willigis to back them up.

Willigis now became deathly pale: he could not negotiate with Falkenberg; he could only kill him, and Guericke knew that too. Guericke knew. He asked Willigis how much time he thought the city still had. Willigis couldn't say; all he could say was that they were out of time.

Guericke, suddenly quite pale himself, but with unshakable calm: "Willigis, shall I take your rapier and pistol for a little while? Remember that it is not Falkenberg to whom you go, but to the poor maid Magdeburg, of whom you spoke yesterday; she cannot find her way to the emperor's lap on her own—she needs you to go and get her, and you don't need your pistol and rapier for that!" It sounded almost as if Guericke was joking, as he once had with little cousin Anna.

Willigis now looked as though he were shivering with a fever. On the market square, they heard the song of the great clock as it rang the seventh hour. The trumpeter instantly leapt onto his horse. They had to go, they had to go—there was no time for the good sir to go to the Rathaus!

"Guericke," Willigis said, "why not just strike me over the head with your sword to silence me, as you did when you exiled me?" Then he shook the other man's hand and jumped on his own horse. "All right, back to the Rathaus, then!" he said, with a glance at the standard.

The horses' hooves pounded through the silent streets, over which the morning sun now hung low, like a farewell kiss—good God in heaven, could the last day be as sweet and fresh as the first? In the distance, an isolated cannon shot sounded—the trumpeter uttered a curse: that was the signal; the marshal wouldn't hesitate a moment longer now!

Willigis, riding with a loose rein, recalled that His Excellency did not actually expect the Council to capitulate until after the assault had begun—the storming of the city could take hours; as long as the Imperials were not yet inside the city, there was still hope. They had now reached the Rathaus; in front of the door stood Colonel von Falkenberg's black horse. Willigis tossed the reins of his gray to the trumpeter and hurried up the stairs.

The ruling gentlemen of Magdeburg sat in assembly, their guarded faces looking ghostly and forlorn—they'd been there half the night, after all. Outside the window the new day had arrived; on the table the low-burning candles smoldered—one of them had already gone out—leaving behind a heavy haze, through which the gentlemen gazed, as though paralyzed, at Falkenberg. There he stood, his face like brass and iron,[17] reading out a letter in an imperious voice:

"And because His Royal Majesty of Sweden has, solely for the sake of this illustrious Magdeburg Virgin, abandoned his glorious campaign on the threshold of Saxony, His Royal Majesty thus implores this same illustrious Virgin by the blessedness of her soul to remain steadfast at this final, perilous hour, giving no credence to those who cunningly seek to disturb her confidence in her royal liberator, because they have no other counsel to offer! For her royal liberator is on his way, and like the bridegroom he will appear at midnight—nay, he stands before the gates even now." It was as though the gentlemen could hear for themselves the brilliant music that Colonel von Falkenberg

[17] Probably a reference to Jer 6:28: "They are all grievous revolters, walking with slanders: they are brass and iron, they are all corrupters."

had heard that very night up on the rampart as it made its ponderous approach—it came from farther away, as though from the Havel and Spree, and yet it was already quite near, for he'd heard what sounded like the trumpet of a small, bold vanguard hailing Magdeburg over the silence of the enemy's guns! And it could not have been anything other than the vanguard of His Royal Majesty of Sweden, for the trumpet had sounded the March of the Finnish Cavalry, which nobody in this country knew. Why, the last time Colonel von Falkenberg had heard it, he was in Sweden! And they all knew how cold and superior Colonel von Falkenberg was; he could not possibly have deceived himself as he'd once deceived everyone else!

Meanwhile, Colonel von Falkenberg was saying to himself: I must have deceived myself; His Royal Majesty cannot bring us succor now—it's too late. Then, mentally removing his helmet, as if to pray: Whether His Royal Majesty comes or comes not, His Royal Majesty shall today and always find me prepared to live or to die, as the cause demands—the fighting here will continue to the very end. This city may be reduced to rubble and ashes, but it must never become an Imperial stronghold!

In the distance, musket shots were now ringing out—the gentlemen looked up in alarm. Then the door of the Council Chamber suddenly opened wide, and a breeze blew into the room, extinguishing the candles still smoldering on the table. Willigis Ahlemann walked right over to the two burgomasters: "Give me the signed capitulation—I must be off!" The gentlemen gazed fixedly at Falkenberg.

Falkenberg casually lifted his head. Speaking curtly and imperiously: "There will be no capitulation here," he said. Musket shots again rang out in the distance.

Willigis did not look at Falkenberg: "The city has already capitulated!" Then, to the two burgomasters: "The signature—I must be off!"

"That capitulation was invalid," Falkenberg said. "The Swedish commandant is the one who commands here, on behalf of his king." Shots.

Willigis, still not looking at Falkenberg: "There is no Swedish king here, no Swedish commandant. This is Magdeburg—Herr Falkenberg has no country." He turned to the burgomasters: "The signature!"

"Yes, this is Magdeburg, where they choose their country and their king for themselves, just as the Magdeburg Virgin chooses her bridegroom," Falkenberg replied.

"They do not choose for themselves here," Willigis shot back. "They are bound by obligation—Herr Falkenberg has no home and no bride." He looked directly at the colonel. For seconds there was silence. And I wanted to kill this man, Willigis thought to himself, but he's not even really alive! Why, he doesn't have a human face of flesh and blood—it's as though he's but a specter of brass and iron. And this was a man Erdmuth could ... Suddenly he felt something like a vault inside him collapsing—Willigis shuddered. Somewhere in the distance, a horn wailed. Hurried footsteps came up the stairs—Otto Guericke appeared at the door. Shots could be heard from all directions.

Willigis screamed at the two burgomasters: "For God's sake, the signature, before it's too late!"

Guericke spoke, his quiet voice trembling, yet remarkably clear: "It's already too late," he said. "The Imperials are inside the city."

The High Gate stood wide open; to the right and to the left of the gate, two houses blazed like wedding torches: the terrible guests rushed into the House of the Virgin, where they were received with violent honors that nearly bowled them over. Once, twice, three times, four times, the raging fury of the savage pageant staggered backward—every so often

Colonel von Falkenberg, atop his black horse, could be seen through the milky-white smoke of the guns; now his face really did look as if it were made of brass and iron, but aglow with the blazing heat of the welcome reception. Then, all of a sudden, there was only the black horse.

As the mortally wounded Colonel von Falkenberg fell from his horse—there was now savage and desperate fighting on all the ramparts and at all the gates—the roaring of the guns and the whistling and singing of the musket balls suddenly began to sound like the clangor of kettledrums and trumpets! From Lakemacherstrasse the Imperial cavalry burst forth, led by Marshal von Pappenheim over an improvised bridge of hoes and picks that took them over the rampart and into the middle of the city; the marshal had found a way around the still-raging and unabating battle to enter Magdeburg with flourish and fanfare! Suddenly, the cry was going up from every direction: "Victory is ours! All ours!"

Colonel von Falkenberg lay dying in the hallway of a small burgher's house; he'd still had strength enough to cover his own face before they'd carried him through the turmoil and laid him aside—no one here could find out that Colonel von Falkenberg had been hit! He now lay away from the fighting—alone, for he'd sent his bearers back into battle—his wound bleeding out like his life slipping away: he saw it rushing past him in vivid detail, from the day he'd broken free from his mother's arms, up to the moment in this city when he'd found himself again desiring life from a woman, the final thrill before death—and she still owed it to him! But what did that matter to Colonel von Falkenberg as he lay dying—the only thing he wanted to know was the outcome of the battle. The uncertainty made death such a bitter prospect that he almost couldn't bear to surrender to it. But the din and clatter outside now floated away so strangely; in his ears he heard but a gentle, distant roar: that had to be the music of death! Colonel von Falkenberg knew he should pray one more time. He did not pray, however, nor did he feel the desire to do so. This surprised him, for he'd spent his entire life fighting for the Gospel and the Faith; how could it be, then, that in his final hour, he found himself unable to pray? Was God not merciful to him? He listened as his senses faded. Suddenly, breaking through the gentle roar that filled his ears like the sea, he thought he heard a sound—far off and yet very near, much nearer than last night up on the rampart, so near that it felt to the dying man as though the effervescent cup of life were being put to his lips: it was the March of the Finnish Cavalry, drowning out the music of death! Why, those were the heavy drumbeats of Ake Tott's Gotland Cavalry! Those were the brilliant tones to which Stenbock's regiments rode—that could mean only that Niels Brahe's troops were approaching with unrelenting speed! Colonel von Falkenberg sat up straight—he went to remove his helmet, which he was no longer wearing, as if to pray: His Royal Majesty has come after all! His Royal Majesty shall find me prepared to live or ... He slumped back. Kettledrums and trumpets now filled the whole house, seeming to blow apart the walls—the room became vast and soaring, and Colonel von Falkenberg lay in an open field, as it were, nestled peacefully against the German soil of his childhood, as though now but a part of it, over which passed the triumphal march of the foreign king.

Pappenheim's troops now drove the city cavalry before them in wild flight from street to street; all the while the trumpeters blared the Swedish march, as the marshal himself had ordered. He now made his entry into Magdeburg like the very "Herr Storm" to whom he'd drunk at the banquet in Hamelin! And now, all of a sudden, the storm was there, unexpectedly bursting forth from the lovely May day, like another army in the heavens coming to enter Magdeburg from above; it chased the sparks from the two burning houses at the High Gate before it like the marshal chased the fleeing riders, lashing the city of Magdeburg with showers of fiery rain.

Willigis and his trumpeter halted on the market square as the cavalcade of horsemen, their coats fluttering like billowed sails, swept past. They'd been unable to get His Excellency's standard out of the city at the start of the assault due to the fury of the defenders, and now they were in dire straits with the Imperials because they did not have the watchword or the day's insignia—the streets were already seething with unfamiliar soldiery, blindly striking down everything in sight! They stopped right before the Imperial horseman, their backs covered by it; Willigis had drawn his rapier, ready to protect the flag, which was being carried by the trumpeter, but soon he realized, rather, that the flag was protecting them; indeed, it was the only protection the two of them had—it was recognized by all. At Willigis' feet there now huddled a throng of trembling women and children, growing larger with each passing moment—it was as if this spot had been established as a place of refuge amid the dreadful horrors of the devastation—and it was apparently the only one! All around them, hell raged; Willigis felt as though all the grief and misery of the earth lay at his feet: he scarcely dared look at the faces of the poor, wretched women who fled to him in tattered clothing, naked and bleeding, and yet he could not help but look, constantly searching for the face that was still missing.

When the generalissimo appeared on the market square with his staff, Willigis was so beset by people seeking help that he could no longer move his horse. His Excellency, recognizing his standard, rode over to him. As Willigis briefly reported how Falkenberg had prevented the capitulation, the marshal came galloping back toward them, reins held loose.

Breathlessly, he called to the generalissimo: This was a victory, the likes of which had not been heard since the capture of Troy and Jerusalem! In no time at all he'd been inside the city, as soon as the signal to storm it had come; he'd left no time during the assault even to think about capitulation! (And His Excellency had hoped that the onset of the storm would force a capitulation!) Like cats his men had climbed the walls, like rats they'd swum across the Elbe, like a pack of hounds they'd chased the city cavalry through the entire city all the way to the Sudenburg Gate, which he'd just now opened for his comrade Mansfeld, who couldn't manage it on his own. Now the whole Imperial army was inside, and he was going to sound the victory trumpets once more!

His Excellency interrupted him: Before sounding the victory, could the good marshal take care to put out the fire that already engulfed half the city?

The marshal looked about in astonishment: indeed, everything was red, as though under an aurora! He shouted to a gang of Croats, already brandishing knives at one another as they divided up the spoils: Everybody to the pumps and squirts at once!

The men he shouted at bellowed with laughter—one called out, drunkenly slurring: "No pumping here—is booty to be had!" On the marshal's forehead appeared the infamous red mark in which his nurse claimed to have recognized two crossed swords when he was a baby. He drew his rapier: "Don't you besotted scoundrels recognize Field Marshal von Pappenheim when you see him? The generalissimo himself commands you to the pumps!"

The drunken men glared at him. One of them, staggering on, shouted at the top of his lungs: "Only the generalissimo give orders here—no one else!"

For a moment the marshal was speechless. Meanwhile, His Excellency—his face like solid ice in the glow of the blaze—commented: "The good marshal wanted to make a show of power at Magdeburg—well, let the marshal make a show of power!" Turning to his retinue, His Excellency commanded that his own old regiments from the League provide fire brigades and stand guard at the cathedral, where they were to bring the women who were still crowding around the standard. Then, speaking to Willigis: "The good sir has done what he could; I now grant him leave to search his native city and save his own—there is nothing further to be done here."

At the lower end of the market square, house after house was now catching fire; Herr Storm danced the dance of the torches for the fair bride of Magdeburg, his wild companions blowing in from above and laying out for her a nuptial bed of flaming debris. Willigis arrived at the House of the High Song to see the wreath that hung over the front door come down in flames—there, amid the blazing woodwork, already half-consumed by the fire, he saw the old inscription for the last time: "Love is strong as death." The interior of the house was a scene of smoke-filled devastation. Willigis rushed from door to door, as though following a desperate cry for help. On the threshold of the last room, a Croat came staggering toward him—he struck him down. Then he picked up the unconscious bride from the rumpled bed.

The vast space inside the great cathedral was like a darkened ship[18] lying at anchor amid a sea of flames, having taken aboard four thousand passengers, four thousand souls in mortal fear. Reflections cast by raging firestorms battered all the windows, like waves spraying blood-red foam into the ship and splashing against the piers of the vaulted ceiling—Bake expected the ship to sink at any moment. His head buried in his hands, he lay on his knees beneath the same pulpit from which only yesterday he had, at Dr. Gilbert's urgent behest, forcefully reminded the wavering Council that eternal damnation awaited anyone who even thought of making an accord with Tilly. And now it looked as if he'd fallen to such a fate himself. He felt that he was no longer witnessing the destruction of Magdeburg but the end of the world itself, the day from which there was no hiding, no escape, as on that day when the tower of the high gate of his soul fell to the wrong side—the day of the last trumpet, the day of the Son of Man, coming in the clouds of heaven to judge the quick and the dead.[19] Bake lay as though already dashed to the ground before the face of the returning Christ, who gazed at him, not as he had on that fateful day, with a look of unfathomable pain, entreating his bride-like soul to say, like Himself: "Father, not my will, but thine be done"; rather, it was now the voice of his Judge that Bake heard, the same voice that had once foretold, in the seventh chapter of the Gospel of Matthew: "Many will say to me in that day, Lord, Lord, have we not prophesied in thy name? and in thy name have cast out devils? and in

[18] The German word for the nave of a church is *Kirchenschiff*, which literally means the "ship of the church".

[19] A reference to Mt 24:30–31.

thy name done many wonderful works? And then will I profess unto them, I never knew you: depart from me, ye that work iniquity!"[20] Bake—the whooshing and crackling of the flames of burning Magdeburg in his ear—believed he would soon face the onset of eternal fire. He felt nothing of the fear of bodily death that filled the blazing hot space and threatened to explode the bow of the ship that sheltered it within its hold. But then there arose a voice:

In the midst of life
We are in death.
Of whom may we
Seek for succor,
But of Thee, O Lord!

Bake looked up to see his dear wife; she stood close to his side, their four little children clinging to her skirt, their little faces, full of fear, all buried in its folds; her small voice sang with great anxiety and great fervor, as though she was preparing her soul to fall, altogether willingly and confidently, into the hands of God, as on the morning when Bake had heard the words of the Gospel: "And woe unto them that are with child, and to them that give suck in those days!"[21] He felt as if these were now his death sentence—for his dear wife's fifth child could arrive at any moment now! Meanwhile, her small, trembling voice continued to sing:

Who for our sins
Art justly displeased?
O holy God,
O holy and strong,
O holy and merciful Savior,
Deliver us not to bitter death. Kyrie eleison.

[20] Mt 7:22–23.
[21] Mt 24:19.

At the last words, a few voices, and then more and more, had joined in the singing—trembling like the first one: the breathless silence of the mortal fear that gripped the room and threatened to explode the ceiling dissolved. It broke, as though above the sinking ship in the storm of flames there arose a lodestar, and Bake suddenly had the impression that he should seek refuge in his Judge as he did in his Savior. This shook him in such a way that he pressed his head—for he still lay dashed to the ground—against his wife's knees, sobbing. But then he immediately felt how they wavered, and when he looked into her face once more, he saw, as through a veil torn abruptly, his fifth child on its way! And now Bake was extricated from inescapable judgment after all, pardoned from eternal death to life, pulled away from the brink of hell and placed at the side of his dear wife, on whose behalf he was now obliged to clear a path through the four thousand trembling souls to a corner of the great cathedral, where she would, at this terrible hour, bring his and her fifth child into the world.

At that moment Willigis Ahlemann pushed his way through the crowd toward Bake and asked that he marry him to Erdmuth right there on the spot; he could not allow her to bear the disgraceful state in which he had found her a moment longer—she was his bride, after all, his property and his inheritance, promised to him by both of their parents; the will of parents regarding their children was the will of God, after all, and Willigis was obliged to fulfill it—he couldn't run the risk of appearing before God without his bride, could he? And who could say what would become of all these people here? Outside, the war now raged over and above the terrible powerlessness of all power to control it—who knew whether His Excellency Tilly, who alone stood upright, would be able to maintain his hold over the fire and the unfettered soldiery here at the great cathedral?

Bake, kneeling to comfort a dying man, promised Willigis that he would perform the wedding ceremony; thus Willigis went back to get Erdmuth, who lay motionless on the ground where he'd laid her after carrying her in, near the tomb of Queen Edith. Like her, the gorgeous, proud Erdmuth Plögen now lay buried, so to speak, leaving but a poor, disgraced maid, utterly broken and covered in misery and wretchedness. It was in this state that Willigis now had her back, in the very same place where he had once abandoned her at their banns—and now they were to be wed! She had nothing on but his big, old riding coat, which he'd thrown over her before carrying her out of the burning house. Willigis proceeded to put it on her properly and button it up; it would have to serve as her wedding gown, after all—truly, what a curious ensemble he now dressed his bride in! She lay there limply, letting it all happen, her eyes closed, as though she could never in her life look Willigis in the face again; he gazed into hers, however—it was such an ugly sight, all black with smoke and soot from the fire. Hot tears welled up in Willigis' eyes—he couldn't take her to the altar like this!

Here and there, the windows began to shatter from the immense heat that filled the space; streams of water poured in from the firefighting teams outside as they doused the great cathedral. Willigis dipped a corner of his ample riding coat into one of the puddles and began to wash Erdmuth's face with it. Then he took her in his arms and carried her before the altar.

Three days—an eternity—had passed inside the great cathedral when Generalissimo Tilly ordered the survivors of this great flood of fire to come out of their ark. Bake stepped forward—he was now entirely given over to his spiritual occupation once more. In the cathedral, he had comforted the dying, he had wed Willigis and Erdmuth, and finally he had baptized his own fifth child, who, amid great suffering and distress, had been born happy into this world. As the portal of the great cathedral opened, Generalissimo Tilly, on horseback, stopped before it. Behind him, where the fair, proud city of Magdeburg had once stood, could now be seen a great, smoking pile of rubble, beneath which lay buried twenty thousand thriving Magdeburg lives; but beneath it also lay buried the victory of His Excellency Tilly and the solid bulwark against the Swede that His Excellency had sought to win here, all of his plans as commander, indeed the entire fate of this war. It could now go on for thirty years, and His Excellency could not hope to see the end of it, nor could he ever again hope to achieve victory in this war. The horror of the blazing torch that had burned here in Magdeburg would drive protesting estates all across the Empire into rebellion, into the arms of His Swedish Majesty. The king had defeated His Catholic Excellency yet again—this time with a crushing blow to his honor. For ages and ages to come, the name Tserclaes, Count of Tilly, would be associated with the fate of this unfortunate city, as the bridegroom gives his name to the bride at their wedding. Even in his grave the crude toast made at the banquet in Hamelin would disturb the peace of His Catholic Excellency; he would forever be the cruel suitor who had strangled the Magdeburg Virgin in her bridal bed. And yet, the icy-gray Excellency had been prepared to treat the city with nothing but paternal care—but he was never given the opportunity! This made His Excellency's lonely eyes turn so hard and his old bachelor's face so dreadfully severe that it looked as though it would freeze and turn to stone—no one had ever seen His

Catholic Excellency like that before. And where was his blue silk standard? Did it, too, lie buried under the ruins of Magdeburg? Or perhaps His Catholic Excellency did not even want to look at the Blessed Virgin and Mother—after all, no one had dared meet his gaze since Marshal von Pappenheim had thought to sound the victory in the middle of the burning city!

As the poor, famished souls staggered out of the portal of the great cathedral, where they had spent three days cowering in mortal fear with nothing to eat, His Excellency was suddenly reminded once more of the terrible toast to the Wedding of Magdeburg. For it was through the Bride's Portal that the wretched train of survivors now dragged themselves toward him; when they caught sight of His Excellency's terrible countenance, the expression on their faces abruptly changed, as though they wished to flee back inside the cathedral!

Meanwhile, Bake had stepped forward in order to speak on behalf of his poor flock. His Excellency looked at him with bitter resentment; after all, Bake was one of those accursed preachers who had thwarted the accord again and again with his preaching of eternal damnation! Bake, scarcely pardoned before the judgment seat of God, now saw himself dragged before the judgment of the world. His easily distressed soul once again ended up in an entirely different place than it actually meant to be: instead of imploring His Catholic Excellency to have mercy for the sake of Christ, Bake in fact found himself reciting to the Papist commander a lovely passage from Virgil about the destruction of Troy. Thus, His Excellency's wrath was stirred up for a third time as he was reminded of the marshal, who'd already come to him—amid all the terrible things that had transpired here—talking about the conquest of Troy! And now the train of poor souls really did flee back into the cathedral, for His Excellency made a face that looked as though in his implacable severity he might have Bake put in chains forthwith. But then the pastor's four young children rushed out of the throng of fleeing townsfolk and anxiously hurried over to their mother, who it seemed was far too weak to move on her own. There she stood beside her husband, the object of the strange, wrathful generalissimo's gaze. She wavered somewhat, the four young children clinging to her skirt; the newborn fifth cried softly; she held it in her arms like the uncertain, unsheltered fate of them all—at once patiently and pleadingly. "Sir," she breathed, "remember your mother!"

His Excellency gazed fixedly down from his horse at the little, haggard girlish face. Suddenly the tears burst forth, as though at that moment a mass of solid stone shattered behind his aged, lonely eyes: Tilly, the icy-gray Excellency, wept like the little, helpless child in the woman's arms. He could utter nothing more than "Give them all some bread!" Then, without taking another look at Bake, His Excellency turned his horse. And then, all at once—indeed, it was really quite strange—His Catholic Excellency looked as though he had his standard back at his side.

The regimental detachments carried their wreath-bedecked standards into the great cathedral to the martial beat of the drums, as they once had at the Wedding House in Hamelin: all the triumphant banners of League and Empire, still billowing with the victory at Magdeburg as they had that night from the storm. Leading the way was the light blue personal standard of Generalissimo Tilly, the only flag that bore no wreath, per His Excellency's orders—why, no one knew, for indeed the Most Blessed Virgin could well have demanded the very first victory wreath; after all, it was her victory that had been won here at Magdeburg! And now they were going to sing the Te Deum in the great cathedral; outside on the ramparts, the howitzers were already in position to fire a salute. In the nave of the cathedral, His Excellency's adjutants were clinking and flashing hither and thither, supervising the display of the flags; His Excellency himself—he'd already heard a quiet Mass—had just been summoned to the sacristy.

In the sacristy, His Excellency and his young priest, who was preparing to say High Mass, stood facing each other, eye to eye for the first time in a long while. His Excellency waited in silence; after all, it was the other man who had summoned him. The priest was not yet vested for Mass; the low-burning flame in his youthful face flickered, as though licking at a veil that had slipped loose. He sputtered: The trumpeters and the drummers of the Imperial cavalry had just asked for permission to participate in the Te Deum, but how could they sing a Te Deum when twenty thousand dead lay buried here beneath the ruins? A Te Deum would be a mockery—a Te Deum with kettledrums and trumpets! Realizing his helplessness—for His Excellency remained silent—he continued: "His Excellency has not permitted them to place a wreath on his own personal standard either!" Even more helplessly: "Nor could His Excellency allow it—this victory is a dreadful defeat!"

In a sober tone, His Excellency replied that yes, this victory was indeed a defeat, but the soldiery demanded that the Te Deum be sung; they could not be denied this request—just as they could not be denied plunder, for they had taken the city by storm.

The low-burning flame in the young priest's face now flared brightly. It caught on the veil of his wondrous self-control, clearing it away as though in a surge of fire: "And they would not have stormed it if not for the Edict!"

For a moment, His Excellency looked as though the implacable wrath of the past several days was about to overtake him again, but then it was past: His Excellency was one with his standard once more, he'd kissed the blue silk and accepted his destiny—and there was no destiny for His Catholic Excellency apart from his glorious banner! Mary did not wish to triumph over religious division with sword in hand; she wished to triumph with the sword of religious division that pierced her heart. Mary had not been granted this triumph, and so His Catholic Excellency was likewise defeated. And this defeat would be even more complete, for the war of religion would go on; the war for the Empire was lost. A victory for Mary would also have been a victory for the *ratio belli*; her defeat was a mockery of the same: the protesting estates were already going over to the Swede! The distorted image of Mary with sword in hand also entailed a distorted image of the Empire: the Empire with the sword knocked out of its hand—brute force within, impotence without! And now His Excellency, at more than seventy years of age, was compelled to enter into the most terrible of all wars, just as he'd been compelled to take Magdeburg by storm—and if not for the Edict, as the young priest had said, they would not have stormed it!

His Excellency spoke, again quite soberly: Yes, if not for the Edict, then it was likely that Magdeburg would have capitulated in time.

The young priest's face now lay bare, like an open wound; his voice, however, still obeyed his accustomed mastery of the will: His Excellency had once entrusted him with the task of seeing the Edict delayed. His Excellency's instructions had been carried out, but in such a way as though they had not been carried out.

His Excellency, with unshakable dryness, remarked that he'd already suspected as much. The other, meanwhile, exploded with passion, as though the flame had now caught onto his voice as well: "Why, we should have thrown ourselves at the feet of His Imperial Majesty and got him to delay the Edict! We should have implored him not to do violence to consciences, to exercise patience until the Spirit overcame the division! But we had no patience with those who had fallen away, just as Luther had no patience with a Church that had grown worldly, and now it is because of the impatience of Christians that Christendom is perishing! Instead of closing the rift, we've opened it up even wider: Magdeburg will never forget this day! Holy Religion will remain encumbered with the fate of this unfortunate city—for ages and ages to come, she will be blamed for this crime! For ages and ages to come, the Edict will be held against her—never will the Holy Church be one again. The Holy Church will be condemned to powerlessness, and from her disunity shall come the ascendancy of the world; all the violence that she perpetrates today in order to establish Holy Religion, the world will revisit upon Holy Religion when her hour is come. And her hour will come: indeed, that is what they're fighting this war for! For it is not possible to fight for Christ using the weapons of this world; rather, when one fights with the weapons of the world, it is for the world that one fights—the only way to win against the world is to overcome the world!" The young priest threw his hands up to his face: "I knew this, but I did not want to know it—I did not want to allow Holy Religion to suffer, and now"—he was shaking with pain—"I have just delivered Holy Religion over to the greatest suffering of all!" His voice choked: "Holy Religion is herself not to blame for this calamity; she did not command the Edict—she did not desire this war; Holy Religion is the mystery of divine patience itself, after all! It is not in fighting against the Cross that Christ triumphs, but on the Cross; Christ can defeat the cross of religious division only *on* the cross of religious division—Christ triumphs only in the mystery of His love! Indeed, this is what Holy Religion proclaims with every offering of the Mass, with every exposition of the monstrance, with every sign of the cross! This is her mysterious counterblow against all the powers of rupture and rebellion, her triumph over the same—the only one that the Bride of Christ can ever have, even if she must wait centuries for this triumph! And then if the world were to snatch from her the last of her power—even then Holy Religion cannot triumph over the world except through the mystery of love; and it is precisely when it lies defeated that this love triumphs! At the very moment at which the world defeats it, it is then that the world is thrust into that space where its victories cease to matter, and where the world is itself redeemed of all its victories—"

Out in the nave, the heavy footfalls of the soldiery could be heard as they marched into the cathedral. The bells began to toll. Suddenly, His Excellency walked over to the door of the sacristy on his stiff knees and closed it cautiously but firmly—he had to attend to his young priest: it was as if his slender figure had been caught in the grip of a storm that shook him like a young tree all the way down to its roots. In the face of His Excellency appeared old Father Tilly.

Graciously, though still tersely (for one could help in such moments only by being firm; indeed, it was the only way in which His Excellency knew to help himself), he spoke: "You must prepare yourself to celebrate High Mass now, Father. They're waiting for us both out there. You are a soldier in the company of Jesus Christ; the true soldier is known by the way in which he behaves in defeat—it is to such a defeat that I, too, must reconcile myself: the Te Deum is a *De profundis* for me, as it is for you."

The young priest shook his head vehemently: There was no need for His Excellency to sing a *De profundis*: His Excellency had sought to delay the Edict. The supreme commander had been unceasing in his endeavors to save this unfortunate city! He paused—His Excellency had been supreme commander. The young priest's quick mind already understood: His Excellency would be held responsible for the destruction of Magdeburg. Before the world of the living and before posterity, it was he who would have to answer for this terrible event. His Excellency, at more than seventy years of age, would face a martyrdom like no other—not the glorious martyrdom of fallen heroes, of which His Excellency would have been equally worthy; rather, if His Catholic Excellency's heart should ever bleed with the noble wound of battle, it would have long before bled dry from the loathsome bite of unjust blame. The unbound flame of the young priest now seized his heart; His Excellency was, after all, the pride of the young Order. Again bursting forth with impassioned pain: "His Excellency is as blameless for the destruction of Magdeburg as Holy Religion is; and now, His Excellency will suffer the same curse as she will! His Excellency will be branded a dark and sinister fanatic of the Faith; the glory of His Catholic Excellency, his humanity, and his reputation as a Christian will be tarnished. His Excellency will have to suffer for crimes which he did not commit—I have delivered the glorious banner of His Excellency up to the same fate as I have our Holy Religion!"

Now His Excellency became somewhat cross, for when it came to his own reputation and his own glory, he was beyond caring, thanks be to God. He had no desire to waste one more word on such things—if only he'd been able to salvage his cause, if only he'd been able to save the Empire! Protruding his lip with some displeasure: "You need to put any concern about my reputation and glory completely out of your mind, Father! As a commander in His Imperial Majesty's service, I am obliged to defend my banner from the enemy to the last breath, but as a Christian, I must not refuse to bear the burden of unjust blame; indeed, in the order of Holy Religion it is only right that I should take such a burden upon myself—as you yourself have said, I cannot triumph with my banner in any other way. What else could you expect from me, Father? Surely you know this better than I." His Excellency broke off somewhat awkwardly and began to look around for the Mass vestments, for out in the cathedral the crowd was already growing noticeably restless.

The priest said, quietly but loudly enough to hear: "Yes, I know, Mary's banner cannot triumph in any other way than Mary's Son. And Mary has triumphed in her Son; in the midst of defeat, there is the victory—that is what it looks like."

His Excellency gave no reply, for it was now necessary to finish up at all costs. Fortunately he'd managed to collect all the vestments, and touching the young priest on the shoulder, he said: "Allow me to assist you; I served at the altar when I was a boy."

Suddenly the priest seized the old soldier's hand and thrust his young face into it. For a moment His Excellency looked as though he were about to become cross again—another such outburst was really unacceptable! However, he felt the moist tears on his palm—why was the young priest still so distressed? Could it be that he still did not understand that His Excellency had reconciled with him? His Excellency gave an almost sheepish look; he was no good with nice words, after all—he'd been too alone for such things for many years now!

His Excellency—in a tone that was truly sobering (and had he forgotten about the soldiery out there, to become so long-winded now?)—explained: Father only ever thought about religious victories, but there was also the world to consider. Now came the lost war for the Empire, into which they appeared to be headed with flags flying, and he could only grit his teeth to take upon himself the responsibility of being the Empire's commander in this war, so that he might thereby at least protect His Imperial Majesty from the very worst; and indeed, he had to take it upon himself, because His Imperial Majesty had no other commander. Suddenly, as though in His Excellency's old, lonely eyes a gate that was tightly shut now opened wide with strange ease, and seemingly by itself: "Will you accompany me on my difficult path, Father, until the bitter end?" he asked.

The priest pressed his youthful face deeper into His Excellency's hand—then, in a soft voice, asked in return: "Will you give me your blessing before we walk this path, Father Tilly?"

His Excellency turned to the holy water font, dipped his old soldier's hand in it, and slowly, almost solemnly, traced the sign of the cross on the other man's young, pale forehead. A few minutes later the High Mass began.

The young priest was reading the Gospel in his very soft, very frail voice when Bake arrived in front of the great cathedral. Bake had felt the need to say farewell before he departed for distant lands with his wife and children: here among the charred and devastated ruins of Magdeburg, there was no place for him and his family anymore. Otto Guericke had managed to procure several small wagons for the poor souls left homeless from War Commissary von Walmerode, who'd provided him with lodgings himself—Guericke was already as good at dealing with the Imperial officers as he had once been with Colonel von Falkenberg. It was now time to load up Bake's estate, all that he had left to his name: his dear wife with their four young children clinging to her skirt, the fifth one in her arms—the little, little girl who'd arrived in this world at the same ghastly hour in which the fair, proud Maid of Magdeburg had died such a wretched and miserable death—this tiny, little newborn maiden—almost the only maid of Magdeburg that was still left a maiden! Bake's dear wife would keep her under her mantle, cradling her on her knees like a slender light of hope as they journeyed into an uncertain future. The four older children could scarcely wait to climb onto the wagon, clapping their hands and shouting with joy, as they had done at the terrible sound of the guns; one might have thought this pitiful exodus was a festive holiday excursion. Amid all the sorrow, Bake had to smile when he thought about how his children seemed to be reproaching him with the verse "Except ye be converted, and become as little children, ye shall not enter into the kingdom of heaven."[22] And truly, it was a verse that Bake needed to remember! For he now stood for the last time before his beloved, great cathedral, in the same place where he had stood on that fateful morning. Inside, the Imperials were celebrating their idolatrous Mass; outside sprawled the scorched wasteland: the city of Magdeburg, now truly like the destroyed Jerusalem in the Gospel from the Tenth Sunday after Trinity Sunday. A wet wind blasted Bake's face with the smell of charred rubble, as well as another, coming up from the buried cellars where the many, many dead lay buried—those who had taken refuge down there and then miserably suffocated. Bake's eyes were not, as on that fateful morning, misty with the darkness of the new dawn but filled with the tears of farewell; yet despite this, today he was able to make out clearly

[22] Mt 18:3.

the stone figures above the Bride's Portal that stood gathered around the Papist Mary being assumed into heaven. No trick of the devil, however fiendish, would ever again be able to fool him into mistaking a foolish virgin for a wise one: he was now able to distinguish them so clearly that he nearly thought he saw poor Erdmuth Plögen once again—not as he'd seen her on that fateful morning seated beneath his pulpit: glorious, proud, and resplendent, but as she'd been when he'd married her at the flame-lit altar of the great cathedral: clothed only in Willigis' riding coat, half-unconscious, her face as bitterly contorted as those of the desperate virgins above the portal! It had seemed to Bake as though there in this miserable parishioner of his, whom he'd shamefully neglected and abandoned to ruin, the poor, foolish, disgraced Virgin of Magdeburg herself lay before the altar, and even though he'd believed himself already released from judgment, he would once more be obliged to look into the face of his guilt in all its gravity. But then during the wedding ceremony, when Willigis had truly given his yes—firmly and clearly, his good, faithful gaze directed at the unfortunate soul at his side, as if he were consoling her in his heart: Whatever else has happened, whatever errors have been made, the bride is still the bride, for love is still love, love makes all things possible—all at once it had been as though the image of Erdmuth had become detached from her image as it actually was and transformed into an entirely different image. Where Bake had just seen the victim of his guilt, his neglected spiritual daughter, an altogether poor, foolish, disgraced virgin, he now saw a parishioner who'd been saved—she was now a beloved bride, accepted with love and honor! And so indeed Bake thought, when he looked back on that moment, it was also to his own soul—which had, after all, denied Christ, its Bridegroom—that those words, "The bride is still the bride," had been spoken, and the love of God had released him from his own guilt toward his poor spiritual daughter and rescued him from the shipwreck of an entire world and placed him in a new world, one where judgment was carried out according to completely different laws than those of the one that had gone up in flames outside before the great cathedral. For there, indeed, fate had been mercilessly fulfilled; there, every wild seed that had been sown had sprouted and grown rampant, no saving miracle had stopped the bloody harvest, no transformation had changed the deadly bitter fruit—for the poor Virgin of Magdeburg, nothing had been remitted, nothing granted! For the kind of miraculous transformation that Bake had experienced in the great cathedral at Erdmuth's wedding ceremony could only ever happen in a place where it was said: "Love makes all things possible." In the world, it was an altogether different matter; for there it was said: "Eye for eye, tooth for tooth, pride for pride"[23]—indeed, what they were truly saying was: "Pride makes all things possible!" And they would soon be saying it all the more: Guericke had related to Bake that the war was about to begin anew—they could expect to see even greater piles of rubble than they'd seen in Magdeburg, and when it was over, the entire fatherland of the German nation would look as this city did! And surely Otto Guericke knew what he was talking about; the top Imperial officers thought highly of him, they trusted him—War Commissary von Walmerode was even supposed to have said that if Magdeburg was ever to be rebuilt, then they should make Guericke burgomaster. But then when Bake had asked apprehensively whether that meant there was indeed no hope of averting such great misfortune for

[23] A variation on Ex 21:23–25.

their poor homeland, Guericke—affable Otto Guericke—had given him the altogether bitter reply that no, there was no hope, not until Christian love had been restored to its rightful place; without it the world could do naught but destroy, as they'd witnessed in Magdeburg! And what Guericke had meant to say by this, Bake had understood quite well—he'd felt as though he were being reproached with yet another Bible verse, namely: "Ye are the salt of the earth: but if the salt have lost his savour, wherewith shall it be salted?"[24] Indeed, Bake was now entirely open and willing to hear the voice of the Lord Jesus Christ everywhere, as ready as he was to place the fate of the precious Faith entirely in God's hands—Bake had at last arrived at the place where he'd actually meant to be all along, where he could say, with the Lord Jesus Christ: "Not my will, but thine be done." He nevertheless shrunk back once more, as he had done before the Papist commander when leaving the great cathedral; for after all that had transpired in Magdeburg, there really could be no peace! On what should such a peace even be based? There was no communion to be had with the Papists—Bake trembled all the while at the thought of having to hear with his own ears the voices of those wanton men who had marched into his beloved cathedral with kettledrums and trumpets in a frenzied victory celebration among twenty thousand fresh and open graves! And yet, everything was curiously silent, and he heard only a soft clinking from time to time, as though behind the smoke-blacked walls the glittering weapons of the colorful soldiery flashed and sparkled.

But then a voice arose: "Credo in unum Deum . . ." The Gospel was finished, and the choir began: "Patrem omnipotentem, factorem coeli et terrae, visibilium omnium et

[24] Mt 5:13.

invisibilium ..." Bake listened: Why, that was the great Christian creed he was hearing, the same which he himself had uttered many times in the great cathedral with great reverence, the precious confession of the faith of all his forefathers, and, God willing, of his children and his children's children! He found it altogether curious that at the very moment of his departure he should hear this precious creed from within his beloved cathedral—he was positively shaken, and for a moment he completely forgot that those singing it were Papists; he could not help but conceive of what he heard as anything other than the sound of his own voice reverberating in a many-voiced echo: "Et in unum Dominum Iesum Christum, Filium Dei unigenitum. Et ex Patre natum ante omnia saecula ..." Or perhaps his—Bake's—own voice had already been an echo, the resounding echo of an immense choir that had rung out and would continue to ring out all across the centuries, such that the vast spaces of the years became as small and constricted as the bedchambers of children, and their thundering footsteps as ghostly and fleeting as the winds flitting by, or like evening shadows, upon whose edges the night already encroached. "Deum de Deo, lumen de lumine, Deum verum de Deo vero, genitum, non factum ..." To Bake, it was as though each of these brief, majestic statements laid bare a vast, timeless foundation on which all those gathered in the great cathedral, and he himself, shut outside yet protected by the little shelter afforded by the Bride's Portal, likewise stood—separated only by the wall of the great cathedral, by just one single wall, built by human hands! And for the sake of this wall, all of Magdeburg was reduced to rubble! "Qui propter nos homines et propter nostram salutem descendit de coelis ..." Bake felt the touch of a soundless storm as it came and swept away all human emphases on the words he was hearing, as though, embedded in this creed, the Eternal Word itself approached his bowed-over soul: "Et incarnatus est de Spiritu Sancto ex Maria Virgine: et homo factus est ..." Bake fell to his knees: for the first time in his life, he was shaken to realize that beyond all the things that separated the confessions, there was one, singular creed professed by all of Christendom—the wall wavered, as though overwhelmed by the immense weight of the shared guilt for this forgetting: Bake thought he saw inside the cathedral the high cross above the rood screen, from which the Lord Jesus Christ now looked down on the triumphant Papists at their kettledrums and trumpets with the same look of unfathomable pain and love with which he had gazed on Bake that fateful morning; and at the same altar where the words "the bride is still the bride" had been spoken to his soul, he now heard the same words being spoken to them. And then, in an instant, all things were transformed: in place of the great site where an immense guilt shared by all of Christendom had been satisfied—the destroyed Magdeburg, forever separating that Christendom—the destroyed Magdeburg now became the hill of Golgotha, where the whole of Christendom was united: "Crucifixus etiam pro nobis sub Pontio Pilato passus et sepultus est ..." The love of the Lord Jesus Christ had been crucified at Magdeburg, and there was no other hope than that hope which all Christians shared: "Et resurrexit tertia die, secundum Scripturas ..." Bake thought he could hear the buried cellars of Magdeburg trembling and quaking, as though the love of Christ that lay buried there with the twenty thousand dead were about to force open its tomb—"Et ascendit in coelum: sedet ad dexteram Patris ..."—not as the betrayed and denied love that had been put to the cross here but as a new, transfigured, and unifying love, resurrected from the dead at Magdeburg, endowed with its power from on high. The transformation engulfed the world: Bake thought he saw the poor, torn, and tormented fatherland of the German nation, having finally arrived at peace once more as a result of all its members reflecting in a fraternal spirit on the shared creed of their fathers and, God willing, of their children and their children's children until the end of time. "Et iterum venturus est cum gloria iudicare vivos et mortuos ..." The buried cellars of destroyed Magdeburg trembled and quaked once more, now with the resurrection of her twenty thousand dead! And now indeed, Christendom had to prepare to give an account of these twenty thousand dead, assembled on the ruins of Magdeburg for the Last Judgment, cast at the feet of Mercy—the all-embracing Mercy of Jesus Christ. "Cuius regni non erit finis ..." This was the pardoning of Christendom, the absolution for the guilt of love broken and torn—of His kingdom there would be no end—the kingdom of His love would overcome all separation! The final transformation began: Bake thought he saw the fair city of Magdeburg as the heavenly Jerusalem, built high and glorious as it had once been, all her towers and battlements raised anew, once more decorated for a wedding, the wedding of love eternal, according to the Revelation of John the Apostle, chapter 19. The soundless storm returned. Bake found himself back on earth, his forehead pressed against the wall of the great cathedral; painful, yet amid the blowing of this soundless storm, it felt as if a miracle must be taking place. "Et in Spiritum Sanctum, Dominum et vivificantem ..." But now, all of a sudden, kettledrums and trumpets began to sound inside: "Et unam sanctam catholicam et apostolicam Ecclesiam ..." The great cathedral roared and quaked, as though the Church triumphant, accompanied by the entire Imperial army, were preparing to march out over the poor ruins of protesting Magdeburg. Christendom foundered. But only for a moment, because now the miracle did occur: lonely, displaced Bake had taken up the common creed, whose words the kettledrums and trumpets inside threatened to shatter. He spoke plainly and humbly, yet also firmly and clearly, as if his lone voice out here outside the great cathedral filled and confessed the vast expanses of an invisible Church: "Confiteor unum baptisma in remissionem peccatorum."